Praise for Howard Odentz's
Dead (A Lot):

"A fun and witty zombie apocalypse narrative that will bring a smile to your face as you discover (or remember) how the teenage mind operates in times of difficulty. The dialog is clever and the characters are realistic."
—*ScaredStiffReviews.com*

"Right out of the gate, the plot is fast-paced and action packed (like any good zombie book should be) and infused with some great humor. It's a fun and entertaining ride and I was sad when it [came] to the end."
—*BookandCoffeeAddict.com*

"Howard Odentz does an impeccable job writing about this world turned dead."
—*BeautysLibrary.com*

Bloody Bloody Apple

by

Howard Odentz

Rae –
What's in your basement?

Bell Bridge Books

Bell Bridge Books
PO BOX 300921
Memphis, TN 38130
Print ISBN: 978-1-61194-557-7

Bell Bridge Books is an Imprint of BelleBooks, Inc.

We at BelleBooks enjoy hearing from readers.
Visit our websites
BelleBooks.com
BellBridgeBooks.com
ImaJinnBooks.com

10 9 8 7 6 5 4 3 2 1

Cover design: Debra Dixon
Interior design: Hank Smith
Photo/Art credits:
Apple (manipulated) © Shawn Hempel | Dreamstime.com
Skull (manipulated) © Rainbowchaser | Dreamstime.com

:Lbba:01:

Dedication

For David

1

EVERY FALL, WHEN the orchards ripen and the leaves begin to die, there are murders. We know it, and we accept it. It's the price we pay for living in Apple, Massachusetts. Our town carves up and spits out a few seeds each year. We all approach autumn with dread because nobody wants to be a seed.

The murders started this season the second week in September, right before people began putting pumpkins out on their front stoops and tying green stalks of corn to their lamp posts. We were just getting back into a routine of classrooms and homework when the senior class president, Ruby Murphy, disappeared.

Everyone took notice of the cop cars at school the next morning. In the fall, cops at school aren't there to bust someone for pot or pills.

In the fall, cops at school mean death.

Ruby's story spread through the hallways until we were all fat and bloated with the news.

Her body was discovered near the railroad tracks behind the strip mall. A meth-head named Junior Ziff found her there. Of course, the cops knew he didn't kill her. Christ, even a kid at the state school over in Bellingham could see that Junior Ziff didn't have the brain wattage to use a butter knife, let alone something sharp enough for murder.

Ruby wasn't raped or anything messed up like that. Someone had just plain stabbed her—over and over again, sixteen times in all—to make sure that every last breath had escaped her body. Nothing about her death could be chalked up to a morbid sexual lust that wrapped blood and sex and gore all together into some maniac's perverse fantasy.

In the end, no one knew why Ruby was targeted—or why she was the first.

As for the second murder, I guess there were more than a few people in town who breathed a collective sigh of relief when a brutal waste of space like Ralphie Delessio finally got what was coming to him. He liked to hit girls. Everyone knew it.

He was hung by his feet in one of the tobacco barns out on Street

Road. His jugular was slit, and his life spilled out of him so quickly that he was probably dead before much of it had a chance to seep into the ground.

In the deep recesses of my mind where no one can see, I hold a bitter thought that Ralphie Delessio deserved something more sinister than a humane slice of the throat.

Over the years, murders in Apple have been much worse. Ralphie didn't live through the agony of having each finger cut off and arranged neatly in a halo around his head. Ralphie wasn't violated with a miniature statue of The Virgin Mary. Ralphie didn't have his skin flayed off while he was crucified with screwdrivers to a tree in the woods.

Ralphie was killed like a lamb or a cow would be, and in the most compassionate way possible.

Kosher-like.

Ruby and Ralphie—murders one and two.

Now there is a third body in the woods, propped up against a tree. It's a girl, but I'm afraid to look. I'm afraid that I'll know her.

The wind picks up, and leaves swirl around Newie, Annie, and me as we stand on the path that we cut through between the high school and the middle school every day after school. Off to our left, much of the greenery has turned color or fallen to the ground so we can easily see through the thicket of trees. I'm immediately afraid, and a familiar burning sensation spreads across my chest and up my neck. I feel hot and nervous and excited all at the same time.

"Jackson, what the hell is that?" Newie asks, but I can tell by the waver in his deep voice that he already knows what it is but doesn't want to be the first to say it.

Annie grabs my hand and squeezes it tightly. I wrap my arms around her, and she buries her face in my shoulder.

"Shit," I whisper.

"I can't look," she says.

I don't want to look either, but my curiosity trumps my fear. I push Annie gently away and step off the path into the woods. The leaves crunch under my feet, and it occurs to me that I'm being loud. I don't want to be loud. A fresh corpse is like a newborn monster. I don't know why, but I feel as though it can be wakened from death with the slightest noise, only to come back as something putrid and evil.

Newie follows me, his big feet making even more noise than mine. Every step he takes makes me cringe. I have a sick feeling inside. What will it be this time—a maiming? Asphyxiation? Something worse?

It *is* something worse.

The dead girl has no eyes. They're missing from her face as though someone has forgotten to draw them in. Black blood weeps from the dark, vacant holes. Her skirt is pushed up, but not too far, and her legs are twisted at odd angles. Her lap is filled with dead leaves, and her hair has a bright yellow one stuck in its dead tangles.

She is decorated by death.

My mouth goes dry. Even without eyes, I know her. She's that girl who sits alone in the library and doesn't talk to anyone. She's not pretty. Her eyes are too far apart, and her hair is too straight. Her mouth is always curled into a frown. She's one of the unnoticed—destined to live out high school without ever going to a party or eating an ice cream cone with friends—or hanging out at the strip mall.

Unnoticed—and now that she's dead, she'll only be remembered for one thing—the act of dying—the act of being murdered.

"Fuck," Newie manages before he moans and barrels away from me and the dead girl. I don't turn around, but I know he doesn't make it all the way back to the path before he vomits. It comes up out of him in a torrent that he can't control. He coughs and moans and coughs again. "Shit."

"Who is it?" Annie cries, but I'm not sure how to tell her that I don't know the dead girl's name. She's always just been there, living at the edges of our lives but never touching them. We've seen her since kindergarten with her ugly, wide-spaced eyes and her straight hair. I feel sick and shallow and horrible, all at the same time—for never noticing her—for never knowing her name.

"It's that ugly girl from history," sputters Newie. "The one with the bug eyes."

Annie stamps her foot on the carpeted path of dead leaves and starts to cry. I don't look, but I know her tears are spilling out of her eyes, and her black eyeliner is dripping down her soft cheeks.

"How?" she sobs.

In Apple, we never ask why a murder has happened. We ask how.

"I can't," coughs Newie. "I can't."

Annie moans. I don't turn around to look at her because I have to stare at the body with the missing eyes and the twisted legs. I owe her that much. It occurs to me that I wish I could somehow turn back time and be nice to her—even once. I wish I could go back and say hi to her in the hallways at passing time, or maybe ask if she wants to sit with us at lunch. I know, if given the chance, I won't do any of those things. Still, I wish I could be offered the opportunity. It would help me make sense of everything—of her—of murder.

After a minute or two, I turn from the dead girl, help Newie to his feet, and go back to Annie on the pathway. Her arms are crossed. Her face is streaked with black as I imagined it to be.

"What do we do?" she asks.

"Tell someone," I say.

Newie closes his eyes and shakes his head. "We have to tell the police."

"No," blurts out Annie. "What if the killer finds out that we're the ones who found her? He'll come after us." She starts shaking, so I pull her to me and put my chin on her head.

"It doesn't work that way," I whisper, thinking of all the other people in all the other years who found bodies in September and October. "People who find the bodies don't seem to get murdered here."

"Why not?" she sobs.

I don't have an answer for her, so I just shrug.

2

THE POLICE STATION is in the center of Apple, next to a doughnut place. The spectacular cliché isn't lost on any of us. Doughnuts and cops seem to go together—doughnuts and cops and death.

When we walk in, we're all pretty freaked out. Annie's makeup has smeared into deep, dark bruises on her white cheeks.

"Newton," Officer Randy nods from behind his desk. It's common knowledge that next year Newie's going to take the entrance exam to become a cop. Being a cop is genetic in Newie's family. His father is a cop, and his grandfather was a cop, too. That's why Officer Randy knows him.

Life's going to be weird when Newie's finally wearing a badge, but he's still getting wasted with us out at Rattlesnake Ridge or down at Pulpit Rock Lake. It's not going to be the same. I can already feel time stretching thin around us, getting ready to snap the umbilical cord between whatever kind of life we're living now and adulthood.

I'm not sure any of us are ready, but I don't think we have a choice.

"Are you okay, miss?" Officer Randy asks Annie. She only shakes her head. A few fresh, blackened droplets splash to the floor.

I turn to Newie, expecting him to say something—anything—to Officer Randy, but he just looks scared. Officer Randy is the cop who's always at school assemblies, lecturing us about the dangers of drugs and alcohol. He's the cop who goes to reading-time at the Apple Library and warns the kiddies not to accept candy from strangers. He's short and fat, with a round, bald head. I try to picture him running down a shoplifter at the strip mall or a bunch of delinquents writing graffiti underneath the railroad bridge on Gully Street, but I can't do it.

"Um, is my dad around?" Newie finally asks, but his words come out like he's a little girl instead of the captain of the football team.

Officer Randy looks at the three of us for what seems like forever, but mostly he's checking out Annie's tear-soaked face. Finally, he puts down the newspaper he's reading and says, "Okay—sure. Wait here a sec."

He heaves his bulk out from behind his desk, rearranges himself in his baggy pants, and heads off down the hallway to Chief Anderson's office. There's a box of tissue paper sitting on Officer Randy's desk. I take two of them and hand them to Annie.

"Here," I tell her. "You look terrible."

"Nice," says Newie. "You're a freaking saint."

Annie doesn't say anything. She takes the tissues from me and wipes her face without the benefit of a mirror. It doesn't work too well. By the time Chief Anderson comes walking in, looking every bit like a Sasquatch—all six feet and ten inches of him, with a huge barrel chest and a great head of shaggy black hair—Annie probably looks worse than before.

"What's this?" Chief Anderson barks, looking directly at Annie's face. Something terrifying flashes in his eyes, and he curls his meaty fists into hammers. "I don't need trouble from you in the fall, Newie," he hisses at his son and takes a huge step forward. "What did the three of you do?"

Newie's not often afraid to speak, but in the shadow of his father he's ten years old all over again. The giant man, with his giant gun, hanging from his giant belt, is the stuff of nightmares.

Annie starts crying even more, so I put my arm around her. My throat is dry, and I can't quite get the words out.

"Answer me, goddammit," demands Chief Anderson. His very presence sucks the air out of the room.

"Um," Newie starts, but can't seem to let the words free from his mouth, either.

Finally it's me who blurts out, "We found another body."

Chief Anderson's arms fall to his sides. They look like massive tree trunks. I can't help but notice that his right hand grazes the butt of his gun, and I swallow something thick and goopy.

"Where?" he says.

Newie finds his voice, but it comes out with a crack. "Behind . . . behind the middle school."

Chief Anderson runs a large hand through his hair. It's exactly like Newie's. It occurs to me that, twenty years from now, Newie Anderson is going to be standing in this very same room. There will be three new kids telling him that they've found a body. It will be September or October, and rows of colored in scarecrow drawings will be taped to the cinder block walls. They'll be from one of the third grade classes, thanking Officer Randy for his discussion on Stranger Danger.

"Shit," mutters Newie's dad. Little veins pop out on his forehead, and the sour stench of sweaty-stress rolls off of him. "Show me," he says, as his lip curls in disgust.

So that's what we do.

3

WE RIDE IN THE back of the chief's cruiser. Newie sits behind his dad, biting his nails. Annie's leaning up against me, and I have my arm around her. We've been dating since the end of ninth grade, so now, at the start of our senior year, we're pretty much a big blob called Jacksannie, instead of just Jackson or Annie.

We were friends before we got together, so hooking up was inevitable. If it hadn't been me, it would have been Newie, but I don't think I could have lived with that. He's shoved his dick in so many holes by now that I'm surprised it hasn't rotted off. Annie's better than that. She's a good girl.

Newie isn't dating anybody, but that's okay. There's a line of Apple trash a mile long—and probably some closet cases, too—who are more than interested in boning him. Annie says it's because he's tall, good looking, and built.

He's just Newie to me. We've been friends forever.

Chief Anderson looks uncomfortable squished into the front seat of his cruiser. He's so big it's unnatural. Newie's already 6'2", but right now he's small and quiet and chewing at his cuticles with a vengeance.

The chief pulls the cruiser down Main Street, past Dippity Doughnuts and Francine's Fire House. It's really not a fire house—it's a burger place—but it has burned to the ground at least twice, so it's been renamed Francine's Fire House. My family doesn't go in there. My mother and Francine didn't get along in high school, and my father once called Francine the Whore of Babylon to her face at church. I don't know why. I think it may have something to do with the fact that she's always shacked up with a different dude. I don't know how she gets them. Francine has a terminal case of leather face. She's baked herself in the sun so much and smoked so many cigarettes that her skin is hard and brown, like a biker's wallet.

We pass Zodiac Tattoo Parlor and a place called Three Penny's. People bring their old clothes and stuff there for resale, especially when it's almost the end of the month, and there's nothing left from their unemployment checks but toilet paper and Bagel Bites.

The chief turns down Carver Street and drives slowly by Bliss Playground. That's where nervous mothers stand in small, tight groups as their children play on the jungle gym or go down the slide. Any other time of year, kids can climb on the monkey bars by themselves, but not in September or October.

That's when mothers don't pull their eyes away from their kids.

Apple's a quiet town. We're in the part of Massachusetts that nobody ever visits. We're not west enough to be in the Berkshires or east enough to be considered part of the Boston metropolitan area. We're not north enough to be near New Hampshire, which doesn't matter anyway because there's nothing there. Way south of us is Connecticut— the desolate part—between Hartford and Providence.

Apple is just in the middle, and nobody ever visits the middle.

Nobody even cares about the middle.

All along one side of town is the Quabbin Reservoir. It's one of the biggest man-made bodies of water in New England. Most of the drinking water for the state comes from there. It's pretty remote. No one ever gave a crap about the Quabbin, except for when it was closed to the public after 9/11. I was too young to care, but I guess the state thought that terrorists were going to put anthrax or something like that in the water, to ruin our drinking supply.

Then we could have called ourselves Poison Apple. That lame-ass joke has been making the rounds for years.

Above us is a nothing town called Hollowton, and beyond that, state forest. Below us is state forest, too, and tobacco farms. That's where most of us work in the summer—in the tobacco fields. We're eager hands for minimum wage. Besides, it's the best way to store up some cash for the fall because no one wants to go out and work then.

People die.

For almost sixty years now there've been murders. There were murders when my grandparents were starting out and when my parents were kids. I used to hear my mom and dad whisper about the ones who are gone, but I remember their names just the same—Jenny Zaiken, Debbie Radcliffe, Coach Heffernen, Felicity Gifford, and her brother Jeffie. The list goes on and on.

When they happen, Chief Anderson investigates the murders just like his father did before him, but nothing ever comes of his investigations. Of course, there are theories as to why people are killed in Apple. Some people say the land is cursed because the early settlers stole it from the Indians. Other people say that people are killed in the fall because it's the Devil's time of year, and he always expects his due. There's even a messed up idea that the local apple crop is tainted with some sort of mold that makes people do crazy things—like what happened during the witch trials in Salem.

I don't hold much stock in superstitions or religious crap, and there's nothing wrong with the apples in the orchards.

They're all just excuses. People like excuses.

The truth is, we stay in Apple for the same reasons that folks stay in California even though there are earthquakes, or swimmers dip in the ocean where there are sharks that can bite you in two. Turning the other cheek is cake. Doing something about it sometimes seems too hard.

Creepy Father Tim seems to think that praying will make the murders stop. Most people in Apple agree, so church is usually packed on Sunday mornings. Still, the truth is, praying isn't going to make things better. Murder just happens here—like teen pregnancy. In the end, someone always gets screwed—like the girl with no eyes.

She got royally screwed.

"How's your dad, Annie?" Chief Anderson asks with a serious look on his face. She shifts uncomfortably in her seat and looks out the window. Annie's dad hasn't worked in a while, and everyone seems to know it. Her mom does check-out at Tenzar's Market and manages to keep their house running, but only barely. Mr. Berg sits on the couch in his T-shirt and underwear and drinks beer. He's been doing that forever. The Bergs have a television, but it only gets a few stations, so he watches whatever's on and smokes cigarettes. Annie's house is always filled with a faint haze that smells like dirty laundry and tobacco.

"He's okay," she says quietly, but she sounds painfully unconvincing. Newie glances over at her with a weird look on his face before continuing to gnaw on his nails.

"What about you, Jackson?" Chief Anderson says to me. I watch his sunglass-shades in the rearview mirror as they tilt in my direction. His sunglasses are so unfair. He can wear them and look anywhere, but no one knows exactly where.

My dad used to be friendly with Chief Anderson, but not so much anymore. They don't go out of their way to avoid each other—they just don't talk. I'm pretty sure it has something to do with the chief's girlfriend. I don't think my father approves. Then again, my father doesn't approve of much.

"What about me, what?" I say. It comes out ruder than I mean for it to sound.

"How's your father?"

"Good," I murmur. I try to think of something else to tell him, but I come up with nothing.

"Is he still woodworking?" he asks me.

For real? It seems like woodworking is all he ever does. I nod, hoping that the chief sees me through his mirrored lenses. I think he does, because he stops talking.

The cruiser finally pulls up to the gate in back of Glendale Middle School. It's open because it's soccer season, and there's practice out on the fields behind the sixth grade classrooms. Some parents have their cars parked alongside the field, so they can watch the practice and make sure that nothing happens—so they can make sure their kids come home tonight.

We all get out of the car. Chief Anderson pulls a toothpick out of his shirt pocket and sticks it in the side of his mouth.

"Which way?" he says.

Newie looks at me and Annie, but we don't budge. He sighs, slumps his shoulders, and moves down the back of the field toward the path. He doesn't move fast. After all, what's the rush?

The girl's dead. She's not going anywhere.

4

CHIEF ANDERSON'S talking on his phone to someone at the station.

"Christ. That makes three," he says, as he looms over her body like a redwood tree. Next to him, the lifeless, eyeless girl seems doll-sized.

Newie watches what his dad's doing. It's his future he's staring at—sooner rather than later. One day, Newie knows it will be him in the woods, standing over a corpse with its nose cut off or its insides scooped out. I wonder if he ever thinks he should be doing something else with his life.

Once again, I feel the tug of time yanking the last days of youth away from me. I don't want to grow up if growing up means dealing with death. I just don't.

Chief Anderson nods his head and says something else into his phone. After a few seconds, he covers the mouthpiece and yells over to us. "You kids know who she is?"

Silence.

None of us know what to say. We certainly don't know her name. For Newie and Annie, she's just that ugly girl with the bug eyes from history.

Newie says, "She's from one of my classes."

Chief Anderson nods and says something else into his phone. I hear him use the word "local" which sort of strikes me funny because everyone who's murdered in Apple is local.

Eventually, more cops appear. One of them has a camera and is taking pictures of the body and the crime scene. Another one is stretching yellow tape around the trees. Soon, there are five men in blue, Officer Randy, and the chief—the sum total of Apple's police force. The three of us start feeling awkward.

Chief Anderson notices and strides over to us.

"You guys go home," he says. Newie nods, but his dad plops his massive paw on Newie's shoulder and sticks his cigar-sized finger in his face. "Straight home, Newie. You feel me?" Then he looks at me and

Annie. "You, too. Straight home." We nod and gladly turn away from him.

When we walk home at the end of the day, we usually cut across the middle school parking lot and out the front gate. Then we meander down through High Garden Cemetery to Dunhill Road. Annie lives in one of the tenements there.

As far as cemeteries go, High Garden is beautiful. It's terraced on a steep incline. Between every row of tombstones are rough brick stairs carved into the hard ground. Everyone calls them the Giant Steps, because most of them are oversized and lumpy. Annie and I have sat on those steps before and talked about some pretty serious things. She's thought of leaving Apple more than once, but I've convinced her to stay. She's talked about Boston and how things must be better out there, and I've reminded her that geography doesn't change problems—it only moves them someplace else. She's even cried in my arms while I've held her and stroked her hair and not asked why.

High Garden is a good place to cry. The sadness seems to soak into the roots of the old trees, helping the gnarled branches let loose their dead until the whole cemetery's covered in leaf litter. All those severed oak and maple leaves are just another reminder that death is all around Apple.

You can never get away from it.

Newie, Annie, and I hop over the low stone fence at the top of the cemetery and begin weaving our way through the gravestones and down the Giant Steps.

"Her name is Claudia Fish," Annie blurts out. It's like her brain has been searching for the dead girl's name since we found her, but up until now, it's been looking for it in the wrong place.

"That's right," says Newie, pointing two fingers at her like a game show host. "I remember now."

"I do, too," I say to them. "Claudia Fish." I also remember what they used to call her. I'm embarrassed and stare at my feet as we walk. "Crawdaddy Fish," I say. "Remember in elementary school? Some of the kids used to call her that."

"Because she had those weird eyes," Annie says softly.

"Not anymore," says Newie.

"That's not funny," Annie snaps. She's right. It's not funny at all.

I reach for Annie's hand, but she pulls away. She's all tense, which is totally understandable—not because of Claudia Fish, but because we're getting close to the bottom of the cemetery. That means the beginning of Dunhill Road, where Annie lives.

Annie doesn't like to go home. Her mother won't be off work until seven, and her father will have been slowly brewing a bender since this morning. If she's lucky, he'll be asleep on the couch. If not, then Annie will shut down and go on autopilot. I don't know what happens to her when she does that. I imagine she goes some place so deep inside herself that she has a hard time finding her way out. At best, she'll hide in her room if she can, until her mom gets off work and comes home. If not, who knows?

I fucking hate Mr. Berg.

Newie's not the brightest, but he can sense the tension building up around us. "Do you want to come to my house for dinner?" he asks her. The hair on the back of my neck bristles. Newie's my boy, but I don't want him alone with my girl. Not a chance. I wish I could bring her home to my house, but I can't. Nobody comes to my house, and nobody ever asks.

Thankfully, Annie shakes her head. "My mom's going to want me home tonight," she says, her eyes turning wet like glass. "As soon as she hears what happened, she's gonna want me home."

We walk a little more in silence.

"I don't have anyone to tell," mumbles Newie. He says it for all of us. I don't have anyone to tell, either. I'd probably be met with a funny look if I did. Or someone might remember Claudia's horrible nickname and say it out loud.

I don't want to hear her name out loud. All it will do is make me remember what I saw—empty eye sockets looking back at me—dark holes where holes shouldn't be.

"Me neither," says Annie. "It's sad."

I reach for her hand again, and this time she lets me take it. Her skin's soft and warm. It's alive. It's not cold and hard and dead like the thing that used to be Claudia Fish.

Crawdaddy Fish.

On Dunhill Road, we all move slowly along the sidewalk, trying to stretch out the amount of time it takes us before we drop Annie off at home. Five houses, four houses, three houses. This is the part of town that most people consider "the other side of the tracks." At one time, Apple was a mill town. There were factories here where they used to make all sorts of things for World War II. We all studied the history of Apple when we were in grade school. I remember writing a report once about the old soap factory. They mixed oils and fats in big cauldrons and combined them with chemicals and lye before pouring the mixture into blocks to cure. Soap was cut, wrapped, and sent overseas to men on the front lines who didn't care about washing, anyway.

They only cared about killing.

Just like home.

The factories died out, but the housing for a lot of the workers was left behind. That's where the Bergs live now—in old factory housing. Some of the attached row-homes surrounding them have been converted into apartments. They now house the Apple residents who don't want, or can't afford, better—the bikers and the tattoo-covered eighteen-year-olds who already have a baby or two on their hips.

Most of the houses have plastic Little Tikes furniture sitting in postage stamp-sized front lawns. It's all throwaway stuff, picked out of sidewalk garbage on trash day or bought on layaway at the Walmart in Worcester. That's the closest city to us—Worcester—and it's still an hour away from Apple.

The funny thing is, there's nothing between us and there. Even though Massachusetts is supposed to be one of the small states, it seems unfathomably large to me. No wonder we have murders in Apple, and no one cares. No one probably knows we're here.

"Home again, home again, jiggity jig," says Newie when we reach Annie's house. She doesn't say anything, but I can see sadness wash over her face. I pull her to me and run my hand through her dyed-red hair. It occurs to me that I like her much better as a blond, but I'm not stupid enough to say anything. She'd be pissed, and she's fine as a redhead, too. She's fine any way I look at her.

I kiss her softly and say, "Are you going to be okay?"

She shrugs. "I'm alive, so I guess I'm okay." She stares at the front stoop of her house, with the crumbling cement stairs and the dirty flowered drapes in the window. There's a lamp on in the living room. She grimaces.

Annie hugs me, punches Newie lightly in the arm, and trudges up to her doorway.

"Remember, you're alive," I call after her, but somehow, I'm not sure if Annie thinks that's a good thing or not. She slides her key into the keyhole and turns the knob.

"Where the hell you get to?" we hear Mr. Berg bellow from inside, as Annie quickly slips through the door and closes it behind her. I can picture him, dirty and drunk, with spittle flying out of his mouth and his hand in his crotch.

Where the hell you been, Annie girl?

In Hell, I think. *That's where we've been. In Hell.*

5

NEWIE AND I WALK in silence the rest of the way to Main Street. I don't want to look at him, because I know he's dying to say something about Mr. Berg. Finally, he can't hold it in any longer.

"Don't you want to fucking pound that guy's head into the ground?" he says.

I spit onto the pitted sidewalk and keep walking. Of course I want to pound him into the ground, but I'm 5'8" and about 140 pounds—s oaking wet. Newie's the walking hulk who hasn't even hit his growth spurt yet.

We both live off Main Street about a half mile down the road. That means we have to walk by every single store and see all the people who are hurrying to finish their errands for the day, so that they can get home and have a locked door between them and autumn.

We pass the police station again and the doughnut place. We pass Francine's Fire House, Zodiac Tattoo Parlor, and Three Penny's. We cross over Carver Street—where Chief Anderson turned down when we took him to see the body of Claudia Fish—and continue walking.

There's a bar there called The Gin Mill, with darkened windows and a bright yellow sign hanging over the doorway. When the sun disappears, the sign will light up and make this part of town look more seedy than it already is. Motorcycles will be parked out front, and big, fat hippies wearing leather vests will descend on the place like flies on dog shit.

There's another bar next to The Gin Mill. It's called Millie's Café. Its name makes it sound like you can get apple pie and a chocolate milkshake there, but don't let that fool you. Millie's is even worse than The Gin Mill. Almost anyone can get in with a fake ID that's marginally realistic. Ziggy Connor sells pills there—mostly Oxy and sometimes other stuff like Valium or Xanax. He also sells pre-rolled joints, too, but he usually wants a boatload for them, and no one wants to pay that kind of cash for skunk weed.

"Yeah," I say.

"Yeah, what?"

"Yeah, I want to pound that fucking guy's head into the ground. He's such a douche."

"No joke," says Newie. "I don't know how Annie does it."

I shrug. I don't know how she does it either, but then again, I'm sure Newie and Annie have had the same conversation about me and my house. I can hear them saying to each other, "I don't know how Jackson does it."

Beats the hell out of me—I just do. Besides, freedom is so close I can taste it. Next year, Annie and I can leave this freaking town. We can say up-yours to Apple and murders and death.

Next year we're eighteen—adults. I don't know what it is about that magic number, but somehow, when you turn eighteen, people don't give a rat's ass what you do anymore. No one cares about another waste-of-space from a low rent town, whose expected life's trajectory includes knocking up his girlfriend, getting a misspelled tattoo on his chest, and applying for unemployment, because that's his best shot at having cash in his pocket.

Not me. I'm getting out of Apple, if I can. Annie, too. We're so gone.

I let that thought swirl around my head as we walk, but it slowly drifts away to the same place dreams go the moment you forget about them when you wake up in the morning.

Sometimes the stories we tell ourselves can seem so real. They seem so real, it's sad.

"Asshole's going to be home late tonight," Newie says about the chief as we stop and look in the window at Nick's Newsstand. Old Nick sells comics there. I'm waiting for the next edition of *Dead A Lot* to come out. It's a zombie serial—kind of dumb—but I like stuff like that when I know it's fake. The last issue, a poodle got eaten, so a whole bunch of animal rights activists from the PTA demanded that Old Nick stop selling *Dead A Lot* in his store, because it sends a bad message to kids.

It was big news in Apple for a day or two—until Ruby died.

I can see from the window that the next edition isn't on the shelves yet. Last month's offense is still facing forward, with its colorful cover montage of dead bodies and carnage. Old Nick's posted a sign next to it that says, *Poodles—you can't eat just one.*

I guess he thinks that's funny. It sort of is.

"Wanna go in?" asks Newie.

"Nah," I say, even though I know he's only stalling because he doesn't want to go home at all—not after what happened today.

"What about Mary Jane?" I ask him. Mary Jane is Chief Anderson's girlfriend. It's sort of a big deal in town that he's dating her, because she dances at the Magic Lantern out on Boston Road. That—and she's a smoking-hot twenty-five-year-old.

Life's cruel to Newie that way. How is it fair that his dad is banging a *Penthouse* babe in the next bedroom over, while Newie's lying in bed with his dick in his hand? It's like he lives in a weird corner of Purgatory reserved for horny teens with blue balls, and the Devil is Chief Anderson.

"She's working," he mutters.

"She's working something," I joke. "Besides, you heard what your dad said." I point my finger up into Newie's dark, brooding face. "Straight home, Newie. You feel me?"

"Shut the hell up," he says, as he slaps my finger away and grabs me in a headlock. My backpack falls to the ground, and we wrestle there on the sidewalk for a minute, like it's any season other than autumn, and there isn't a foreboding sense of dread that's permeating everything around us.

"I can take you, ass-wipe," I squeal as he practically lifts me upside down to deposit me flat on my head on the cold concrete.

"Who you calling ass-wipe, ass-wipe," he laughs. Then we're both laughing, until the door of Nick's Newsstand opens and Old Nick, looking older than death, limps outside to yell at Newie.

"You let him go, Newton Anderson. You let him go right now, or I'll tell your father."

Newie, still laughing, deposits me back on my feet and brushes off my shirt as if he's soiled it in some way.

"Aw, Nick," I say. "I was beating the crap out of him."

"You can both beat the crap out of each other for all I care," says Old Nick, as the wrinkles on his forehead crease down deep into his mottled skin. "Just do it someplace else. I know your parents, too, Jackson Gill. Don't think I don't."

I scoop up my backpack and punch Newie in the arm. Old Nick hobbles back into the Newsstand, and we continue to head toward home.

"I'd come over if I could," I tell him, as our footsteps fall in line again.

"I'm fine," he says, but he doesn't sound very convincing. "I hate it when shit like this happens. Asshole's going to be out until late, and when he comes home, he's going to have all the pictures that were taken at the crime scene, and you know what he's going to do?"

"No," I say, but I do know. He does it every time.

"He's going to spread them all over the kitchen table and stare at them for hours. Before I go to bed tonight, he's going to call me downstairs and ask me to look at them to see what I think. How the fuck am I supposed to know? I'm not a cop."

"Well, isn't that what you're going to be?"

"I don't know," he shrugs. "What if I want to do something else? What if I want to go into the army or go to culinary school or be a paramedic?"

"Culinary school?" I snort.

"You know what I mean."

I throw my hands up in the air. "Hey, by all means. Feel free to have a heart to heart with the chief and tell him that you don't want to follow in his footsteps. Great idea. Then we'll have four murders in town instead of three."

Newie kicks at the ground as we walk. "You're not helping."

Across the street, a little boy, all alone, peddles his bike the other way. "Hey," I yell out to the kid. "Go home. Somebody else was just killed."

I want to tell him to lock his bike up in his parents' garage, go into his house, shut his bedroom door, and hide underneath his bed. At least it's safe there.

The kid flips us the bird and keeps going. Great—another white-trash, Apple victim-in-the-making.

I turn to say something snarky to Newie about the kid, but it turns out I don't have to. I can tell he's thinking roughly the same thing as me. His eyes look sad and a little scared. I don't blame him one bit.

"I'd have you over to my place . . ." I start, but then trail off.

"I don't think so," says Newie. "No offense, but I'm already freaked enough."

"None taken," I say, mostly because I don't have anything I *can* say. You can pick your friends, but you can't pick your family.

If you could, I certainly drew the short straw.

6

NEWIE AND I LIVE on Vanguard Lane. My parents have an old two-family that my great grandparents built a million years ago. We're on the first floor, and my grandfather lives upstairs. There are two staircases that lead to the second floor—one in the living room and one in the back of the house, behind the kitchen. The doors upstairs are usually open, in case my grandfather needs us. It's easier that way, because he hasn't been doing so hot for the past few years—ever since my grandmother was—ever since my grandmother died.

The Andersons live diagonally across the street from us in an old Victorian that the chief bought when Newie and I were little.

When they moved in, we became fast friends, mostly because we were the only boys our age on the street. Vanguard Lane is short. There are only about twenty houses before the dead end, some woods, and the railroad tracks. Newie and I used to go back there and put pennies on the rails and collect them the next day. They would be flattened by the trains that go whizzing by like clockwork. President Lincoln's head would be gone—smoothed out by tons of metal.

Newie's mother got sick and died before he had a chance to remember her. She had that thing that people name in whispers when they talk about it—cancer—as it barely leaves their lips in conversation—*cancer—cancer*.

Apple has a cancer.

We don't talk about that either.

As we walk down the sidewalk, Newie hikes his backpack over one shoulder and straightens his back. I can't imagine what it must be like to come home every day to an empty home. I can't image what it's like to come home to peace and quiet. Sometimes I wish that it was like that at my house. I would bask in the silence. I would walk around naked. I'd fart when I want to—but I can't do any of those things at my house.

It's a different sort of place.

"You okay?" I ask Newie as I begin to cross the street to our two-family. The trees tower over us like giants and their multi-colored dandruff washes down on the sidewalk. Fall is such a funny time of year. It makes death so pretty.

He doesn't answer me, so I turn and look at him and realize that Newie looks like a man, not a boy. He's going to go home and pull something frozen out of the freezer. It's either leftover Chinese food, or worse, something Mary Jane concocted.

I know that Newie should be happy that his dad's found someone. It's just that he doesn't want another mother right now, especially one that looks like Mary Jane. I think it would be worse if Mary Jane officially lived with them, so it's a good thing she doesn't. Still, Newie has to put up with her when she's around. He has to eat her food, which he says tastes like something bad made in Life Skills.

Life Skills is for the stupid kids—the ones who drop out senior year and can't even find work in garages or on street crews. They end up living in Annie's neighborhood and breeding more mental giants just like them. That's where Mary Jane's from. She's a Life Skills dropout with big tits and a killer ass, who grew up in the tenements below High Garden.

I doubt Chief Anderson and Mary Jane have the kind of relationship where they do a lot of deep talking. I think he just uses her—and she likes it.

"I'm cool," Newie says. "I'll catch up with you later."

I watch him go. Part of me wants to follow him right up his front walk, climb the stairs, and go directly in his front door. It would be better than going home to my house. Almost anything would be better than going home to my house, but I begrudgingly turn and face the old two-family.

My parents have tried to spruce it up a little, but old is old. There's fairly new white vinyl siding on it that was put on about three years ago. They've updated the windows and added a new front door, with a fancy glass cutout and a gold crucifix sandwiched between the panes.

Still, beneath it all, it's an old two-family house in the very core of Apple, Massachusetts.

I trudge across the street, my mind rehashing the last few hours and wondering how they could have played out differently. Newie didn't have football practice this afternoon. Coach Nickerson was out today, so Newie blew off laps around the track so we could hang. If he hadn't been around, Annie and I might have found a quiet corner some place in school to fool around for a while. We do that a lot. I'd like to think it's because she's really into me, but sometimes I think it's because Annie doesn't like to go home.

We might have even walked down to the reservoir and found some place really quiet where we could do whatever we wanted. I know it's not smart to go off by ourselves in the fall, but it's really beautiful this time of year, when it isn't too cold, but the leaves have started to change color.

On days when the sky is robin's-egg blue and the wind isn't blowing, the surface of the reservoir looks like a mirror with a double set of multi-colored trees lining the shores—one that stretches toward the sky and one, upside down, that reaches into the depths.

Annie likes it by the reservoir. It's away from town and Dunhill Road and everything else. When we're there, sometimes we talk about where we're going to go next year when there's no place for us *to* go. High school will be over. The invisible shackles that chain us to Apple will be gone.

I suppose it's funny how we never talk in terms of us going someplace together, but we talk about our dreams just the same. Annie says she wants to go to Boston. I want to travel. I want to get out of this town and out of Massachusetts. I want to see what else is out there, like that mountain with all the presidents' faces carved on it or the Grand Canyon or maybe the Crystal Caves in Pennsylvania.

I have a cousin who lives down there whom I talk to online every once in a while. She says that the Crystal Caves are caverns that seem to go on forever. She says you can get lost in them, and it makes me wonder what it would be like to be lost in the cold, hard earth surrounded by nothing but darkness.

That's what's going to happen to Claudia Fish. She's going to be lost in the cold, hard earth forever, and she's going to be surrounded by nothing but inky blackness for comfort.

I take a deep breath as I reach the other side of the street and open the gate to my front yard. Without Newie to distract me, my mind doubles back and lands squarely on an image of the dead body we found. Behind my eyes, I see her deep, empty sockets boring into me, accusing me of never noticing her. Bile begins to rise in my throat, but I can't tell if it's because of the memory of her dead body or because I have to walk inside my house.

Finding Claudia Fish is one kind of horror. Walking into my house is another.

I sigh and hop up the short flight of steps to the front porch. My mother has a rusted, old antique crib filled with dead potted plants sitting up against the left-hand railing. There was a time when bright red and orange flowers were crammed into the crib this time of year. My mother would count her pennies and save all summer to buy fall mums. My father would yell at her for spending the cash, though they were only something like three for ten dollars at Bilton's Farm Stand at the edge of town.

Mom loved the way they looked. I remember she used to buy funny-looking gourds, too, and a few medium-sized pumpkins. For a split second, I imagine what it would be like to carve a jack-o'-lantern again, but it only makes me think of the person who carved great, gaping holes where Claudia's eyeballs used to be.

I'm not going to sleep much tonight. Empty faces are going to dance around my mind. They're going to stare at me with dark, hollow sockets and blame me for murders that I have no way of stopping.

I pull my key out of my front pocket and reach for the screen door. We never keep our door unlocked. In a place like Apple no one keeps their doors unlocked—not even the rest of the year, when the only thing bad that happens is that someone gets hauled in for drunk driving or beating on his wife and kids. The key slides into the lock, and I turn it as quietly as I can, but it doesn't matter.

The screaming starts as soon as the tumbler clicks.

7

IGNORING THE INCESSANT, never-ending noise is like ignoring a dead body in the woods. You want to make believe it's not there, but you can't. You want not to listen, but something compels you to—no matter how horrible what you hear may be. It slices through you like millions of tiny razors, leaving you in tattered ribbons, but still intact.

I drop my backpack at the door and hang my jacket on the coat rack that my father made out of an old post and some rusted hooks he found at the Haddonville Flea Market. My dad's handy like that. He likes to make things—like a carpenter.

He used to have a workshop in the basement, but he doesn't work down there anymore. He has a workshop out in the garage, and he spends all of his free time there. It's his sanctuary. No one goes in there but him.

For a while now, my father's been making crucifixes. I suppose there's something comforting to him in making them. He uses all different types of wood—some hard and some soft. He even gets lucky sometimes and scores pieces of spalted maple or scrap ebony.

His crucifixes are all over the house. They cover the free spaces on the walls, hanging between pictures and hiding the dingy patterned wallpaper.

I've lost count of how many crucifixes we have. They seem to multiply like mice. If you've seen one, then you know there are ten—if you've seen ten, you know there are a hundred. That's what the crucifixes are to me—vermin infesting the house.

I hear cackling from beneath my feet, then another scream. I just close my eyes, tilt my head from left to right, and pop the tight vertebrae in my neck. I take a deep breath and walk through the living room into the kitchen.

My mother's there. She's sitting and smoking a cigarette, although she's promised everyone that she's going to quit them all together. Her promises are only words. I know that now, so I don't blame her for lying. Her dark hair is tangled and matted and in desperate need of a brush. The bags under her eyes are terrible and bloated. She's wearing a pair of sweats and one of my dad's old T-shirts. I'm sure she hasn't taken a shower today. Instead, she's spent hours listening to the cacophony of sound as it assaults her ears, probably grinding her teeth without knowing that she's doing it.

"Hi, Mom," I say as I kiss her head, then go to the refrigerator and grab a carton of milk. I make sure to turn it around in my hands so I can check the date. I always have to check the date on the groceries in the refrigerator. Things go bad here.

Things have been going bad here for a while.

My mom doesn't say anything to me. She sucks on her cigarette again and stares into the air as if it's a tangible thing. The date on the milk is expired. I pinch open the top and smell it. The all-too-familiar stench of something sour fills my nose, so I pour it down the sink then go back to the refrigerator again and look for something else to drink. There aren't many choices, so I pull out a bottle of soda and pour myself a glass. I sip at it, knowing that the fizz is long gone, but that's okay. I'll sip it slowly. It will give me time to prepare myself.

My mother's cigarette is burning between her fingers. The ash at the end is about as long as the eraser on a pencil. I pull out one of the green vinyl kitchen chairs and sit down next to her. The kitchen set is old, like everything else in the house. There are small rips in the vinyl, and little tufts of dirty white stuffing bleed out of the gashes.

My mother doesn't move. She continues to stare at nothing. I hate when she gets like this. My grandfather's going to want his dinner soon, and my dad isn't home from work yet, so I pull the cigarette out from between her fingers and drop it in a juice glass that's sitting on the table. She's been using it as an ash tray.

Taking her cigarette away seems to wake her up a little.

"How was school?" she whispers in the hoarse voice of someone who hasn't used their mouth to speak for the whole day. She swallows and clears her throat. "How was school?" she asks again.

I don't want to tell her about Claudia Fish—not when she's like this. I smile and say, "It was good. I like school."

Another scream, prolonged and painful, cuts through the house, but my mother doesn't blink. She brings her fingers to her mouth again, as if the cigarette is still between them. After a moment, she realizes that it's not there and puts her hands down on her lap instead.

"What time is it?" she asks me.

I look at the clock over the range. The oven is fairly new, so the display is digital. The glowing green numbers look out of place in our kitchen with its stained walls and old deep double sink filled with dishes.

"A little after five," I say. She nods and licks her lips. They're so chapped and dry. "We're going to have tuna noodle casserole for dinner. Is that okay?"

I have a little repertoire of things I know how to make when my mom gets like this, which seems to be always. It's easy, and my dad won't get angry when he gets home and finds that my mother's been sitting here doing nothing, and there's no dinner on the table. Besides, my grandfather needs his dinner, too. My grandfather and Becky.

Becky.

Becky is my sister—sometimes. Today she's Not-Becky—a shrieking, wailing thing in the basement, screaming incoherent obscenities between bouts of almost lucid, maniacal banter.

Becky used to be my sister all the time. She used to have long red hair and bright blue eyes that sparkled when she laughed. Her cheeks used to be ruddy and covered with freckles. She used to be fun, and I wanted to be around her all the time.

She used to be my big sister, but today Becky's not my sister at all. Today she's something else.

I take another sip of the flat soda before getting up and walking into the pantry. I pull a pot out from one of the cupboards while scanning the shelf for a box of macaroni and the three cans that have become all-too-familiar to me—peas, tuna, and cream of mushroom soup. It's amazing what you can do with cream of mushroom soup. It's amazing how that little can of processed goop can help you masquerade as your mother so your father doesn't need to acknowledge how bad things really are.

It's amazing that he knows anyway, but won't, or can't do anything about it.

In minutes, I have the water boiling on the stove and the three cans mixed together into a sloppy mess so I can add it to the macaroni and pop it all into the oven.

More wailing comes, and my mother shifts her eyes to the basement door.

"Mom?" I say to her. "Why don't you go take a shower and get dressed?"

She slowly pivots her head and stares at me with red-rimmed eyes that are all but uncomprehending. I sigh, open the cabinet above the sink, and reach for the little orange bottle with the white top that says

"Jolly's Pharmacy" on it. I twist the cap until it snaps open, shake out two capsules, and hand them to her along with my glass of flat soda.

Slowly, very slowly, my mother peels them off of my palm and puts them on her tongue. She takes a long swallow of the sugary water without any fizz and forces them down.

"I suppose you're right," she says.

"Good. Dinner will be ready soon," I tell her. "It smells really good. You must have been cooking all day."

Laughter, like crazy wildfire, runs up the stairs and floods the kitchen, so I close my eyes and wait for it to stop.

I help my mother to her feet and gently turn her toward the hallway. She shuffles forward into the darkness, and I walk behind her, making sure to flip the hall light on so she can see where she's going.

"You're such a good boy, Jackson," my mother whispers softly as I guide her down the hallway. When she gets to the door to her bedroom, she stops, her thin fingers holding the doorframe so she won't fall over right on the spot. "I'll be okay," she says to me. "I'll be okay." That's another lie, like the one about the cigarettes. How many lies can someone tell before the difference between what's true and what's not becomes blurred?

She steps into the darkness of her bedroom, which always has a vague odor of my father and dirty clothing. I'll have to strip their bed tonight and maybe do a wash. I can probably get to that between dinner and homework, although homework is rapidly falling down my list of priorities. It's disappearing into the abyss of my youth. Every time I skip an assignment or forget to hand in something, a little bit of my future gets erased.

All I can see in front of me is Apple, and it makes me sick.

With my mother safely in her room, hopefully getting into the shower instead of under the sheets in her unmade bed, I jog back down the hallway, through the kitchen, and up the back staircase. I take the steps two at a time, ignoring the piles of newspapers climbing the treads.

"It's a fire hazard," my dad used to tell my grandfather.

"Then don't light a match," my grandfather would say back, but my grandfather doesn't say much anymore. He's locked in a prison inside his head, much the same way as my mother, but I have to believe that my mother still has a chance for a "Get-Out-Of-Jail-Free card."

I think my grandfather's done playing that game. Most eighty-five-year-olds are probably done playing any kind of games.

At the top of the stairs, I rap once at the open door and call out into the gloom. "Old man? You hiding on me? I can hear your dentures chattering from here."

I listen for the squeak of his wheelchair and pinpoint him in the living room. My grandfather's sitting there with the remote control in his hand and static on the television.

"It's a piece of crap," he mutters as I walk in.

"You want me to try?"

"What good are you?" he grumbles. "You're useless."

I have to bury his words as quickly as they dance off his tongue. Every once in a while, bad things come out of his mouth, but he almost always forgets as soon as he says them.

"Hey, buddy-boy," he chirps when he looks up and realizes that it's me. "Can you help me get this contraption to work?" I walk over and pick up a second remote that's on the coffee table and change it to channel three. Immediately, a picture springs to life, and my grandfather's happy again.

"How did you do that?"

It's useless to try and explain a remote control to him. His ability to understand technology died a long time ago. "Magic," I say. "It's all in the wrist."

"Humpf," he snorts. "Maybe you got the Devil in you, after all." He stares down at the larger remote in his hand. I can tell that there are too many numbers and symbols on it for him. No amount of teaching is ever going to help him get it right. He's too far gone to get things right anymore. He's just a shell in a wheelchair, living out the remainder of his days in his empty rooms, probably wondering where my grandmother has gotten to.

"Dinner will be soon," I say to him. "You hungry?"

"I can eat."

"Okay then. I'll be back soon with a plate."

As I turn to leave, he says, "Jackson?" His brow furrows like he is trying to remember something. "Where's your grandmother?"

My throat tightens, and my heart becomes hard in my chest.

"She not here," I tell him, trying not to look at the picture on the wall of the woman who has Becky's eyes. One of my father's crucifixes hangs above it.

By the time I leave, my grandfather's probably forgotten he's even asked.

8

I GO BACK DOWN the stairs, past the piles of moldy newspapers, sure that amongst the fading, yellowed newsprint are stories of the dead—like Ruby or Ralphie Delessio. In the kitchen, I check on the macaroni to see if it's soft yet, which it is, so I pull the strainer from the pantry and drop it into the sink on top of the dirty dishes. Then I strain the water out and plop the mixture of soup and tuna and peas into it.

As an added treat, I pull a can of processed grated cheese out of the refrigerator and dump a third of it into the pot, stirring the goop until everything is coated in white. I spread the mixture into a casserole dish and put it in the oven to get brown and bubbly.

After I wash the dishes in the sink—the ones that I created and the old ones that have been sitting there since this morning—I dry them with a ratty old dishtowel that used to be decorated with orange flowers and yellow daffodils. The pattern is now all but invisible on the faded cloth.

I do everything possible to avoid my sister, but she's started to scream again, and I have to go and see her. If I don't, she'll never stop.

Finally, I gulp down the last of my flat soda, wash the glass, and put it back in the cupboard. Then I take a deep breath and do what has to be done. I go to the basement door and swing it open.

Whoops and squeals come from the dankness below, but, as I slowly descend the wooden staircase, they change to a sinister laugh. It smells wet and foul in the basement, and I try to remember if it always smelled like that or only since everything started with her.

At the bottom of the stairs the laughter abruptly stops, and I hear Not-Becky begin to chant.

> *"Momma had a baby that I killed when it cried.*
> *Momma had a baby so I sliced its neck wide.*
> *Momma had a baby who I stabbed with my knife.*
> *Momma had a baby who must pay with its life."*

Not-Becky goes on and on like that, but I'm not scared. I'm used to it by now. I'm used to the madness and the incessant, never-ending taunts. I'm used to the thing that's no longer my sister.

The basement is dirty and old like everything else. It seems like a room that is waiting to move on. There are wooden pallets with boxes on them, filled with things that no one wants anymore, but are afraid to get rid of. A single light bulb burns in the middle of the room, hanging from one of the exposed ceiling joists. Straight ahead of me are the washing machine and the dryer. There are clothes on the floor in a pile of mixed colors. That's my fault. I got as far as bringing the laundry downstairs late last night. I haven't separated it yet, and I haven't started a wash.

In our house, laundry magically gets done. It's too bad that I'm the one providing the magic.

"Stab it, slice it, scoop it out," Not-Becky laughs from behind the door at the far left of the basement. There's a window in it with heavy bars that break the small opening into a vertical mosaic. Underneath the window are the locks—three of them in all. One is a chain, another is a dead bolt, and the third is meant for the key which hangs on a nail, sticking out of the railing at the bottom of the stairs.

My hands curl around the toothy piece of metal, and I palm it carefully in my fist.

"Becky, it's Jackson," I say to the door.

"I know who you are," it hisses back—Not-Becky—the one who stole my sister from me. I take a deep breath, walk across the basement, and stand in front of the door. Light pours through the barred window, and I can see most of the room from where I'm standing. It's painted pink, with nice white furniture and a rocking chair in one corner. Becky's teddy bear, Rusty, is sitting on the cushioned seat, wearing a little red cap that's sewn to his head. My sister's had Rusty since she was a little girl. I feel sorry for him and his beady glass eyes. If they could show absolute, abject terror, they would.

On her bed lie a lacy quilt and about a dozen different-sized pillows. Becky made them after taking a sewing class in eighth grade. She became obsessed, for a time, with pillows, and that year, everyone got one as a gift from her. I have a Patriots pillow up in my room that she sewed for me. My father put some chicken-shaped ones in the farmer's co-operative where he works in Haddonfield. He manages the warehouse there and sometimes handles the ordering—mostly grain and stuff. That's why he was able to put Becky's pillows in the store. He's kind of in charge of what goes on the shelves. I remember when her first chicken pillow was sold, and he handed her ten dollars over dinner that night. Her eyes sparkled with happiness.

I miss that Becky—the one with the happy eyes.

As I peer through the bars, I see the dog chain attached to a thick metal ring that's bolted to the wall behind her bed. The chain trails over the headboard, across the lacy coverlet, and off the side of the mattress. It snakes across the carpet toward the door.

"Where are you?" I say through a mouthful of cotton. I hate Not-Becky for making me scared.

"Where are you?" the thing that's not my sister mocks me with a voice that sounds like it's buried in gravel. It's deep and guttural and slimy.

Not-Becky is right below the window, huddled against the door, waiting for me to come—waiting for its chance to scare me because it knows it can.

Tonight I'm not in the mood.

I hold my head back as I undo the chain and twist the dead bolt until I hear it click. It's become deathly quiet on the other side of the door. Not-Becky must be holding its breath in anticipation. It's waiting for me to play the game—for me to slide the key into the tumbler, turn the lock, and twist the knob so it can come charging out at me, only to get yanked back inside by the chains around its manacled wrists.

This is the jewelry it's worn since my sister failed to graduate Apple High two years ago—two long years ago.

Still, I slide the key into the tumbler, turn the lock, twist the knob, and open the door, because that's what brothers do for their sick, sick sisters.

Thankfully, it's Becky sitting there after all, cross-legged on the plush burgundy carpet that my dad bought from the carpet outlet in Three Rivers and meticulously cut and installed with care—to make an exact duplicate of her room upstairs.

Her red hair sprouts out of her head in sparse clumps. The rest of her scalp is bare and scabbed over. She looks like an old doll that's lost the little knotted horsehair strands used to craft its silky locks. Today, Becky's drawn big circles around her eyes with a makeup pencil in broad, black strokes. My sister's skin is pale white—so white that it's almost blue, but that can't be helped. Becky hasn't felt the sun on her face in forever. I feel as though I'm looking at a dead thing instead of my sister.

"How was school?" Becky asks, like she truly is my big sister and not some sort of monster we hide away in the bowels of our house.

"Good," I say as I walk past her into the room with an almost audible sigh of relief, because when my sister is Not-Becky, it can be dangerous. It can scratch and bite. It can say awful things.

Becky's bathroom light is on, and I notice that her makeup kit is out, and the light around her small, round mirror is on.

"Good good or just good?" she asks. My sister always asks me the same questions. She knows that I hate chemistry and that I'm having a hard time in math. When Becky was in school, she was in all the advanced placement classes. She knows that she can help me with my homework if I ask, and I guess that makes her feel good.

"Good good," I say and plop down on her bed. Becky stands, and her chains fall to the floor. She softly pads across the carpet, her long toenails curling into the sea of burgundy, and sits down next to me, one leg folded under the other.

I don't want to look at her, so I stare at my feet. My sneakers have been getting tight, and I'm going to have to get a new pair soon. I'd ask Newie if he has any hand-me-downs, but he hasn't worn my size since the seventh grade.

"I was bad today, wasn't I?" Becky asks. She won't look at my face, either.

"Yeah," I say to her. There's no reason to lie. "Mom's upset."

"I'm sorry," she says.

Becky reaches up and pulls at the tatters of her scalp. "I wish she'd come and brush my hair. I used to like it when she brushed my hair."

I don't know what to say, so I change the subject. "We're having tuna noodle casserole for dinner. Is that okay?"

"Sure," she says. "That's fine." She unfolds her leg, gets up, and walks across the room. Her back is to me, and I can't help noticing how thin she's gotten. Part of it's her medication. I know it makes her not want to eat—but part of her deterioration is the thing inside of her that's wearing her skin like a costume.

Two years. It's been two long years since Not-Becky came to roost inside my sister's head like a rabid bat. It's been two years since my life took an unexpected turn to the left, and my older sister went mad. Sometimes I fantasize about something horrible happening to Becky, like what happened to Ruby or Ralphie. I'm not sure if that would fix everything that's wrong with my family, but it would be a start.

As I begin to spiral into the toilet bowl of my own sick thoughts, I almost miss Becky's shoulders slump. I almost miss her head droop down and forward.

Immediately, I'm off the bed and bolting for the door, the key in my hand.

"Of course," Not-Becky chortles, its scratchy, grating voice returning to invade my sister's mouth. A sinister tone colors its speech. "We could have Crawdaddy Fish instead."

Crawdaddy Fish. What the fuck? How does she . . . ?

I'm up the stairs and out of the basement before its crazed laughter has a chance to grab hold of my heels.

9

IT'S AFTER SEVEN before my father comes home. I hear the rumbling of his car, with the Jesus-fish sticker on the bumper, pull into the driveway. He needs a new muffler but is avoiding getting one. There are so many other things we need that a new muffler has fallen close to the bottom of his list.

Now, the list is filled with things like medication for Mom, Becky, and my grandfather, oil for heat, electricity, and gas to go back and forth to work.

Food is on the list, too. It's way above where a new muffler sits.

My father bought the car from a huge fat guy named Mr. Howard, who used to squeeze himself into one of the back pews at church. He carried a handkerchief with him and constantly mopped the sweat off his forehead. People avoided him on Sunday mornings because he sort of smelled. I know that's an un-Christian thing to do, but people do a lot of un-Christian things, then think that praying their sins away will erase away what they've done.

I've already brought a plate of dinner up to my grandfather and put it on a TV tray in front of his television. He doesn't say anything to me when I bring it to him, but a confused look comes over his face, because I think he's still expecting my grandmother instead of me. I tuck a napkin into his shirt and kiss the top of his bald head before going back downstairs.

My sister's finally stopped screaming. I mashed the contents of her medicine capsules into a plate of food about thirty minutes ago and brought it down to her. She doesn't get a fork or knife with dinner—only a spoon. As I held the tuna-noodle goop and peered through the barred windows on her door, Not-Becky was still there, glaring at me from the bed. I performed the ritual of the locks, opened the door, and slid the plate of food inside before quickly locking up again.

I heard the quiet clinking of chains, so I knew it retrieved the plate. The fact that my sister's finally quiet means she's doped up. Hopefully it'll work and keep her calm for the night. It usually does, but not always.

As I rearrange the plates and silverware on the dinner table, like my mother always did, my dad comes in the back door, his face pale.

"Jackson," he says, almost in a whisper, and motions for me to come out onto the back porch.

I glance down once more, to make sure that everything's set properly for dinner, before following him into the night.

"Hi," I say. That's an epic monologue for me. We don't talk much. We used to talk more, but lately, there doesn't seem to be anything left worth sharing.

My father rubs the stubble on his face. "Chief Anderson called me," he says. "He told me what happened."

"Oh," I say. I'm not sure if that's a good thing or a bad thing.

"Does your mother know?"

I shake my head no. "Becky's been screaming." Our unspoken conversation is filled with subtext. No, I didn't tell my mother about Claudia Fish. I didn't want to upset her. She already has too much on her plate. Eventually everyone has a breaking point.

My father licks his lips. "Becky?" he whispers.

I know what he means, so I shake my head again. "Not-Becky."

It's funny how we talk about the other one as "Not-Becky." I suppose that makes my sister's illness easier to understand.

Becky was always different, but she managed to hide most of the differences for years. I remember her coming into my bedroom when we were little and talking in a strange voice.

"My name is Suzie Zickle," she would say. "I like to play games." I used to love playing with Suzie Zickle, until she would abruptly stop, mid-checkers or crazy eights, and say something like, "Why are you in my room?" even though we were in mine, then storm out like I had done something wrong.

Other times, she would spend hours up in my grandparents' apartment, then come downstairs and read the Bible like an obsessive nun, rocking back and forth, her lips mouthing every word.

When the shit really hit the fan two years ago—when Not-Becky appeared—a doctor in Boston diagnosed my sister with that disease that used to be called multiple personality disorder but now has a fancy new name—dissociative identity disorder—DID.

My mother and father probably nodded their heads like they always did and stared at their hands in their laps, instead of at the doctor.

When they came home from Boston, they got on their knees and prayed, right there in our living room. They made me pray, too, although

I'm not sure that what I was doing could be called praying. When we finished, my father got his tools and started building my sister a duplicate bedroom in the basement.

My parents don't think that Becky has dissociative identity disorder at all. They think that she has something else—something evil.

They think she's possessed.

That's all a bunch of horseshit to me. Becky's nuts—plain and simple. Her disease is something in our genes—nothing more—or at least, that's what I believe.

The alternative is too messed up and sideways. That's someone else's life in a Stephen King movie, not mine.

"Where's your mother now?" my father asks.

"Inside," I say. I'm not sure why he's asking. Where else would she be?

"Okay," he says. "Good." He leans against the porch railing, pulls out a cigarette, and lights it. The pack, one of the cheap, new ones that isn't a name brand, gleams in the light of the porch bulb. He sees me staring at it and offers me one. I shake my head. I don't want to tell him that smoking a cigarette would take me one step closer to being just like him. He shrugs, puts the cigarettes back in his pocket, then breathes sweet, acrid smoke into his lungs as he stares at the rough floor boards.

Finally, I turn to head back inside. "Dinner's ready," I say as I pull open the door.

"Jackson?" my dad croaks, as I'm about to close the screen. I turn and look at him. "You fine with everything?"

I don't know how to answer him. I'm not sure what he's even asking. Am I fine that my mother's almost catatonic? Am I fine that I have to take care of the demented old man upstairs? Maybe he means about Becky. Am I fine with the responsibility of having a psycho for a sister? Am I fine with mashing her drugs into her food like an orderly on a mental ward?

"What do you mean?" I ask him. My voice is coated with something sticky—maybe anger or sarcasm. Maybe indifference.

He shifts his feet and takes another drag on his cigarette. "About the body in the woods—you okay with all that? The chief told me it was pretty bad." He spits off the porch and shrugs, as if to say there are worse things in the world.

I look at him for a moment, a sad middle-aged man living a sad middle-aged life. "Oh, that," I say in all seriousness. "I almost forgot."

10

THANKFULLY, MY mother is dressed for dinner—nothing too fancy, just a pair of jeans and a light fall sweater. She's even put a little bit of makeup on. It's all part of the fantasy that there's nothing wrong with our lives, but that's okay. Whatever works is better than something that doesn't work at all.

While my mother pulls the casserole out of the oven, I walk quietly down the hall into my parents' musky bedroom, strip their bed, and throw everything into a laundry basket. I fold their blanket at the foot of the mattress, walk back down the hall, open the basement door, and softly tiptoe down the stairs.

I leave the basket on the bottom step, not even bothering to chance a glance at Becky's door. Sometimes Not-Becky is there, holding onto the bars with its thin fingers and staring at me like it wants nothing more than to make me hurt. Other times, it's only Becky, and she wants a book or something from up in her bedroom, because this room isn't her bedroom, at all. It's a doppelganger. It's a copy that looks like the real thing but isn't. Just like Not-Becky isn't my sister. It looks like her, but it's only a cheap imitation.

Back upstairs, my father's still hiding on the back porch, finishing his second cigarette. I've never asked my parents why they don't smoke in front of each other. My mother will only light a cigarette when my father's at work, and only when she slides into darkness. My father favors the back porch. It's outside of the house, which he prefers. His ritual is to smoke at least two cigarettes after he pulls into the driveway, but before he comes inside.

Maybe he does it to wind down from the day. Personally, I think he does it to mentally prepare himself for what he has to walk into.

Like I said, I don't smoke cigarettes, so I don't know.

When he finally comes in, my mother has a smile plastered on her face. It's as though she's pulled it out from a cupboard and pinned it to her skin. My father kisses her on the cheek—a fake and automatic gesture that makes me wonder why he does it at all—then walks into the living room to hang his light jacket on the coat rack he made.

"What's for dinner?" He doesn't look at me when he asks. He looks directly at my mother.

"Tuna noodle casserole," she says. "With extra parmesan."

"Great," says my father, as though he's reciting lines in a play where the actors all suck on stage, and every word they utter is stilted and boring. My mother puts the casserole on the table, but I can't help noticing the two hunks I scooped out of it for my grandfather and the thing in the basement.

Our dinner's not whole anymore, like our family—like Claudia Fish.

How does Becky know about Claudia Fish?

I close my eyes and bite down hard on the inside of my lip. We clasp our hands together, and my father says, "Before we eat, we turn our attention to the bountiful harvest before us." I hope I draw blood. I want to taste copper and salt. I want to feel alive. "We are truly thankful for this meal and for the richness of our lives. May this food nourish the bodies of all who partake in this meal." I press my teeth down harder, until I feel my eyes burn from the pain. Somehow, I feel like I can't stop until my father finishes talking. I have to endure the pain until he shuts up for good. "Finally, dear Lord, please nourish our spirits."

It's over. I relax my teeth and rub my tongue along the inside of my mouth, tasting for blood, but there isn't any. We all say, "Amen," and pull our hands away from each other and back into our own private Hells.

I've noticed that my father has changed the prayer that he usually recites. I've heard it all my life. He's supposed to ask that this food nourish all those that we love instead of just all those who partake in this meal. Maybe he forgot, or maybe what Chief Anderson told him has shaken him, and his mind is preoccupied in thought.

I don't say anything, and my mother doesn't seem to notice.

A thought scurries through my head. It leaves a residue that hints to the unspeakable idea that maybe my father doesn't love us anymore, but I brush it away and quickly forget it was ever there.

As we eat, my mother takes her food in delicate bird bites. My father wolfs his down and scoops a second helping onto his plate before I've made a dent in my first.

As he shovels forkfuls in his mouth with a vengeance, I tentatively break the silence. "I have to do my laundry tonight, and Mom's been washing and folding all day," I say. "I'll finish up for her. I'll have your sheets ready before nine, if that's okay?"

He tilts his head to the right, to let my words funnel down into his ear, before quickly nodding and continuing to eat. When he's done, he gets up and puts his plate in the sink. "I'm working out in the garage tonight," he mumbles.

"What are you working on?" my mother whispers, without lifting her eyes. She asks the same question every night.

"The Lord's work," my father answers. "I won't be in until late."

"Okay, dear," my mother says, as she takes another little bite of tuna, peas, and macaroni.

My father walks out the back door, reaching in his pocket for his cigarettes as he goes. As I push mush around my plate, I realize that this is a good night. There isn't any craziness coming from the basement, probably because Becky is flying high on whatever I mashed into her food.

My mother's medication doesn't seem to have kicked in. She's only a shadow of herself. My dad is no different than always. Sometimes I think he hates us, but I know that's not true. I think he's damaged inside, so he hides in the garage every night to tinker on himself with rusty tools and prayer.

He'll never get it right, though. Some things are just too damaged to be fixed. No matter how normal they appear on the surface, they'll always be broken underneath. I think my dad is like that.

He's broken underneath.

I clear the table after dinner and wash the dishes. My mother sits on her green vinyl chair, staring at nothing. When I remove her half-eaten plate, she suddenly brushes my arm and catches me with glassy eyes. "You're such a good boy, Jackson," she says for the second time since I got home. I stop and search her face to see if there's anything in there that's still my mother. Her hand falls away, and her eyes go dim.

Nope. Not a damn thing.

11

"IS THE CHIEF home yet?" I ask Newie, as I separate clothing in the basement while talking to him on my cell. I know we're poor, but phones are the one thing we all splurged on with the dough we got from picking tobacco all summer.

It makes us feel less alone.

"No," he says. "How's it over at your place?"

I look over at Becky's door. "Same shit, different day," I tell him. "Becky was flipping out when I came home, so I guess it's a good thing you didn't come over, anyway."

"No kidding, dude. I've had enough creepy-ass shit for one day. As it is, I'm not going to be able to sleep tonight."

"Yeah, I know what you mean." I look at the piles of laundry. "Listen, I'm going to be up late tonight, so if you get the willies, just text me or something."

"Thanks," he says. "I appreciate it. Really."

I hang up and finish stuffing a load of whites in the washer, along with my parents' sheets. As I turn the machine on and get ready to leave, I hear crying coming from the bedroom in the basement. It's Becky, not the other one. Over the past two years I've learned to tell the difference. There's something menacing behind Not-Becky—something corrupt. No matter how well it thinks its hiding, I can hear the evil in its voice.

I leave the empty laundry basket on top of the dryer and cautiously walk over to the barred window. Becky is sitting on her bed with her bony knees drawn up to her chest and her head down.

"You okay?" I ask her.

She nods as she stares at the floor.

"No, you aren't," I say. "You're crying." Becky rubs her face against her folded stick arms but still doesn't look up at me. It's hard for me to see her like this. It's hard to realize that two years ago my mother was happy, my grandmother was alive, my grandfather wasn't nearly as far gone as he is now, and my sister was still crazy but somehow normal.

Normal—I hardly remember what the word means.

The first time Becky really went off the deep end was after Margo Freeman was murdered. That was two years ago, but it seems like yesterday. Margo was Becky's best friend. She was this little mousy thing with buck teeth and long brown hair—definitely not a looker—but Margo Freeman was one of the most popular girls in town. Newie said it was because she'd put out for almost anyone. She even screwed him one day after school. That was before the chief started dating Mary Jane, and Newie was alone in his big, empty house. He told me he lay back on his dad's bed and let her go to town, with her buck teeth and long brown hair.

"Christened Asshole's sheets," he said the next day. "I christened the shit out of them."

After he told me that, I couldn't help but notice Margo every time she was over at our house doing homework with Becky or goofing off.

That last day—right before everything happened, she caught me staring at her as she and Becky were watching TV in the living room, and I was sitting at the old oak desk in the corner doing homework. That was back when I still cared about school—when I still thought working hard was my ticket out of Apple.

They were both wearing their varsity cheerleading outfits and going on about which guys on the football team they'd like to bone.

Margo kept saying, "Check, check, double check," and Becky kept saying, "Slut, slut, you're a slut," like I wasn't even in the room.

As they were talking trash, I caught a glimpse of Margo's legs out of the corner of my eye. They were long and shapely, and her skirt barely covered what was supposed to be covered.

I guess she caught me staring, so I glued my eyes to my book. It didn't matter.

"Hey, Jackson," she said. "You still a virgin? Because, you know, if you are, maybe you don't like girls at all." I could feel my face burning hot. Becky was in hysterics. I guess she thought Margo was funny or something. I didn't think she was funny at all. Besides, I was already dating Annie by then, and we'd fooled around—not that it was any of her business.

"Shut up, Margo," I said—big words that meant nothing.

Becky could hardly breathe, because she was laughing so hard. I turned around. Margo was sitting on the floor with her legs open wide and her arms stretched out behind her so I could see everything.

"Slut," giggled Becky as she watched me squirm.

Margo just grinned. "Maybe I'll show Jackson the ropes. What do you think about that, Jack-off?"

I didn't know what to think. I didn't know what to say. So, I left my homework on the oak desk and walked out. I spent the next twenty minutes in the bathroom trying desperately to ease the itch that burned in me, fueled by an image of Margo Freeman's open legs.

That was the last time I saw her alive. Somewhere between our house and hers, which was about a mile away from us, someone had counted her as number three and the last one to die that year.

Her murder was gruesome. Bits and pieces of her were left on porches and in gardens all over town, fashioned into horrific scarecrows.

On Mikey Boutin's front stoop was one of the straw-stuffed bodies. It was wearing a gore-splattered letter jacket that Margo had scored from an upper classman named Charlie Farga. I think Charlie banged her once or twice before letting her wear it, along with his class ring. Margo's head was shoved rudely onto a sharpened branch, and dried blood was clotted in her hair.

Another scarecrow was found on the porch of Foster Crudup, one of the nicest guys in town. That one was wearing Margo's knit sweater. It had a stuffed head and stuffed legs and Margo's bloody torso, complete with Charlie's class ring still on her dead white finger.

Mr. Crudup ran Toys-for-Tots around Christmas and can drives for the poor nearly every other month. He even organized a blood drive along with that lady, Sandy something-or-other, who worked for the Red Cross. I guess the shock of finding only a chunk of Margo was too much for him. He ended up at a hospital out in Redding. When he finally came home, which was about six weeks after Margo Freeman's body parts had been laid to rest, he hid inside his house with the shades pulled down and the drapes hanging loosely in the upper windows.

He was afraid of Apple. Who wouldn't be? Finally, one day, Mr. Crudup flat-out disappeared, but Newie said the chief let it slip that he got locked up someplace that had pillows for walls and served lots of pudding. Mr. Crudup didn't have any family, and no one's ever come to sell his house. It's still there, cold and empty, with its shades drawn and dark stains on the front porch.

The lower half of Margo Freeman was found at a third home, where a girl with Down syndrome lived with her mom. Margo's creamy white legs were sticking out of a pillow of straw, with twigs for arms and hay for hair. That morbid piece of human folk art was placed neatly in their garden, nestled between a display of gourds and pumpkins. I guess the girl's mother didn't believe her about the scarecrow with the pretty legs.

She completely ignored her daughter as she walked her to the short bus that morning—the one that takes kids like her to the state school in Bellingham.

Her mother believed her once she walked back home and found Margo's pretty legs for herself.

When all the pieces were found and Margo Freeman's body was identified by her grief-stricken parents, a very stressed out Chief Anderson came over to our house and spoke quietly to my family in the living room.

I still remember the more he lowered his voice, the more Becky wailed and tore at her beautiful ginger hair. No one could calm her down—not even my grandmother, whom she loved more than anything.

Then she started in with that maniacal laughter that turned into obscenities.

"You fucking think I did it, don't you, you fucking cocksucker cop," she snarled at the chief as she crouched on the ground and foamed at the mouth like a rabid dog. "Maybe *you* did it," she cackled as she pointed her finger at him. "Maybe it was you."

"Rebecca Ann," my mother cried, but it wasn't Rebecca Ann she was talking to anymore. It was Not-Becky, a new personality born out of the shock of knowing that Margo Freeman was brutally hacked to death. Suzie Zickle was gone. So was the obsessive, Bible-toting nun. Now it was only this evil thing that looked like my sister, but wasn't.

The chief was so blown away, he didn't know what to say—and trust me, startling that beast into silence is a rare feat.

"Every cock in town's had the chance to break that bitch in two," Not-Becky laughed. My face burned. My father and my grandparents were varying degrees of white and red. "So what? Someone finally split that whore wide. No fucking loss."

I couldn't believe those words were coming out of my sister. Margo Freeman was her best friend. How could she be talking like this?

It only went on like that for a short time. She spun in circles, pulling hunks of hair out of her head, and screaming in ways that would embarrass even the bikers at The Gin Mill. Finally, the chief pulled my father aside and told him that he should bring her to a hospital and get her a sedative or something.

He kept saying, "Think about the boy. Think about the boy." I'm not sure what he meant by that, because I was fine. I mean, it was weird that Margo died and all, but I wasn't the one going nuts over it.

Becky was.

Finally, my father agreed, and my mother called 911. They came and took her away for a while.

Becky was never right after that, and the episodes got worse and worse and creepier and creepier. Somewhere along the way, my parents stopped believing what the doctors told them about my sister. They refused any diagnosis of hysteria or dissociative identity disorder. Instead, they came up with their own conclusion about what was wrong with her.

It involved the Devil.

Now, two long years later, here I am, staring through a barred window at my ruined sister, sobbing in her duplicate bedroom.

How does she know about Claudia Fish?

My heart wants to break, but I think there's a layer of icy fear over it that's making it practically shatterproof.

"Becky, what can I do?" I ask her as she cries. Finally, she stretches out her legs and lies back on the bed.

"Can't you come in?" she pleads. "I want to show you something." My face begins to tingle. I don't want to go through that door. I don't want to see what she has to show me.

"I don't think so," I murmur.

"Please," she begs. "It's important."

She sounds so pitiful that I finally give in, even though I'm probably being a major idiot. I go to the stairs, take the key off the nail, go back, and open the door.

Becky's still lying on the bed, rubbing the yellow T-shirt she's been wearing for at least the last three days. A dirty stink rolls off of her, along with the funky stench of the casserole that I served her for dinner. The plate is sitting on the floor. It doesn't register until I am already at her side that she hasn't touched it at all. The spoon is still clean. The mound is still a mound.

Her medication is still inside.

Her medication.

Becky's bony hand shoots out and grabs my wrist. I try to pull free, but her strength is so furious that even Newie wouldn't be able to break free. As the sweat pops out on my forehead, her eyes roll up in her head.

"It's important," she gasps.

With her free hand, she lifts up her shirt over her belly button, rolling it back over her white skin. "I have to go now." In a flash, she's gone, and Not-Becky is there instead. It starts laughing and whooping like it's just pulled the best trick ever. It drops my hand and howls as I stare down at my sister's bare midriff.

In the skin, in angry red welts, it says the words, *Five will die*, and I know immediately what Becky is trying to tell me.

After all, this is autumn in Apple.

Five will die this year—five in all.

12

NOT-BECKY IS STILL laughing as I bound up the stairs to the kitchen. I leave the plate of food on the floor. Maybe it'll eat the casserole after all, and the drugs will ooze through its body and soothe the madness.

One can only hope.

The house is quiet. My mother has retreated to her bedroom. She's probably changed back into her sweatpants and my dad's T-shirt and is now huddled on a bed that has no sheets.

My father's disappeared into the garage. I won't see him again until tomorrow morning, when we'll both grab breakfast in silence. He usually eats cold cereal, so I know I have to quickly ride my bike to the BD Mart up by the gas station to get milk.

It's not a real market like Tenzar's, where Annie's mother works. It's just a place where you can get cigarettes and condoms and the other absolute essentials for a place like Apple.

First, I head up the back stairs to the second floor, knock on the door, and slide in to collect my grandfather's dinner plate. He's watching a game show on television. Rather, he's sleeping in front of the moving pictures, his stomach full and his mind empty. I tiptoe into the living room where he's dozing and take the plate from him. Then I turn off the overhead light and leave him to slumber in the soft glow of a table lamp that has a shade with Canadian geese on it.

Sometime later, my grandfather will wake up and maneuver himself into the bathroom, then into his bedroom. One day soon, I suspect that I'm going to find him on the tiled floor next to the toilet, or beside his bed, because he reached out the wrong way or bent over too far. He'll be laying there with a broken hip, or worse. When that happens, I'll know that it's the beginning of the end for him.

I'm not sure what I think about that. I suppose I'm conflicted. Everyone gets old, but when is someone's life not worth living anymore? Is it when they first stop leaving their home? Is it when they begin to lose their mind, and simple things, like the names of the people in their family, disappear out of their brains? I don't know, but I do know that when my grandfather eventually slides away, my father will get even quieter, and my mother will become that much more detached. Who knows about Becky? If she's herself, maybe she'll cry. If she's Not-Becky, maybe that thing will laugh or let loose with a foul eulogy that will make my face burn hot.

Back downstairs, I finish the dishes and dry off my hands with the faded dish towel. When I'm done, I quietly open the back door and carry my bike off the porch and down to the ground. My mother doesn't care if I leave. My father would care if he knew, so I won't tell him. I'll only be gone twenty minutes at most. The BD Mart is only across Main Street and up a couple blocks.

It'll be fine, I tell myself. I'll be okay. Besides, I know it's understood that my mother isn't doing any of the things that a mother should do, like grocery shopping or making dinners, or doing the wash, or even cleaning the house. Deep down, my father knows it's me who's doing all those things, but as long as he doesn't see me doing them, he doesn't have to acknowledge how screwed up everything is under his roof.

Maybe that's why he leaves grocery money on the counter every week, instead of giving it to my mother. She wouldn't know what to do with it, anyway. As for me, I take the cash and keep it inside a tin of saltines in the pantry, because nobody in the house eats saltines. They're one of those foods that everyone has but no one eats, like wax beans and bouillon cubes—or those big tubs of Crisco. No one uses that either, but everyone seems to have a can in their house.

It's not that cold out, so I don't take my jacket. The air is still, and the night has closed in around Apple, making me feel almost claustrophobic. I madly peddle my K-Mart mountain bike down Vanguard Lane, cross over Main Street, and pump feverishly up the slight incline to where the BD Mart and the gas station sit like lonely sentinels on opposite corners at the top of the hill.

As I peddle, I see things in the shadows. I imagine dark creatures crouching in the bushes and figures with hooded eyes, gazing at me from underneath porches or fading into the shadows next to cars. These are the images that are going to haunt my dreams tonight, filling them with heinous visions of bloodcurdling deaths that can only be imagined and executed by someone with a seriously messed-up mind—deaths that include maimings and gougings and rough-cut amputations—burnings and beheadings and all manner of pain.

I pump my legs harder, not stopping until I come to the top of the hill, peddling my wheels too quickly into the BD Mart parking lot, skidding to a stop in front of the big glass window.

Julie Dopkin is working inside. She's a senior at Apple High, too. Julie plays field hockey, and I'm guessing she wants to be a gym teacher someday.

"Yo, Jackson," she says in her gruff man-voice when I walk in, out of breath from my mad cycling up the hill.

"What's up?" I ask her.

"Did you hear?"

My heart flip flops in my chest. I'm sure she's going to tell me about Claudia Fish, but she's going to say Crawdaddy Fish, because that's how everyone knows the ugly girl with the wide-spaced eyes. "Hear what?" I ask, feigning indifference.

"About Annie Berg?" she says. "Geez. I thought you guys were dating."

No, not Annie, I think. Nothing can happen to Annie. My mind reels with the thought of someone breaking into her house, stepping over her drunken, worthless father, and taking a knife to her in her upstairs bedroom, splattering the walls with her warm, red life.

"What about Annie?" I ask a little too quickly. My eyes open wide. I swear I can hear the blood pumping through my veins and sloshing between my ears.

"Chill," she says. "It's nothing bad." Julie reaches down and pulls out a piece of paper. I had forgotten that Annie filled out a work application at the end of the summer, before school started and the murders began.

"She got the job here," says Julie. "Three nights a week."

I'm so relieved that I almost hug her right on the spot.

I know it's only a minimum wage job, but it means more than that to me. Five will die this year, but not Annie. She's going to be working. She's going to be too busy to die. That's what I keep telling myself as I pull a carton of milk out of the refrigerator, drop a few crumpled dollars on the counter, and thank Julie for the news.

I even whistle a little as I zoom down the dark hill at night, heading toward Main Street with the carton clutched in one hand.

Five will die, I keep telling myself, but not Annie. She's going to be working at the BD Mart.

13

BECKY HAS EATEN dinner. She's curled on her bed with her chains looped lazily around her legs, like snakes basking on hot rocks in the sun. I'm too tired and too wired to retrieve the plate from inside her room. Instead, I sit on the bottom step of the basement stairs and call Annie on my cell phone. I usually text, but I think I need to hear her voice. Normally I'd call in my room, but Becky is dead to the world, so it doesn't matter.

"Hi," she says as she answers the phone after the first ring. "Why didn't you text?"

"I just didn't," I tell her. "I wanted to talk to another human being, so that counts my family out. Are you okay?"

She's quiet for a moment. "Okay because of Claudia?"

"Well, yeah."

Annie sighs through the phone. "I was, until you just reminded me. I guess you're not?"

"No. Not really."

There's a brief pause on the other end of the phone. Then Annie says, "Jackson, it's not your fault, you know. You didn't kill her."

The problem is, there's a small part of me that thinks I did. "I know," I say. "I can't stop thinking that I wish I was nicer to her."

"She'd still be dead," says Annie.

"I suppose," I say, as I sit in the gloom of the basement. "I guess."

I don't really believe my words. I didn't know Claudia Fish, but maybe underneath all the ugliness, she was a really nice person. Maybe we could have been friends. That way, she wouldn't have been caught alone in the woods. She would have been with me and Annie and Newie, making her way through High Garden and scaling down the Giant Steps like the rest of us.

She'd still be alive.

"My mother wants us to move in with my aunt in Springfield," says Annie. "She says Apple's a death trap."

"Yeah, because Springfield's such a safe place," I grumble. "Isn't that where that crazy guy stabbed that girl in the bus station because she laughed?"

"He thought she was laughing *at* him," Annie reminds me. It's true. She laughed. He thought she was making fun of him, so he gutted her in front of her friends, then sat and ate Funyuns while people screamed and the police came.

"Crazy is crazy," I tell her as I steal a glance at Becky's door. "She could have been laughing at lint. He still would have messed her up." Annie doesn't say anything, so I change the subject to one that's probably as depressing as Claudia Fish. "How's Daddy-Prick? He was pretty hammered when we dropped you off."

Annie sighs through the phone. I can almost hear her rolling her eyes. "It takes a lot to get my dad wasted," she says. "He's had lots of practice. I think he's built up a tolerance."

"Yeah, but have you?" I ask in all seriousness. "How do you stand it?"

"Same as you," she says. "How do you stand the freak show you live in?"

"Good point," I say. "Becky was off the wall when I got home." I tell her about my mom and dad and about Becky yelling and screaming, but I don't tell her about the welts on her stomach. I don't want to scare her, and part of me doesn't want to believe her warped message anyway. *Five will die.*

"Newie's dad called and talked to my father," Annie whispers.

"Really? What happened?"

"The chief told him about Claudia and about how we found her. He said my dad should keep an eye on me until everything blows over."

"Yeah, right. What did your dad say?"

Annie licks her lips. I can hear her do it through the phone. "He said, 'What's to watch?' and that I'm too much of a piece of white trash for a murderer to waste his time on."

The words hang in the little space between the phone and my ear, and in that split second, I have a debate in my head about which one of us actually has it worse at home, me or Annie. In the end, I decide that we both have it pretty bad.

"I'm sorry, Annie," I say. The truth is, I'm sorry for both of us.

I think she starts to cry, but if she does, she puts her hand over the phone so I can't really tell for sure. Finally she says, "I wish we could just leave."

"You and me both," I say. "But go where?"

"I don't know," she murmurs then says it again. "I don't know."

The truth is, I would love to leave Apple. I would love to leave all this craziness behind and have a do-over, maybe in a place like Longmeadow or Littleham, where we both come from nice homes with nice families, and each of us has golden retrievers or one of those spastic little lap dogs that look like a fuzzy rat. Annie can be a cheerleader, and I can be on the soccer team, because I don't have to take care of everyone.

In my fantasy, Annie and I are still together. I guess that's the one good thing I have going for me in my life right now. I have Annie.

"Next summer," I tell her. "We'll both be eighteen. Then we're out of here."

"To where?" she asks me in all seriousness.

"I don't know," I say. "Cape Cod, maybe. There's always work on the Cape."

"Oh, okay," Annie laughs. "Sounds like a plan."

"Or maybe we'll get married," I say.

Annie laughs again. I love when she laughs. It's about the only thing that brightens my day. "Get married?" she says. "Sure, why not. Then I can plop out about a dozen rug rats and get really, really fat."

"I wouldn't care," I tell her, because that's what guys are supposed to say to their girls. I try to picture Annie fat, but the image doesn't come. "Besides, this is my fantasy. You don't ever get fat in my fantasy. You stay perfect, just like you are."

A deep, throaty chuckle comes from behind the barred door.

"I'm gonna fucking puke," Not-Becky spits and sputters. "If you don't shut your fucking pie hole right now, I'm gonna puke all over everything, and you're going to have to clean it up . . . Jackson."

I hate it when it says my name. It doesn't sound right coming out of its mouth. It sounds dirty, and wrong, and evil.

"Annie, I have to go."

"Text me later," she says. "I love you."

"Me, too," I whisper then the phone goes dead. I don't get to ask her about the job at the BD Mart. I don't get to talk to her about a lot of stuff.

Not-Becky makes a retching sound, but I don't hear any wet splatters, so I know it's only messing with my head. It likes to do that—just like with the welts on Becky's skin. It's all a game. It's all just a sick way of screwing with me, but I won't let it.

The welts aren't new. They've happened before. There have been unspeakable things written on my sister's skin, but that only fuels my father's insistence that the worst has happened to his daughter, and she's possessed. Of course, that only serves to throw logs on the pyre of my mother's depression.

I know they're wrong. I've even looked it up on the Internet. Writing on skin is something called dermatographic urticaria or dermographism. Some people also call it Paper Skin. It's not all that uncommon. If you have it, all you need to do is trace images or words on your skin, and they'll pop up in angry, red welts that last for about fifteen minutes.

Believe me, it's scary as hell, but that's all part of Becky's illness. My parents can believe whatever screwed-up crap they want. My father can hang crucifixes all over the walls and go to church on Sunday mornings and pray like someone who desperately needs salvation—but it won't make a lick of difference.

My sister's sick, and she needs real help—not prayer or tranquilizers or the kind of help that my parents think comes from their God. If she doesn't get it soon, something's going to give. I can feel it in my gut. I can taste it in the musty air of our creepy-ass basement.

Still, the one thing I can't figure out is how she knows things—like Claudia Fish. How does she know that her murder is pressing on my mind like a vice?

There has to be an explanation, because if there isn't, the only other answer is too frightening to think about, so I don't.

I go to the dryer and pull out the whites, along with my parents' sheets, fold them up in a wad, and head toward the stairs. I'll gently coax my mom from her fetal position and dress their bed with hospital corners and everything, like she used to do for me before Becky got sick.

Of course, before I can do that, one more little piece of horror has to be piled on top of my Jenga of a day. One more piece that threatens to topple me over. As I start up the stairs, Not-Becky says a few last words that chill me to the bone.

"What scares you, Jackson?" it sputters in a pea-soup voice, like that fat, piggy girl in the movie where she puked all over a priest. "What . . . scares . . . you?"

14

I DON'T REMEMBER dozing off last night. Sometime between grabbing a handful of cookies, playing with Betty Palm and her five sisters, and rereading old comic books full of blood and violence, sleep overtakes me. I'm carried away down a deep, dark hole filled with disturbing images.

First, there's Claudia Fish reading a book, all alone, in the library at school. She doesn't have any eyes, but slimy, congealed jelly oozes out of her empty sockets and plops down on the pages.

Then there's my mother, holding her hands against her ears to seal them from the insane ranting of the thing that she birthed, that's now locked away in the basement.

As she fades away, my grandfather comes into view. He's sitting in his wheelchair, grousing about nonsense to my grandmother, who's been dead for two years. She's doing cartwheels behind him, with her head flopping back and forth, left and right. My grandparents disappear, only to be replaced by my father, feverishly rubbing oak-stained wax all over a freshly carved crucifix. His hands are raw and bloody, and he keeps saying, "Jesus was a carpenter . . . Jesus was a carpenter . . ." over and over again.

As he dissipates into smoke, I see Becky. She's alternately pulling bloody handfuls of red hair from her ruined scalp, while absent-mindedly tracing vulgarities on her bare arms and legs. The words become three-dimensional, like those pop-up pink hippos and dancing alligators in that old Disney cartoon. *Ass-wipe—cocksucker—motherfucker.* They sail off her skin, leaving gaping wounds clear to the bone, before flying away into the maelstrom of my nightmare.

I fall further still, plummeting past Chief Anderson, who makes a haphazard attempt to grab me as I fly by him. Then I see Newie, who's biting his nails as the brown head of Margo Freeman bobs up and down between his legs. Finally, I plunge by Annie's open front door. She frantically reaches out for me, but dozens and dozens of drunken dirty hands are grabbing and clawing at her, pulling her inside and away from me, forever.

I wake with a start. My neck is a knot of pain, and I know my cheek has a flat, red palm print pressed into it. My hand is numb from sleeping on it all night, and the skin beneath my damp T-shirt is slick with sweat. The clock says 6:10. Normally, I'd sleep another twenty minutes before getting up for school, but I don't want to fall back into my nightmares, so I pull myself out of bed, scratch lazily at the hard-on that every guy has in the morning, and wait for it to deflate, so I can get up and take a leak.

Thankfully, I don't have to worry about my grandfather or Becky in the mornings. My father begrudgingly took over that responsibility after what happened to my grandmother. He doesn't get along with my grandfather. I've never fully understood why, but I think it has something to do with faith. Simply put, my grandfather thinks my father has too much of it. My father thinks my grandfather has too little. I think it's funny how faith can build a wall instead of tear one down.

My father spends the first thirty minutes of each day in prayer, on his knees in the living room, his hands clasped together so hard that if there was a piece of coal between them it would turn into a diamond. When he's through, he brings a tray to my grandfather and another to Becky. He also brings a Bible with him when he sees her. It's the same Bible he's had since he was a child.

He stands outside her door and reads passages to her while she eats.

I can't think of anything more painful. Frankly, I think it screws with her mind. It would definitely screw with mine.

I quickly take a shower and pull on a fresh T-shirt with a Mr. Jones logo on it. Mr. Jones is a local band. They're pretty good for Apple standards, and sometimes you can see them for free if you can catch a ride out to Finnegan's at the edge of town.

By the time I spread some peanut butter on toast for a quickie breakfast, it's almost 7:00. I pull out my phone and text Newie.

You walking? I ask him.

He immediately texts me back. *Asshole's driving. He says come with.*

Annie, too? I text back.

Si, senor.

I text Annie and tell her that we'll be by to pick her up. She sends me back a heart which speaks volumes. Roughly translated, it means, *Oh, my God. Thank you so, so, so, a thousand times, so much. I didn't want to walk through High Garden and up the Giant Steps by myself, and I certainly didn't want to go through the path between the middle school and the high school. That's where we found the body, you know. I'm not sure if I'm ever going to be able to walk down that path again. How am I going to get to school? Am I going to have to walk all the way around? I don't want to do that. It's like three miles that way . . .* it goes on and on and on.

My father's in the shower, and my mother's still in bed when I leave. I grab my jacket off his coat rack in the living room and quietly slip out the front door, noticing as I walk down the steps that our little front lawn needs another cut, even though it's getting late in the season and the grass isn't growing as fast as usual.

I mentally scribble down *cutting the lawn* on a list of chores I have for the weekend, then swing open our gate and trot across the street to the Andersons' house.

The chief's cruiser is parked along the curb. There's another car in the driveway. It's Mary Jane's. She must have stayed over last night.

I'm right, because she opens the door and almost bowls me over as I'm about to walk in.

"Watch yourself, Jackson," she purrs, then squeezes by me closer than she needs to be. She lingers a moment, her tits crushed up against my chest, before sliding past me and out to her car. Only then does it register that she's only wearing an oversized man's shirt and nothing else. I watch as she opens the side door and bends over, the shirt riding up and showing a major portion of her slutty ass. Mary Jane grabs a gym bag from the back seat and slams the door shut. Then she giggles as she pulls the shirt down and straightens it, before leisurely walking back across the lawn and up the stairs. "Forgot my clothes," she pouts like it's the opening line in a porno movie on the Internet.

"I see that," I say. She only smiles and saunters past me into the house.

Poor Newie. Poor, poor Newie.

I notice Mrs. Owens from next door, staring out at me through her kitchen window. Her hair's neatly done up in curlers, and she has a disapproving look on her face. She slowly shakes her head back and forth. Is she judging me or Mary Jane? Who knows? I suppose lust is a sin, but as I turn away from her wrinkled, leathery skin, that will never be young again—that will never be caressed by another living soul unless you count a coroner—I remember that envy is a sin, too.

"Jackson," Chief Anderson growls and nods at me as I walk inside and drop my book bag in the hallway.

"Thanks for driving," I say to him. "You don't mind picking up Annie?"

He gives me a look like I'm the village idiot, then stuffs his shirt into his pants and checks his huge mop of hair in the hallway mirror. While he stares at his image, he yells up the stairs. "Get your ass moving, Newie." His booming voice cuts through me like the speakers at Finnegan's.

"I am, I am," I hear Newie call down from the second floor. Seconds later, there are footsteps, and Newie is flying down the old curved staircase wearing his letter jacket and carrying his football bag. "Can I at least grab a bagel or something?"

The chief doesn't answer. He stands in front of the mirror and begins tying his uniform tie. I watch him as he admires his reflection. A smug, self-satisfied look slowly creeps across his face. I suppose I'd be pretty pleased with myself, too, if I regularly got my knob polished by someone as hot as Mary Jane.

Newie must go to bed at night with cramps.

"I talked to your dad last night," the chief says, as he loops his tie over and around and back through itself.

"He told me." I look self-consciously anywhere but at his eyes.

"Did he say anything to you?" I hear dishes clattering in the kitchen, and Chief Anderson is momentarily distracted. "What the fuck are you doing in there?" he yells after Newie.

"Sorry, nothing," Newie yells back like a ten-year-old instead of the linebacker that he is.

"Fucking idiot," mutters Chief Anderson and shakes his head. Once again, he shifts focus back to me, staring through the mirror like he did yesterday with his reflective glasses on. He opens his mouth like he's going to say something, then he closes it and slightly shakes his head.

It's like I know what he's going to say, so I silently pray that he doesn't. If he does, it will probably be something about how sorry he is that it had to be Annie, Newie, and me that found Claudia Fish's body—not because Newie is his son, or because Annie has a drunk for a father.

He wants to say he's sorry because of me.

He wants to tell me that it's not my fault that my grandfather's brain has turned to mush, or that my mom has crippling depression, or that my father's born again. He wants to tell me that Becky isn't my fault either. Sometimes things just happen, and we have to suck it up and move on.

Maybe he doesn't want to tell me any of those things. He just wants to ask how soccer's going this year. If he does, I'll have to tell him that I had to drop the team. He'll know why, and the vicious circle will start all over again.

The chief finishes tying his tie, turns, and puts his heavy paw on the bannister.

"Mary Jane?" he yells up the stairs.

"Yeah." I hear her silky voice wafting down from the second floor like fluffy dandelion fuzz dancing on the wind—pretty—to hide the fact she's an invasive weed.

"We're out. Lock up when you're done."

Newie comes out of the kitchen with half a bagel stuffed in his mouth. He didn't shave today, so he looks more like the chief's younger brother than his son. As a matter of fact, he looks like the one who's banging Mary Jane instead of his dad.

"Okay, sweetie," she calls down from the second floor, and Newie winces like it's the last thing he wants to hear. As the chief turns around to put on his jacket, I look at Newie and mouth *Sweetie?* at him. He rolls his eyes, then we're all out the door and in the cruiser to go pick up Annie.

Although he doesn't say it, I know Newie's relieved that I'm with him.

I'm relieved he's with me, too.

15

ANNIE'S DYED HER hair back to blond. It's almost the original color, and I like it better than the red. At least it's not pink or black, because if it were, I'd think we'd have to talk.

"Thanks for the ride," she murmurs to Chief Anderson as she opens the back door. Newie and I slide over to make room for her. The chief only nods his head and gives her a long look through his rearview mirror. I'm beginning to think that mirrors are what he uses to intimidate people. Staring at him head-on is scary enough. Catching his eye in a mirror can make you pee your pants.

Newie gapes open-mouthed at Annie's new hair. Finally she says, "What? I needed a change."

Neither of us truly believes her lame excuse. She might as well tell us the truth—that she needs to be someone else right now instead of Annie Berg—the girl with the alcoholic father and the sad, overworked mother—the girl who found Claudia Fish's cold dead body in the woods less than twenty-four hours ago.

"Okay," Newie shrugs and stares out the window. As for me, it's not her hair I'm thinking about. She's wearing her gray sweater, the one that she shouldn't be pulling out of her closet until November, when the air gets really nippy. The sleeves are extra-long, so only the pink tips of her fingers are sticking out.

Shit.

Before she can stop me, I shoot out my arm and peel back one of the gray knit sleeves.

"Quit it," she yelps, as she yanks her arm away from me and pushes her sleeve back down, but she's too late. I see the bandage wrapped around her wrist and snaking up her forearm.

"Everything okay back there?" the chief barks as he pulls along the bottom of High Garden and begins the long climb up the hill.

"Fine," Annie says, folding her arms and sinking back into the seat.

That familiar burn starts in my chest and crawls up the back of my neck. I can feel a rush of blood pouring into my face.

"Damn you, Annie," I whisper through clenched teeth. The words are tiny—almost inaudible. "You promised."

Annie doesn't say anything. She looks out the window the same way Newie is looking out his. How can the three of us be so together and so alone at the same time? How can we be so lost?

I close my eyes and force myself to take a deep breath. The air feels good, so I let it out and breathe deeply again. A few more times, and the burning inside is reduced to embers. Any anger I have is replaced by a deep and profound sadness—for me, for Annie, for all of us.

Tentatively, I reach out and rest my hand on her leg. She doesn't pull away, which is a good thing. After all, we've been through this sort of thing before.

Why does it have to be bandages on her arm? I thought we were finished with that part of our unbearable adolescence, but who I am kidding? In Apple, terrible things have a way of creeping back into our lives, like vermin that sneak through the cracks in our foundations when it starts to get cold.

"You said you stopped," I whisper to her so quietly that I'm not sure that she even hears me.

"I did," she whispers back.

"So what happened?" Our exchange is all but inaudible. Newie has no idea that we're having a Lifetime moment two feet away from him. Besides, he's tapping his leg to some nameless beat that's going on in his head.

Annie doesn't answer me. She shoves one of her fingers in her mouth and sucks on it, probably to keep from screaming.

The idea of her sealing herself in that dingy little bathroom on the second floor of her house makes me sick. I can almost smell the vague stench of alcohol and vomit as it leaches through the walls, while Annie pulls out a fresh box of razor blades from the medicine cabinet.

Why does she have to do that to herself? She's so pretty, even with the thin white lines on her arms that have almost faded to nothing. What's going on in her head that makes her believe that doing that will somehow help? I have no earthly idea, except that an image of Becky yanking hunks of red hair from her ravaged skull flashes across my mind.

At the top of the hill, the chief makes a left. Soon, we pass the entrance to the middle school and continue on Glendale Road, past the woods where we found Claudia Fish's body. There are already a few cop cars parked out in front of the middle school. Inside, I can imagine

Officer Randy standing behind a big glass window in the office, telling Principal DesRoberts what happened.

Principal DesRoberts is probably shaking his head back and forth and tenting his fingers in front of his face, not only to cover the frown on his mouth as he hears the news, but to hide his embarrassment for not quite remembering who Claudia Fish is in the first place.

There will be more police officers at the high school, and homeroom will go uncomfortably long. Finally, someone will come and hand a folded white piece of paper to each of the teachers for them to announce what happened. A brown-noser from Key Club or student government will dash out to the flagpole in front of the circle where everyone is dropped off and lower the flapping fabric of red, white, and blue to half-mast.

After that, Claudia Fish's name will be passed from student to student like a game of telephone, until someone remembers her stupid nick-name and passes that along, too.

Crawdaddy Fish. Crawdaddy Fish.

Chief Anderson slowly drives his cruiser into the high school parking lot. Thankfully, he doesn't drop us off at the circle. Instead, he pulls into one of the empty spaces where the teachers park their cars.

"Have to go inside today," he mutters, as he opens his door and unfolds himself to his giant stature. His silver gun scrapes against his seat belt as he gets up, and I wonder if he's ever going to shoot it at the person who's responsible for all this misery. I wonder if one of his little slugs of lead will ever find its way to the heart of the evil that's plagued Apple for so long.

Newie opens his door a little too forcefully and lightly grazes a tiny Hyundai parked next to the cruiser.

"What the fuck do you think you're doing?" his father roars and cuffs him upside the head with a sharp *thwack*. Annie tenses—so do I.

"Ow," cries Newie. "Ow." The chief leans over and examines the little car to see if Newie left any marks. Thankfully he hasn't.

"You're lucky," growls the chief. "Or I'd be running that plate right now to find whatever ass-wipe teacher parked this piece of crap here, and you'd be shelling out your summer savings to fix what you did." His nostrils flare, and he curls his upper lip. "Dumb fuckwad."

Newie says nothing. He rubs his ear, pulls his backpack and his sports bag out of the back of the cruiser, and lightly closes the door. He does it so daintily that he has to pull it open again and close it a little bit harder so it will click shut.

"Idiot," the chief seethes, then hikes his belt up and swaggers away from us toward the front entrance to the high school. There are no goodbyes or catch-you-laters—no father and son high-fives—only a lingering sort of animosity that permeates the air between Newie and his father.

It's always been like that, like the chief somehow blames Newie for everything wrong in his life.

As we walk into school behind Chief Anderson—way behind, so we look like we have no connection to him at all—I can't help but think that the three of us are alone today. We're together, but alone, and the thing that binds us together is a dead girl lying on a slab somewhere in a coroner's office, waiting to be carved up to see how badly she suffered before she died.

My guess is she suffered a lot.

16

"I DON'T WANT TO talk about it anymore," Annie hisses at me. Her words hurt, because Annie doesn't hiss. She's sweet and easy. The last thing I'd be doing is dating someone who hisses, but she does it just the same.

"Talk about what?" asks Newie.

Annie practically stumbles over her words as they pour out of her mouth. "What do you think?" she snaps at him, giving me a dangerous look that means that she really doesn't want to talk about *it* anymore.

"Oh," he says, because he thinks we're talking about bloody Claudia, not bloody Annie. The three of us are in the cafeteria before homeroom, so Newie can have his second breakfast, and I can down a cup of black coffee. He spreads his arms wide. "Good luck with that," he says as he gestures to the room. "Everyone's going to be talking about it pretty damn skippy."

I sigh and take a sip of my coffee. I wish I knew what to say to Annie, but I don't. There isn't anyone to talk to about what she's doing—about the cutting. Everyone in Apple is as messed up as she is or I am, or even Newie. We all live with monsters. At least Annie has a release from it all.

I decide to change the subject, mostly because I have no choice. "Why didn't you tell me about getting the job at the BD Mart?" I ask her.

"You're going to be working up at the BD Mart?" exclaims Newie as he shoves a huge cruller into his mouth. "Score. Free shit. Sweet."

"I don't think so," she says to him. "You'll get me fired, and we, I mean I, need the cash."

I know full well she means that the Bergs need the cash, because her mother isn't pulling down enough at Tenzar's, and Mr. Berg is drinking whatever is left over.

"Besides," I say to Newie. "You'd hoover the place."

"Hey," he says. "I can't help it if I've got a red-hot metabolism." He slides his giant hand through his hair and shakes his head like he probably does after he shaves and takes a shower in the morning. He's probably even imagining that he's doing it in slow motion for a GQ photographer.

The thought makes me want to throw up a little in my mouth.

Just then, Newie catches sight of Erika Tenzar as she saunters into the cafeteria. She's followed by three other girls who all look the same, with long blond hair and perfect bodies. He sighs and shoves the rest of the sugarcoated pastry in his mouth.

I follow his gaze. "Give it up," I tell him. "I thought you weren't into 'bitch.'"

"'Bitch' is right," Annie says as she liberates the cup of coffee from my hand while making sure that the sleeves on her sweater don't slide up to reveal the recent resurgence of her most dangerous hobby. "Hate her."

"I don't care about her personality," says Newie as he wipes his mouth on his letter jacket. "She's hot."

Annie rolls her eyes. "You're a man-whore," she says to him.

"Guilty." He shrugs and heads off to secure his future weekend activity. Of course he'll say something all smooth and macho, and she'll turn ripe for the picking. He'll ask her if she wants to hang out after school. She'll say yes, and Newie's thoughts will be eaten up with images of whatever Erika Tenzar will allow him to get away with, which is literally everything, because she's a total skank.

I shake my head as I watch him go, then turn to Annie and take my coffee back from her.

"I didn't plan not to tell you," she whispers. "About the BD Mart, I mean. I sort of forgot. Between Ruby and Claudia and that Ralphie guy, I'm not exactly happy about getting the seven-to-eleven shift three nights a week."

"When do you start?" I ask her, dreading that I think I already know the answer.

"Tonight," she says. "I'm training with Julie Dopkin. You know her, right?"

"Yeah. She's the one who told me."

Annie looks puzzled. "When?" she asks.

"Last night," I tell her. "I had to go grab some milk. The stuff we had in our refrigerator was nasty."

"You went out last night?" Annie hisses again, like it's starting to become a habit. "After everything that happened, you still went out last night?"

"I had to," I say. "We ran out of milk. If my father found out, he'd be pissed, and he already has too much on his plate."

I take another sip of coffee and think about what I just said. Between my grandfather, my mom, and Becky, he *does* have too much on his plate, but instead of doing something about it, he's shutting down and building crucifixes in the garage—and praying.

He's freaking praying.

I shut my eyes and shake my head. What part of praying does he think is going to help Becky? She's sick, and he's fooled himself into thinking that there's something more sinister going on with her than her illness.

Screw that. The only thing evil and wrong in my house is what my father's allowed to happen to my sister. Hell, what he's allowed to happen to my mother.

They both need help, real help, not the kind that comes from his biblical book of fairy tales.

"It's getting bad, isn't it?" Annie asks me.

I could be a complete asshole and ask her the same thing, but I don't want to open up that can of worms again, so I only nod. The demons under my roof are no worse than the demons under hers. Besides, it doesn't do any good to get into it with her about my family, just like I know it doesn't help to say anything about her absentee mother and her pickled, handsy father—or the box of razors she keeps in the upstairs bathroom.

Across the cafeteria, Newie towers over Erika Tenzar. He's got his hands on his hips, exactly like the chief stands. Erika's banished her court to one of the cafeteria tables, just far enough away so that she and Newie can talk.

I see her make a fake pouty-mouth as she looks up at him. He brushes her arm with his hand, which makes her smile. Then he starts bobbing his head up and down like he's totally into what he's saying—performing the mating dance of the American Blue-Balled Teenaged Quarterback. I'm surprised she doesn't mount him right there. That's what animals in heat do on the Discovery Channel.

After a moment, I see her drop her arms and step back from him—only a little—and fold them across her chest. She shakes her head as she looks at him intently. All the time, Newie is getting more and more animated, and Erika's turning rigid like a yardstick.

"Oh, no," I say under my breath as I watch that big, stupid idiot kill a free lay with one of the hottest girls in school.

"Oh, no, what?" says Annie. I tilt my chin over to where Newie and

Erika are talking, and Annie immediately figures out what's going on.

"Wow," she says. "It he really that stupid?"

"He's your friend," I tell her, ignoring the fact that he's been my friend longer. When he's stupid, he's her friend.

Erika Tenzar covers her face with her hands and runs out of the cafeteria. Newie stands there like a moron, not knowing what he said or did to make her run away like that.

His father's deep, booming voice echoes inside my head. *Dumb fuck-wad.*

Newie's told Erika that we found Claudia in the woods between the middle school and the high school. It's not like everyone isn't going to hear the news as soon as Chief Anderson talks to the administration, and they get the word out to the teachers. The thing is, the chief doesn't know that his brilliant son has just done his dirty work for him.

He's told Erika, and Erika will tell Dina Bridge or Heidi Baker, or worse, Zina Butterfield, whose mouth's been stretched open so wide by any guy with a jockstrap that the news can't help but pour out of it.

Within ten minutes, the entire school will know. It'll be like electricity, shocking everyone who hears it, followed by the numbing realization that there are no longer two murders in Apple this year.

There are three.

Newie finally puts his hands down, shrugs, and lopes back to us through a sea of heads that, at best, reach up to his shoulders.

"You're an idiot," says Annie, as he reaches us.

"What?" he says with that dumb Newie look on his face. It's the one that probably infuriates the chief the most.

"What?" I repeat to him. "You really have to ask?"

"Yeah," he says, getting all huffy. "I really have to ask."

I shake my head, grab my backpack, and reach out for Annie's hand. "You know when you almost scratched that car in the parking lot, and your dad called you a dumb fuckwad?"

"Yeah," says Newie, as he gathers his things together.

"He was right," I say.

We all leave the cafeteria and head off to homeroom, where we'll sit there for way too long, until someone comes in with that damn piece of white paper to confirm what half the school is going to be talking about in the next few minutes.

"Why?" Newie whines again as he follows us, but I can already see the looks on people's faces. Some have turned the color of ash, and others are filled with cheerful relief that it wasn't them who got killed.

"Just shut up," I say to him as we walk, a growing buzz forming around us like a cloud of flies. "Just shut the hell up."

Eventually he does.

17

AFTER THE BELL for homeroom, there's an announcement telling everyone that first period will be delayed. Fifteen minutes later, when there's a simmering murmur about another murder, there's a knock on the door, and one of the senior hall monitors quietly steps in and hands the teacher, Mr. Robbins, the dreaded piece of white paper.

Mr. Robbins is from Ludlow, which is over an hour away from here. He makes it a habit of telling anyone who'll listen that he drives that far to teach in a shithole like Apple because he's committed.

He should be committed. Only someone crazy would do that.

I'm numb through the announcement, and I cringe when I hear a few people say things like "Who?" and "Crawdaddy's dead?" Finally, we're sent off to first period.

As I head out the door, Mr. Robbins stops me. "Mr. Gill?" he says. He always calls everyone Mr. or Ms. instead of by our first names, like a normal person.

"Uh huh?"

He holds out a yellow slip of paper. I take it from him and mumble a thank you. He stares at me without smiling, then pushes his glasses up on his face and goes back to his desk.

I unfold the yellow slip of paper as I walk out into the hall and read the words written on the pre-printed lines. I'm being called to the guidance office. It says I have to go immediately. I have to skip first period, which is gym, and go directly to the guidance office and ask for Ms. Hutch.

She's my guidance counselor, but I don't like her much. The last time we talked was two years ago. That was after Margo Freeman was murdered, and everything happened with my grandmother and Becky. I didn't want to talk about it then. I was really angry at the world. Now, two years later, I'm still sort of angry at the world, and I still don't want to talk about it.

Ms. Hutch is fake. She has ruby red lipstick and an out-of-the-bottle blond dye job that makes her look like some sort of caricature instead of a real person. She also has a hard time making eye contact when she talks.

It's creepy, but I guess I don't care. I don't plan on making eye contact with her, either. I know she's going to ask me things that I'm not prepared to deal with, like feelings and crap.

What a total waste of time.

As I walk down the hallway, I see Newie's massive head rising out of the moving current of students.

"Fuckwad," I yell out. His shoulders slump and he stops.

"You're a douchebag," he mutters when I catch up to him. Then I notice that he has an identical yellow slip of paper between his fingers. I roll my eyes and hold up my own.

"Annie's got one, too," he says. "Right when we were leaving homeroom. She went to the bathroom, though. I think she needs a couple minutes of girl time."

The air momentarily leaves the space around us, and I'm afraid to breathe. All I can picture is Annie pulling a razorblade free from wherever she secreted it away, going into one of the stalls, and sitting on the dingy toilet. Even worse, I can picture her cutting herself too deep with the shiny bit of metal, and everything that makes up who she is dripping down her jeans and pooling on the tiled floor.

Someone foul, like slimy Tawny Sanders, who gives blowjobs to guys on the Giant Steps for pills, will probably find her sometime later and poke at her lifeless body with her foot, before sauntering down to the custodian's office and telling Mr. Meekham, the one-armed custodian, that he's got a cleanup in the girls' john.

"What's with you?" Newie asks, because he probably sees the weird look on my face—half terror and half something else.

"Nothing," I say, trying not to think the worst about Annie. "This sucks." I shove the yellow slip of paper into my pocket and push past him. I figure if we take our time, Annie will catch up to us, because she's not stupid enough to hurt herself in the girls' bathroom. Everyone has their standards, and no matter what her father says about her, she's better than that.

We slowly walk down the newly polished linoleum floor and up a short flight of stairs to the main hallway where the gym, principal's office, and guidance offices are. Still, by the time the river of students thins out to nothing, and the bell sounds, Annie's nowhere in sight. Almost before we know it, we're standing in front of the guidance office with Newie's big hand resting on the doorknob.

"Let's get this over with," he grimaces.

"Fine," I say, trying to remember that the horrific Annie-images in my mind aren't real. Still, all I can imagine is her slouched down on the floor of the girls' room as a scarlet river pours between her fingers, and her eyes grow dim.

Newie pushes through the door and is immediately ushered away by his guidance counselor, Mr. Colton. Mr. Colton's a withered, old husk of a man, inordinately wrinkled, with teeth so gnarled and yellow that people actually talk about how nasty they are. He's been a guidance counselor at Apple High for millennia. He's a permanent fixture here—something that took root a long time ago.

As they walk away, Mr. Colton swivels his head and stares back at me through his half-glasses. He smiles a little, but nobody wants to see that, because even if it's genuine, he has a sinister grin—all teeth and bite.

Seconds later, I hear a voice, high and lilting. "Jackson?" it says.

It's Ms. Hutch. Her white-blond hair is curly and pinned up today, and her lipstick is the color of Hollywood blood—fake, just like her. She stares at a point somewhere past my head, roughly around where some bulletin boards are decorated with college pamphlets and trade-school brochures—all places that most of us will never go.

I make an effort to stare right at her, to see if she really can't look directly back. Maybe it makes her feel uncomfortable, like she might catch whatever I have if she stares right into my eyes. Maybe she thinks my eyes are like Claudia's, but then I realize that can't be it because, you know, Claudia doesn't have any.

I mumble something that's barely audible and hand her the yellow slip of paper.

She takes it from me, smiles, and says, "Thank you for coming." Ms. Hutch looks down and mouths the words on the piece of paper as she reads it over, as though it's brand new to her—like she's not the one who filled it out in the first place. Then she spins on her heels and starts walking back into the depths of the guidance office. "This way, please," she chirps, so I follow her.

We walk down the opposite hall from where Newie and Mr. Colton went, make a quick turn, and go into Ms. Hutch's corner office. There's a big window there that looks out on the parking lot, and I make a mental note that Chief Anderson's cruiser's gone.

"Sit down," says Ms. Hutch as she slides by me and closes the door almost all the way, but leaves it open a crack. That's a trick that teachers use these days to make sure that they don't get blamed by students for doing inappropriate things—leaving their doors open a crack—but inappropriate things happen anyway.

The same old story goes around each year about one of the senior girls and the band director, Mr. Russo, or the personal tutoring sessions Miss Fricke, the art teacher, conducts because she's just like that and all the jocks know it—or Coach Johnson who likes to grab the crotches of quiet underclassman boys who seek him out for help in the weight room.

Newie says Johnson likes his johnsons. I guess he thinks that's funny, but I don't.

It's sad.

"I'm so sorry," Ms. Hutch says in a plaintive, mewling voice as she maneuvers herself around her desk and sits down. Of course, I know what she's talking about, but I don't say anything right away. She's still not looking at me. Instead, her gaze is oddly positioned to the right of my head. It gives me the uncomfortable feeling that she really *is* looking at me, but has something really messed up with her eyes.

"Whatever," I finally say to her. It's amazing how much of a prick you can be with just one word.

I expect her to get the hint that I'm not in the mood to talk, but she doesn't take the bait. Instead she says, "How are you holding up?"

She stops and waits. The silence pushes in on me, and I know that I have to fill it with something, or I'll be sitting here all day—or worse, she might make me go to the school nurse.

"Okay," I mutter, but it doesn't seem like it's enough to shut her up. I search for something else to say, but what comes out sounds a little worse than it did in my head. "I mean, it's not like I knew her or any-thing."

She bends slightly forward, like I've suddenly said something that's vitally important. Then I realize where she's going to go with it, and my stomach begins to twist itself into knots. Still, when she says what I know she's going to say, I'm not prepared. Her words feel like I've been punched in the nuts by Newie.

"You mean it's not like your grandmother?" she says.

Yup, she went there, and the memories come flooding in.

18

MARGO FREEMAN had been dead for under a month. Becky had gone batshit crazy and was freaking everyone out.

My mother wasn't quite doing laps in a pool of black depression yet, but my father was starting to go nuts about the religious crap, forcing the entire family to read passages from the Bible every day. He took off time from work and spent hours on his knees asking God what was wrong with his little girl.

He even had creepy Father Tim come over to the house and pray with us, which was a stretch for my dad because I knew he didn't like Father Tim very much. My dad thinks that a man of the cloth should know more about the Bible than his parishioners. That's a tall order, because my dad knows a lot. Besides, Father Tim looks shifty, like the kind of guy who judges everyone else then goes home and yanks his chain to pictures of little boys on the Internet.

I hated praying with them. It meant nothing to me. To be honest, I was pissed at Becky for being so weak. In some ways, I still am, because I don't quite get "crazy." You'd think in a place like Apple I would, but the truth is, letting yourself go FUBAR is taking the easy way out. Big deal, your best friend got chopped into pieces and left all over town. Shit happens. Grow up.

I remember my dad telling Father Tim that something sinister was happening in our house. That's the only time I ever thought of Father Tim as anything other than creepy. He actually did everything he could to try and steer my parents clear of the belief that there was something demonic going on with Becky. He told my parents that there were services available to her—for low income people—for mentally ill people.

It didn't do any good. The best that Father Tim could do was to tell my father to have faith, so my dad did—all over the house.

My father spent weeks in the garage building and painting crucifixes. He even hung an extra big one in the living room over the television and forced me to get on my knees to pray for Becky's salvation, like it was my fault—like I'm the one who did something wrong.

The night that everything happened with my grandmother, my parents brought Becky up to the second floor to talk with her. Grandma was convinced that she would be able to soothe the hurt that was making my sister so mental, and my parents were about at the end of their ropes.

It was after Halloween, and Apple had simmered down into normalcy, because the murders were through for the season. Of course, no one really knows for sure, but Halloween always seems like the end—like the license to kill has expired.

It was raining out that night. I only remember the rain because I wanted to be anywhere other than home, but the world had gone cold and soggy, and there was no place to go that didn't feel fungal.

My parents were sitting in the living room, nervously doing nothing. My father was lost in thought, and my mother was slowly turning the pages of her Bible and reading the words with her mouth slightly open and her lips moving—like Becky's nun.

Upstairs there was screaming. We hadn't quite got used to Not-Becky's mouth just yet. It was foul. Its words made my face turn red, because my sister never really swore like that. Other people in town did, like Margo Freeman, but somehow, Becky never weaved that kind of language into her vocabulary. She confined herself to words like "jerk" or "crap" or maybe the occasional "slut," only when she was joking around, like she did with Margo the day she was killed.

I sat at my father's desk in the corner, reading a comic book. I can't remember which one—I think *Wicked Dead*, maybe. I'm not sure. I do remember it was filled with blood. I don't know why guys like that kind of stuff, but we do. Who cares about Archie and Veronica? I want to see gore and body parts, and maybe a little skin.

Anyway, I was fake-flipping through the pages because I couldn't concentrate on the story. What I was really doing was concentrating on the commotion upstairs. They were being so loud, like it wasn't just the three of them up there, but a whole bunch of people who had somehow snuck past us through the front door and crept up the stairs.

Something thumped heavily across the floor in my grandparents' apartment, and we all stopped what we were doing—my father, my mother, and me—and looked up at the ceiling. None of us knew what it was, but it sounded like something big. It was followed by more screaming and moaning from Not-Becky, but now my grandmother and grandfather had joined in.

"What the . . ." my father had time to say before there was another jolt. This time, a small piece of plaster let loose from the ceiling and crumbled to the floor in front of my mother. Her eyes grew big like saucers, and she gave my father one of those soundless looks that conveys volumes. My dad clutched the arm of the couch, as though he was getting ready to propel himself off the orange print and dash up the front stairs to the second floor.

Then the upstairs door slammed open—hard. Later, after everything happened, we found a dent where the doorknob hit the wall.

"Stop it," I heard my grandmother wail.

My grandfather cried, "I expel you. I expel you. I expel you." His words were followed by a coarse laugh like the one that comes from Not-Becky.

"Heaven help me," screamed my grandmother. "Noooooo . . ."

The next thing I knew, someone was cartwheeling down the stairs and slamming into the front door.

I'll never forget the horrible sound that came out of my mother's mouth when she saw who it was—my grandmother—all bent and broken, with her head twisted almost completely to one side and her legs contorted like legs should never be contorted.

My father ran to my grandmother, but it was too late. Her eyes had glazed over as her life spilled out of a deep gash in the back of her head. Only it wasn't a gash, it was worse than that, because there was pink and white stuff, too—bits of brain and bone. A chunky, soupy mess pooled around my grandmother's gray hair

My heart pounded in my chest. I wasn't sure what to think or what to do. All I knew was that my grandmother was dead for no reason, and now Not-Becky wasn't screaming anymore. It was alternately laughing and cackling and wailing like my mother—the painful sound of a wounded cat that had lost a fight with a stray dog.

My father's face was twisted in agony. He took the steps three at a time, leaving bloody shoeprints on the treads. "No," my mother screeched. "Don't." Her words tore through me as surely as a hot knife tore through Margo Freeman when she lost her head and her legs and every other part of her.

Somehow, I found myself outside, dashing across the street to Chief Anderson's house. The next thing I knew, I was in Newie's foyer, babbling incoherently to his giant father. The chief's shirt was off, and a huge tattoo of a skull with a snake crawling through its eye socket was inked around his arm and shoulder. Newie stood there with a bag of chips in his hands and that vacant look on his face that he always has when he doesn't know what to say.

Chief Anderson grabbed his shirt off the bannister and pushed past me, down the front steps, and across the street to my house. As I watched him go, I saw my sister glaring at me from the second-floor window with a face that wasn't her face, and a stare that wasn't her stare.

She wore the face of the thing that I came to know as Not-Becky.

She wore the face of evil.

19

MS. HUTCH STARES at me, waiting for me to respond, which really means that her googly eyes are probably staring at a point on the wall somewhere off to my right.

"No," I tell her. "This wasn't like my grandmother." I look out the window and chew the skin on the inside of my cheek. I can feel my insides beginning to boil. Who the hell does she think she is?

Ms. Hutch reaches down, opens up her desk drawer, and pulls out a bag of lollipops, the generic kind with the chocolate in the center. She pulls a purple one out of the bag, which is probably the grossest of all the colors next to green, and noisily peels back the wrapper.

"Want one?" she offers and holds the bag out to me. I shake my head. I'm not in a lollipop mood.

She shrugs and sucks on the purple head for a moment. I can only imagine what Newie would have to say about that. Finally, Ms. Hutch clears her throat and says, "How are your friends holding up? Newton Anderson and"—she opens up a manila folder on her desk and quickly rifles through some notes—"and Annie Berg? Aren't you two dating?"

I don't know why, but I say, "Do you keep track of how many times I jerk off, too?" My nostrils flare, and I look down at my feet. If Newie can be a fuckwad sometimes, I guess I can be a prick.

Ms. Hutch flinches slightly, like she's been slapped in the face by a hummingbird.

"That's inappropriate," she says thinly.

I sigh and shift in my seat. "Look," I say. "It's been a really long day, and it's only like nine in the morning. I just want to go to my classes and see my friends and pretend that I never found Claudia Fish in the woods." It's about the longest stretch of words I think I've ever spoken to Ms. Hutch.

She sucks on the purple lollipop some more. *Yeah, baby, yeah*, I hear Newie's voice in my head.

"That's understandable," she says.

My shoulders, which I didn't even know were tense, let loose a little.

I reach down for my backpack and pull myself to my feet.

Ms. Hutch closes the folder in front of her and folds her fingers together in that weird "here's the church, here's the steeple" sort of way, but her fingers crisscross over each other instead of under, and her thumbs touch together like a little spire, which means if she opens the door to see all the people, no one will be there.

That's fine by me. It's not like the church has ever done anything to help me, anyway.

I pause for a second, because she hasn't given me the mental nod that I'm dismissed. Ms. Hutch takes the opportunity to ask another humdinger that I don't want to answer. "How are things at home, Jackson?"

I let my backpack drop to the floor and clench my jaw.

"It's my job to ask," she says, and I realize she's right. Somewhere buried in her files is that fact that my grandmother, who lived with my family, died two years ago, and my sister has some sort of grave medical condition—but Ms. Hutch doesn't really care.

She's just doing her little job, in her little office, in her little life, in this little messed up town. She's going to go home tonight to her little apartment, where she doesn't even have a cat. She probably has a gold-fish named Frank or Joe or Steve or the name of any number of losers who picked her up at The Gin Mill, said they loved her while screwing her brains out, then never called again. She'll take a frozen dinner out of the freezer and pop it into the microwave and spend the remainder of the night in a housecoat that she probably sewed herself, crying at sappy movies on cable.

Ms. Hutch doesn't care about me. She cares about checking my name off her to-do list.

"Fine," I say. I don't offer her anything more than that, which is just as well.

She sucks on the lollipop a few more times, probably mentally counting how many licks it actually takes to get to the Tootsie Roll center. "That's it, then. Do you need a pass for class?"

I do, so she scribbles one out on her pass pad and hands it to me. "You know if you ever need to talk, I'm right here," she says.

I don't even give her the courtesy of a nod. How can she help? How can I possibly tell her what's really going on at the Gill house? What skills did she pick up from her guidance counselor correspondence course that can give me a leg up on dealing with my family?

As I turn to leave her office, I notice the bag of suckers still sitting on her desk. "Any brown ones in that bag?"

Ms. Hutch stares off into space for a moment, like she's not sure what I'm asking, but something brings her back to reality, and she says, "Oh. Let's have a look." She reaches her painted nails into the plastic bag, rummages around, and pulls out two lollipops. "Today's your lucky day," she says and stretches out her arm.

I take them from her. Then I'm out the door, down the hallway, and out of the guidance offices all together.

As I shove the lollipops into my pocket, I mumble, "Yeah, today's my lucky day all right. La-de-freaking-da."

20

I DON'T SEE NEWIE and Annie until lunch, but I do see eyes everywhere, because everyone knows by now that the three of us found Claudia Fish in the woods, and no one has a problem staring me down like I'm the one who killed her.

Between classes, I walk with my head straight down, praying to avoid any idle conversation that will inevitably lead to death, but prayer has never been my strong suit.

"Is it true?" asks Mark Zebrowski as he catches up to me in the hallway between second and third period.

"Not now," I say to him.

Mark's annoying, but he has his uses. He always has weed because his sister's screwing Ziggy Connor, so he doesn't have to pay for the pre-rolled crap Ziggy's selling.

"No probs," he says and lifts his hand to high-five me. Only then do I notice that he's got a flat spliff between his fingers. Like I said, Mark's annoying, but he has his uses. I high-five him and quickly palm the joint and slip it into my pocket. "For Crawdaddy," he says. "Stay cool, man." Mark winks as he turns down the hallway toward the library.

When the 11:40 bell rings, I head straight for the cafeteria. Annie and Newie are already there, sitting at a table by themselves with their heads hanging down. I'm guessing they've had about as much fun today as me.

I slide in next to Annie, and she pushes up against me.

"Fun times?" I say to both of them.

"It'll be over soon," says Annie. "They're like lemmings—all of them. Something new will happen, and everyone will forget about us and go jump off a cliff after someone else."

Newie stares at her like he doesn't understand, because he probably doesn't. I half expect him to ask what a lemming is, but then I feel bad for thinking he's as dumb as he is. Maybe he's just been tackled one too many times on the football field, and he's got a dent in his head.

"Huh?" he says.

Annie snorts. "Never mind."

"So what's the deal with Erika Tenzar?" I ask him. "Are you getting laid this weekend, or did you kill your chances this morning?"

"She's going to hang out after school and watch football practice," he says.

"Uh huh," says Annie. "And after?"

"Who knows?" Newie says. "Depends on how horny I am."

Annie rolls her eyes, but I feel him loud and clear. I change the subject. "What happened with you and Mr. Colton?" I ask him.

Newie shifts the way he's sitting and straddles the long bench sideways. "I kept expecting him to croak right in front of me," he says. "He's like seriously older than dirt."

"And?"

"And nothing." He shrugs. "He asked me if I was okay and shit. I told him I was used to stuff like that because, you know, Asshole's my dad and everything. Then he let me go."

I turn to Annie. "What about you?"

She shrugs. "I saw Ms. Hutch," she says. "I didn't tell her much. There wasn't much to tell." Then she says, "Oh," and pulls out a handful of lollipops from her knapsack and drops them on the table. "She gave me these."

Newie grumbles, "I didn't get candy." He stares at the jumble of oranges, purples, and greens. "Where's the chocolate?"

I reach into my pocket—not the one with Mark Zebrowski's joint in it—but the other one, and pull out the two chocolate suckers that I got from Ms. Hutch. "Ta da," I say and add the brown wrappers to the growing collection on the table.

"Wow," says Newie, then stretches out his arms and looks to the ceiling. "Where's a hot babe?" Annie giggles. It's a genuine laugh, and I realize that we're going to be back to normal soon. We all will.

By the time the bell rings at 2:15, I'm more than ready to leave the brick prison.

I catch Newie as he's going into the locker room to get ready for football practice.

"Hey," I say to him. "Annie's starting at the BD Mart tonight. I'm going to hang there for a little bit, you know? At least to make sure she gets home okay. You in?"

He shrugs. "I don't know yet. Erika has a car, so we might be doing something." My eyebrows rise slightly, and he smirks because he knows exactly why. "But if I can, I'll try to be there for closing time. When does she get out?"

"I don't know," I tell him in all honesty. "I guess eleven."

"You got it, bro," he says, then pushes through the door into the gym.

Annie is waiting for me outside the front of the school. As soon as I see her face, I know what she's going to say.

"I'm not walking through the woods," she blurts out as she looks across the parking lot toward the entrance to the path between the high school and the middle school. My shoulders slump. It's a far walk down Glendale Road if we don't cut through the woods, and I still have to go buy something for dinner before my dad gets home. I've already started compiling a list of other things I have to do, all unpleasant, before the sun sets.

"Come on," I say. "There's nothing there anymore, except maybe the tape where the police blocked off the area." I look at her, with her new blond hair and her sweet smile and her gray, oversized sweater and can't help thinking that I want to kiss her.

"Can't we please go around?" she pleads one more time, but I already know that she's resigned herself to walking the gauntlet with me. I grab her hand, pull her close, and kiss her softly.

"It'll be fine," I whisper. "Honest."

I only hope I'm right.

21

IT'S STILL WARM out, which is weird for Massachusetts, but not too weird. We're the only state where you have to put the heater and the air conditioner on in the same day. I'm sure it will be nippy by sundown, and tonight I'll be breaking out the freaking flannel.

I guess dealing with menopausal weather is all part of being a Masshole.

I hold Annie's hand as we cross the parking lot to the path and ready ourselves to dive into the woods. Leaves are falling off the trees in front of us and whispering against the ground.

Die. Die. Die.

I'll always think of this small stretch of woods as death now—death and murder. I don't suppose I'll ever feel comfortable walking through here again, but the alternative, which is almost a three mile hike, pushes me forward. I squeeze Annie's hand, and she squeezes mine.

"Yo, wait up," we hear and turn to see Mark Zebrowski crossing the parking lot toward us.

"What does he want?" grumbles Annie. She doesn't like Mark very much. Last year he puked on her shoes during a keg party at Stephanie Martini's house. Her parents were away, so her older brother bought the keg and invited a bunch of waste cases to help him tap it. Probably half the school ended up there. To call the party epic would be an understatement—until Newie's dad showed up, and we snuck out the back, more than a little wasted.

We had to weave our way through town, over the stone wall at High Garden, and down the Giant Steps, to get home without getting caught.

"He gave me a joint," I whisper to her. She just rolls her eyes.

"Did you take a whiff of that weed?" Mark asks as he trots up to us. "It's primo shit."

"I didn't whip it out in the middle of class, if that's what you're asking."

His face clouds over. "Oh," he says, like I've genuinely hurt his feelings. "Well, if you guys are cutting through, can you at least show me where you found her?"

Annie grumbles, "That's gross, Mark."

"Aw, come on," he whines. "I've never seen an actual crime scene before." He pushes past us and enters the path. "I promise I won't hurl on your shoes again. Honest."

Annie shoots me a wicked glance and I shrug, but we both follow Mark into the woods. As he walks, he pulls another joint out of his pocket and lights it, stopping for a second to shield his lighter with his hand. He takes a deep drag, holds it, and lets out a cloud before handing it to me.

"No, thanks," I tell him, although I really want to. "I got a lot of stuff to do."

"Your loss," he says. "Annie?"

She shakes her head. "I'm starting a new job in a couple of hours. I can't."

Mark looks at her like he has absolutely no idea what she means. He stands there, holding the joint, waiting for one of us to take it, but we don't. "Pussies," he says and takes another hit. Even though Mark Zebrowski lives on the hill where all the rich people live, I don't think he's ever going to make it out of Apple. Some of the rich kids' parents actually send them to one of the state schools out in Westfield or North Adams, but most of them flunk out and end up right back where they started.

Mark's like that. He's too entrenched in our way of life here—numbing himself to forget how screwed up we all are.

A noise slices through the woods—maybe an animal—maybe people. We're not quite sure. Mark looks down the path and catches the unmistakable light-blue flash of a policeman's uniform.

"Shit," he squeals and drops the joint into the leaf litter at our feet, stomping on it hard until it's completely destroyed. He cups his hand over his mouth and breathes. His eyes widen. "Do you have any gum or something? My breath reeks." Annie sighs, unzips the pocket of her backpack, and hands him a lollipop, courtesy of Ms. Hutch. He takes it from her, un-wraps it, and pops it in his mouth. "Thanks," he says. "You're a lifesaver."

"Whatever," Annie mutters.

We continue on the path, the faint stench of pot dissipating the further away from where Mark lit up that we get. The trail of dead leaves eventually curves to the right, and we see the police-tape marking off the area in the woods where we found Claudia Fish.

Officer Randy is there, along with two other cops, but I don't know their names. One of them has plastic gloves on and is examining a tree like he's performing a delicate operation. Something about them being in the woods right when school lets out seems a little too convenient, but then I realize that they're probably there by design.

Loads of kids use the path as a cut-through. They certainly don't need a tourist attraction, and they sure as hell don't need anyone messing up the crime scene.

As we get closer, I hear the cop with the gloves say, "Here's another *L*," then after a moment, "And an *E*."

An *L* and an *E*? What does that mean? I notice Mark starting to hang back, first a couple of steps, then farther and farther behind.

"What's with you?" I snap at him, but I know what's with him. His brain cells are being saturated by the weed, and he's starting to freak out. He's practically quivering out of his skin.

"I . . . I gotta go," he blurts out, then turns around and scampers off the other way, just loud enough for the cops in the woods to hear.

Annie and I continue walking with our hands glued together, like paper-doll cutouts that have been scissored out of a piece of construction paper.

"Pick up the pace. There's nothing to see," says one of the cops as we get close. I recognize him from around town, but I don't know his name. He's one of the younger guys, but he has a full head of white hair, which makes him look old.

"Hey, Joe," says Officer Randy. "They're fine. They were the two with Anderson's kid when the body was found."

"It's the only way to get home," Annie stammers. "We have to cut through here or go all the way around to the middle school. It's too far."

"Are the woods closed?" I ask. I don't mean to be a smartass, but I think it comes out that way. The officer with the white hair looks over at Officer Randy like he wants permission to shoot me.

The other one with the gloves says, "And an *F*. Add that to the *V* and *W* and . . . um . . . what were the other letters?" The three cops momentarily forget about me and Annie and gather around the tree that the cop with the gloves is crouched in front of.

While they're all distracted, we take the opportunity to quickly walk past them with our eyes straight ahead. Maybe if we don't look at them, they won't look at us, and we'll be home free—but nothing's ever that easy.

"Hey," Officer Randy calls after us. "Hold up, will ya."

"Shit," I whisper under my breath. I can feel the three officers' heads swivel, their eyes on us like crawling bugs

Officer Randy, with his stubby body squeezed into his uniform, comes over to us. He's smiling, like he does in his lectures about sexual predators—like he's trying to make the subject as palatable as possible, pretending it's not so gross. "I have a couple of questions, if you don't mind."

We both bob our heads a little too vigorously.

"Sure," I manage. Annie squeezes my hand even tighter.

"You were both with Newton Anderson yesterday, when Claudia Fish's body was found, right?"

I don't know why he has to ask, because he already knows. Still, our heads nod.

"Did you happen to notice anything strange in the woods before you found her? Maybe someone walking around off the path?"

"No," says Annie. "I mean there could have been, but everyone uses the woods as a cut-through."

"Right," says Officer Randy, all long and drawn out. He rubs his chin with one hand and gives us both a slow once-over. Finally he says, "Hey, do you mind if I show you something?" We look at each other and shrug. It's not as though he's going to present us with another dead body. Claudia's long gone. This is just one of those "day too late" crime scene sweeps that the cops are required to do but never find anything.

At least not in Apple.

Officer Randy brings us over to the tree where the other officers are looking. He puts his hands on his hips and says, "See that?"

Annie and I squint. "See what?" we both say at the same time.

"There." He points.

"Here," says the gloved guy and puts his finger right on the bark. Annie and I step a little closer. There's a little V carved into the tree. It's very small and precise, like someone actually rolled the gnarly bark into an old-fashioned typewriter and hit the shift button and the V key at the same time.

That familiar burning starts—this time at the base of my spine. It races up my back before fanning out, making my skin feel as though fire ants are crawling right beneath the surface. I can feel the heat and the sweat curl around my neck, and I swallow hard.

In my mind, I hear the officer with the gloves saying that he found other letters in the trees, and a laundry list of them dances through my head—a W and an E, an F, a V, and an I.

A long time ago, before I knew there were murders in Apple, while my grandmother was alive and my grandfather wasn't so senile, Becky and I used to have Sunday morning breakfast with them before we all went to church.

My grandfather would read the newspaper and sometimes cut things out with a pair of big black scissors that I couldn't even wrap my hands around. My grandmother would make waffles and eggs, or sometimes she would bake apple pie with cinnamon and nuts and let us eat some for breakfast while it was still warm.

After, when we were more stuffed than we had a right to be, I would sit on my grandfather's lap, and we would do the word puzzles in the back of the newspaper. They were next to the colored comics, and my eyes would flit back and forth between the funnies and the word games.

"You're a smart boy," my grandfather would say to me, then let me figure out the easy crossword clues, like the four letter word for something that lives in a bowl of water.

"Fish," I would exclaim after way too long.

Claudia Fish.

"Excellent," he would tell me, then write the answer in the cross-word with blue pen. Pen was important, because only the words that were absolutely right were written in pen. The rest were in pencil—until he was sure.

After the crossword puzzle was done, and my grandmother had washed the dishes and put them away, we would all gather around the paper together and work out the anagrams—shifting the letters around in our heads until we got them right.

Then we would all go to church and see creepy Father Tim, because even back then I thought that Father Tim was freaky.

"Is this part of some sort of game the kids are playing these days?" asks the officer with the gloves. "You know, like Dungeons and Dragons or some sort of scavenger hunt?"

I shake my head, because I don't know. Annie does the same thing, but deep inside, my mind is making anagrams like mad. It's rearranging the letters and leaving openings where the blanks are—but it doesn't matter.

"You're a smart boy," my grandfather would say.

I know what the letters are going to spell out. The burning creeps up my cheeks to my ears. It might take the cops a little bit to find them all, and when they do, it might take a couple gallons of coffee and a box of stereotypical doughnuts for them to put the pieces together.

Still, I know what the letters will spell out, and I want to puke.

They'll spell *FIVE WILL DIE* on the trees, just like the words welted up on Becky's milky white skin.

Five will die.

Five will die.

Five will die.

22

ANNIE AND I DON'T talk as we make our way through High Garden and down the Giant Steps. We don't hold hands either. Mine are shoved in my pockets, and I'm trying not to think at all. Thinking will only make my head hurt and my brain more confused than it already is.

How does Becky know about the trees? It doesn't make any sense. How did she know to scratch *FIVE WILL DIE* into her skin last night? For that matter, how did she know about Claudia Fish?

I'm confused, and I can't think about this right now, so I start humming "La Cucaracha" in my head, because it's sure to give me an ear worm. There's nothing worse than an ear worm to totally consume your thoughts. The only way to get rid of an ear worm is to find an equally annoying song like "It's a Small World" to replace it.

Annie's not talking either. She's lost in her own thoughts, and I'm positive they're totally different from mine. She's probably hoping that, when she gets home, her dad is passed out. If he's not, who knows what could happen? I'm sure all she wants is a couple hours of peace before she has to report to work at the BD Mart, but sometimes the monster inside Mr. Berg won't let her have peace.

She never talks about him—her father—but she doesn't have to say a thing. I can see it in her eyes—the hatred and self-loathing. I can feel her tense when we're blessedly alone, and she lets me explore her body.

I know about human scum like Mr. Berg—or Ralphie Delessio, who liked to hit girls. They're the ones with mothers that never taught them to keep their hands to themselves—to not touch what isn't theirs.

What was it that Newie said to me yesterday? *"Don't you want to fucking pound that guy's head into the ground?"*

The truth is I do. I want to grab a hunk of his graying hair and twist my fingers into it until it gets all tangled—and when I have a really good hold, I want to drag him to his knees and drive his head into the floor, over and over again. I don't want to stop when his nose cracks and drives splinters into his brain, and I don't want to stop when the ground becomes slick with blood and his mouth can only make a sopping, gurgling cry.

I want to pound his head into the ground over and over again until his hair falls away from my grip, because there's nothing left for it to be rooted to but a bag of mashed pulp.

But sometimes we can't have what we want.

"I'd walk you to work tonight if I could," I say, breaking our shared silence. "I just can't."

"It's okay," she whispers, but I can tell from her voice that she's already nervous.

"I'll be there at eleven to walk you home," I say. "Newie, too, if he can pry his dick out of Erika."

Annie snorts. "Who are you kidding? Newie's going to have that Tenzar slut on her back all night."

"He'll be there," I assure her. "He's Newie. He told me he'll be there, so he'll be there." That's the one thing about Newie. He might only have two brain cells fighting for territory, but if he says he'll do something, then he'll do it. Besides, he'll most likely chicken out and not do anything with Erika, anyway. She's carrying half the diseases we read about in that thick book from health class, the one with the nasty pictures and the warning labels about how this could happen to you.

"Your mom's at Tenzar's?" I ask her as I unconsciously reach into my shirt pocket to make sure the grocery money is there.

"You making dinner again?" Annie asks me. She sounds sad when she says it, like she's commiserating with me about how both our home lives suck.

"Yeah," I tell her. "Probably something easy like frozen pizza. Everyone seems to like that." In my head, I hear myself sigh with relief, because you don't need any utensils to eat a frozen pizza—not even a spoon. That means Becky's eating with her hands tonight, which makes me feel a little less uneasy about her.

As we reach Annie's house, she leans over and gives me a quick kiss before turning away.

"Hey," I yell after her.

"What?"

"You okay?"

"About as okay as you are, I guess."

She turns to head back into her house again, and I say, "Don't do anything stupid, please." Annie stops. I see her back go stiff. I think I've plucked a nerve, the one that feeds her need to lock herself in the upstairs bathroom for a little alone time with a razor blade. I'm immediately sorry for saying anything. I already snagged her this morning. I don't have to dredge it up again this afternoon. She turns around and walks back to me.

"Can't you just leave it alone?"

I want to. I really do—but the simple answer is, no, I can't leave it alone. "What do you want me to say, Annie? You can't keep doing that to yourself, or someone's going to wise up and throw you in the state school over in Bellingham."

Her eyes narrow into slits. "You mean like where Becky should be?"

It's like getting a slap in the face. Her words come out of nowhere and they sting. Sometimes we hear stories about Bellingham State—about how the patients are left to sit in their own urine for days on end—about how they shit themselves until their giant diapers are full and fat.

"That's not fair," I tell her. "I can't do anything about that."

"Well, I can't, either," she says. "Becky can sit in your house and go freaking crazy if she wants to, but I've found a way that helps me make sense of it all. Don't tell me to stop doing that, because if you tell me to stop, you're going to end up making me go crazy—like your sister."

I want to tell her that, in some ways, she already is, but it won't do any good. I just have to take a deep breath and hope that, eventually, Annie can exorcise her demons with something other than a sharp piece of metal.

I close my eyes and try to summon up the ear worm in my head again. I want it to eat up every bit of the past twenty-four hours and help me find peace, but no matter what I want, it doesn't come.

All that's left are Annie's words cutting into me like a knife, and the only thing I hear myself saying is, "You'll never be crazy like Becky, Annie. Trust me. Never like her."

23

I BUY TWO FROZEN pizzas at Tenzar's and endure a conversation with Mrs. Ruddick, who used to play canasta with my mother. There's something about her that screams "not from Apple." Middle-aged women here don't dress up to go grocery shopping. They're more likely to be wearing sweats and oversized shirts to hide the fact that they're losing the battle of the bulge. Some even go out with curlers in their hair.

"How's your mother, Jackson?" she purrs in that damned superior voice of hers that makes me feel like I'm scum. I'm standing in front of the freezers, deciding between hamburger and pepperoni, and trying to remember if my grandfather doesn't like one or the other.

"Okay," I tell her. Mrs. Ruddick isn't the kind of person you lie to. If she doesn't like what you have to say, she'll make up something else and spread it around like summer mulch—the kind that encourages weeds to grow through it.

"We haven't seen her out and about lately."

I'm not sure who the "we" is that she's referring to, unless she's talking about the "royal we."

"My grandfather's in a wheelchair now," I say. I'm still not lying. I'm just dancing with words. "He needs a lot of help." I'm hoping that Mrs. Ruddick goes away soon, because I don't want to endure any more questions. I already got interrogated by Ms. Hutch this morning. That's about my limit for the day. Besides, the last thing I want is for Mrs. Ruddick to ask about Becky, because she's exactly the kind of person who'd pry like that.

I'm pretty good at switching the subject.

"Do you know which one of these is better?" I ask, as I hold up two different brands of pizza with pictures on the boxes that don't look anything like the flash-frozen disks inside.

"I'm afraid I can't help you," she says, which is exactly what I expect her to say. "We always buy our pizza fresh. It's so much tastier that way."

Of course you do, you stuck-up bitch. Go back to Boston or

Springfield or wherever you're from, because you're certainly not from around here. "Thanks, anyway."

I put the more expensive one back in the big freezer and take two of the cheaper ones. "I'll tell my mom you said hello."

"Yes, please," she calls after me, but I've already gone down the snacks aisle.

I see Annie's mother at the registers. I feel sorry for Mrs. Berg. She wears her long gray hair in a ponytail, and her face is dried up and mottled like a piece of old fruit. Her lips are cracked, and I can tell she's jonesing for a cigarette. Mrs. Berg's been working at Tenzar's ever since I can remember. When I was a kid, she used to turn the other way when Newie and I swiped candy bars from the rows of crap next to the registers. I thought she was cool like that—but more likely than not, letting us commit petty larceny was just her way of giving her middle finger to the Tenzars for being rich people from up on the hill who still paid her next to nothing.

When she sees me, she waves her hand and calls me over, brushing a few long strands of hair out of her face and pulling on her shirt to make the wrinkles disappear. I go stand in line at her register. She's running groceries through for a fat lady wearing dirty sweats that are way too tight. They're almost flesh-colored, which makes her look like she's naked from the waist down. It's not a pretty sight. I look at the bounty she's buying and note things like Pop-Tarts and Oreos and butter—lots and lots of butter. I wonder if she applies it directly to her thighs to make gaining weight more efficient.

Mrs. Berg takes a handful of coupons from the fat lady and runs them through the scanner, then waits patiently while the fat lady slides her debit card through and punches in her access code—five digits long, the same number of people that are going to die this fall in Apple.

Five will die.

Five will die.

Five will die.

I grimace and try to recall the ear worm, but Mrs. Berg brings me back to reality. "Jackson?" she says.

"Hi." I put the pizzas down in front of her and fish around in my pocket for the grocery money.

"How are you doing, honey?" she asks with tired eyes and a sad smile. I know she's really asking how I'm doing since finding Claudia Fish in the woods.

I shrug. "Okay, I guess." I don't want to talk about death anymore.

I don't want to think about it. I search around my head for something else to say, and thankfully, it comes easily. "So Annie's starting at the BD Mart tonight?" It's not really a question, because I already know the answer. I just want to make conversation that's not about murder.

"Yes, she is," says Mrs. Berg. "I really wish I could drive her, but I have to work late." Tenzar's is open until eleven on Friday and Saturday nights because it's about the only place around where you can buy groceries on the weekends.

I like Mrs. Berg. Something inside of me urges me to ease her pain. "I told Annie I'd meet her after work," I say, mustering about as much cheerfulness as I can. "I'll make sure she gets home okay."

Mrs. Berg stops what she's doing. She reaches out and touches my cheek for a moment. It's a little weird. "You're such a good boy, Jackson."

Her words feel like déjà vu. My face gets hot, and I think I turn a little red. "Newie's going to meet us, too," I blurt out.

"That's good," she says. Mrs. Berg finishes sliding the pizzas under the scanner and tells me how much they are, which is way cheaper than buying the fresh crap that Mrs. Ruddick says is so much tastier.

"She'll be fine," I reassure her as I bag the pizzas myself. Mrs. Berg smiles that sad smile again, which really isn't a smile at all. It's a novel written on her face about lost lives and abusive marriages and unspeakable things that go on behind closed doors.

As I leave, right before the exit, there's a bell hanging on the wall with a sign above it that says, *Ring if you've received good service.* I guess I did, so I ring it as I go. The check-out people at the registers, all four of them, stop what they're doing and clap a few times.

It's weird, just like Mrs. Berg touching my face.

I feel smothered in Tenzar's, with its depressing people going through their depressing lives. People like Mrs. Ruddick, who must have one hell of a story to tell about how she ended up in the armpit of Massachusetts, or Mrs. Berg, who doesn't realize she's already in Hell, running a cash register and ringing up food on a black conveyor belt without end.

People like me, who find dead bodies in the woods, and it's not even the worst part of their day.

I make my way up Main Street, past some nameless stores, and try not to look at anyone. I need to mentally prepare myself for whatever I'm going to find at home. Will it be screaming today? Will I find my mother slumped over at the kitchen table, her expression vacant and far away? Will my grandfather be upstairs, cursing out the remote because he can't remember that you have to set the television to channel three in order to make the cable box work?

When I pass Francine's Fire House, I absentmindedly look in the window. It's not quite dinnertime yet, so only old folks are in there. They're buying the early-bird special before five, the one that comes with salad and dessert that they'll wolf down as quickly as they can so they can get home and hide from Apple.

I pass Zodiac Tattoo Parlor, with its darkened windows and its ever-changing bulletin board filled with photographs of arms and legs and chests that have been permanently scarred for some stupid reason. Of course, all the burnouts and addicts think it's funny to get a tattoo of an apple with a razorblade stuck in it and blood dripping out. There are other winners, too, like zippers that are half-open showing peeled back skin and bits of guts, or skeletons with snakes squirming through their vacant eye sockets.

Just like the chief's.

Through the window of Three Penny's, I see a young mother with two little kids looking at hand-me-down coats for winter. She seems familiar, like maybe she graduated when Becky was supposed to, or dropped out because she got knocked up. I try to imagine Annie in there instead of her, but I can't. I don't want that for her.

When I walk by The Gin Mill and Millie's Café, I quicken my pace. I don't like the biker dudes that hang out front. Normally, I'd stop at Nick's, but Newie and I were both dicks to Old Nick yesterday, and knowing Old Nick, he'll need more than a day to cool off.

I brood most of the way home. I don't remember walking down the rest of Main Street or turning onto Vanguard Lane, but once I'm in front of my house, reality comes crashing down, and I realize that I don't want to go inside. I don't want to know what I'll find there.

It turns out I'm right.

I don't.

24

THERE'S A CANDLE lit and sitting on the oak desk in the living room. It's one of those scented ones that smells like fall. The label's been peeled off, so I can't see what flavor it is, but it reminds me of what the house used to smell like when my grandmother made Sunday morning breakfast—like baked McIntosh and cinnamon and caramel all mixed together.

Anywhere else in Massachusetts, it would smell like autumn.

In Apple, autumn smells like death.

I don't know why my mother lit it in the first place. Back when she was still my mom and not a sad shell hiding in the dark, she had this thing she did after she cleaned a room. She would light a candle. Sometimes Becky and I would come home from school, and we would find a clean house and a different scent burning in every room.

I loved that—my mother's little cleaning ritual—but my mother doesn't clean anymore, so leaving a candle burning in the living room is only a tease. Life here will never be like it was before.

I blow out the candle and watch the end of the wick turn from red to black. A trail of smoke rises up into the air and vanishes, just like the memories of a time when my life was relatively normal—back when my sister was just Becky, Suzie Zickle, and the obsessive nun—back before Not-Becky.

The house is quiet, which is good, but there're unwashed dishes in the sink from breakfast. There's also white stuff all over the kitchen counter that looks like sugar. If I didn't know any better, I'd think my mother tried to be normal for a change and bake a batch of cookies or a pie. After all, she did light a single candle. Maybe there's hope for her yet.

I drop the grocery bag on the kitchen table and immediately go into after-school mode, which means washing the dishes and tidying up the kitchen to get ready for dinner.

I run a couple of paper towels under the faucet and wipe the white stuff off the counter. Some of it gets on my hand, and I absentmindedly stick my finger in my mouth.

I'm right, it *is* sugar.

I look around to see if there's actually any evidence of baked goods, but it's been two years since my mom's done stuff like that. There's not, so I only shrug and wash the dishes in the sink before putting them on the drying rack. Then I open the freezer and put the two pizzas on the shelf, because it won't be dinner time for a couple more hours.

When I'm done, I quietly make my way down the hallway to my parents' room and lightly knock on the door.

Nothing.

I knock again, but there's still no response, so I softly push it open. My mother's cocooned in blankets on the bed. She's sleeping. I can hear her faint snores in the darkness. I take a step into the room and sniff to make sure she didn't fall asleep with a cigarette in her hand. She actually did that once before and only woke up when her fingers started to blister against the heat of the smoldering ash.

I spent three weeks rubbing her hand every day with an over-the-counter cream from Jolly's Pharmacy, because she refused to leave the house to see a doctor.

My mother doesn't leave the house for anything anymore. She hides in her black pool and only comes up for air when she has to eat or put on a face for my dad or creepy Father Tim. She always puts on a face for Father Tim, slipping on a fake, cheery skin-mask over her own.

Thankfully, I don't smell any smoke in my mother's darkened room today. It smells of something else though, like a mixture of illness and despair. I've come to realize that both have a distinct odor—like the faint stench of my grandfather's apartment upstairs—but his is also flavored with a touch of resignation. Old people's homes all smell like that.

"Screw this," I whisper under my breath, loosely translated as "I'm outta here—this house, this town, everything," but I know I don't mean it. Sure, I'm angry at my mother, but I'm madder at myself for being pissed. She's sick, like my sister. Still, it's all I can do to keep from shaking her. If she would only wake up from her stupor long enough to remember that she has a house and a family to take care of, maybe every-thing would get better—but who am I fooling?

Instead, I leave her in that dark room, clicking the door closed be-hind me and padding back down the hallway to the kitchen. Without really knowing why, I open up the cabinet where all the medications are and pull out one of the orange bottles with the white lids. It's covered with sugar, too, so I know she's taken her pills today—I just don't understand why they don't work.

She's supposed to take them to keep the darkness at bay, to not let it in like a stray cat that curls around her head and smothers her brain.

Her pills are useless. Why doesn't my father see that? Maybe he's waiting for his precious God to notice for him.

I still have other chores to do, like checking on my grandfather, so I open the door to the back staircase and slowly climb the narrow stairs to his apartment.

The candle scent has permeated the whole house. It makes my nose tingle and reminds me that I once thought the smell of apple was nice. Now it only reeks of rot.

"Pa?"

He doesn't answer.

"Grandpa Gill?"

"What . . . what . . . who's there?" I hear him say from the living room.

"I've come to rob you blind," I call out as I walk through his kitchen.

"Too late," he croaks. "I've already spent all my money on women and liquor. I'm going to be damned to Satan forever and a day."

My grandfather's sitting in his wheelchair by the big window in his living room, the one that looks out onto Vanguard Lane.

"Is that you, Mother?" he asks. I think he's talking about my grandmother, or at least I hope he is. His own mother's long dead, and I'd hate to think he's forgotten that, too, along with most of the rest of his long life.

"No," I say as I walk over to him and bend down on one knee in front of his chair. "It's me."

He studies my face, and a flicker of comprehension flashes through his eyes. "Benny Boy?" he says, calling me by my father's name. I slowly shake my head, because I won't lie to him. I refuse to do that.

"Nope," I say. "Try again."

His eyes seem so small. They've shrunken into his face over the years. Now they're barely buttons sewn onto his thin, wrinkled skin.

"I know you," he says.

"That's right, you do."

My grandfather stretches his thin arm out and runs his bony knuckles along my cheek, stroking my face just like my mother and Mrs. Berg. He stares at me for a long time with his little eyes and his old, loose skin hanging around him in folds. Finally, the little black centers grow big as he reaches into his mind for the name he knows is there. I can see it in his expression. He wants to drag it onto his tongue and bring it to life.

When he finally does, the room grows cold.

"You're Crawdaddy Fish." he says. "You're Crawdaddy Fish."

25

SICKENING LAUGHTER erupts from the air vent in the corner—the one that sinks straight into the basement where my sister's locked away. Becky and I used to talk through the vents when we were little. She'd hide downstairs, and I would come up here, and we could hear our voices echo to each other—telling secrets—giggling all the way.

Now, all I can see is Not-Becky curled up against the grate in my sister's duplicate room, listening intently to my conversation with my grandfather.

"Who told you that name?" I bark at the old man.

He looks scared and leans back in his chair. The wheels creak against the floor boards. "What name?" he says with a tremor in his voice.

"Crawdaddy Fish. Who told you that name?"

His lips quiver as he cocks his head to one side, like he's listening to something far, far away. "It's the mice in the walls," he whispers. "They talk to me."

I hear the obnoxious chuckling again. It drifts out of the vent like smoke. It's Not-Becky playing messed-up head games with our grandfather. It's whispering horrible things to him, the only way it can—through the cracks in the house—through the cracks in his foundation.

"Shit," I say under my breath, but my grandfather hears me anyway, and suddenly, the flat palm of his hand is sailing through the air. He strikes me on the cheek, harder than I think he's able.

"Don't use that language in my house," he growls with utter clarity. I'm stunned and sorry at the same time. As penance, I let the sting work its way into my face without rubbing the hurt away. I deserve it. I deserve whatever punishment he sees fit to dole out while I'm living under his roof.

"I'm sorry, Grandpa," I say to him.

He leans forward in this chair. "Sorry doesn't cut it," he sneers. "When was the last time you went to confession, Benny Boy? And don't you lie to me. I'll know if you lie. I always know when you lie."

"Crawdaddy Fish," cackles the thing in the basement. "Crawdaddy Fish, Crawdaddy Fish, Crawdaddy Fish."

"I'm not Ben," I say as gently as I can, trying to shut out the rant coming from the vent. "I'm not Ben, Grandpa. I'm Jackson. I'm Ben's son."

More laughter rises from the floor, so I take a lumpy pillow off of the couch and put it in front of the little metal grate. It's not perfect, but it cuts out most of the noise.

"I'm going to make the mice go away," I tell him. "They won't whisper to you through the walls anymore, Grandpa. Would you like that?"

He shakes his head yes, but I can already see he's confused. "Who will talk to me, then?" he cries. His eyes are wet. I don't know what to say to him. The truth is, there's nobody left to talk to him. My grandmother's dead, my mother is lost inside herself, and my father hides in the garage.

If I take her away from him, then who will be left besides me?

I can't do it alone. I don't have it in me to do any more than I already do. I feed him and make sure his clothing's washed. I fix his television when he thinks it's broken. That's all I can do. I can't be there for him any more than I already am.

I just can't.

I look at the lumpy pillow I shoved up against the grate and reluctantly pull it away.

"There," I say. "I'll let the mice talk to you, okay?" Secretly, I pray that sometimes it's my sister who reaches out to him instead of Not-Becky.

My grandfather nods, but I know he doesn't understand what I'm saying. Besides, he's so far gone, what harm could come from letting my sister whisper to him through the air ducts? What can she possibly say? What can she possibly do?

Not-Becky's laughter goes silent, and my grandfather sniffs. He wipes his eyes with his sleeve. I know he's relieved I took the pillow away from the grate. It's like his lifeline—his telephone. The truth is, my grandfather and my sister share an old-fashioned connection through the walls, like two prisoners in a dungeon who pass each other notes between a chink in the hard-packed mortar.

I suppose there's some kind of comfort in knowing that neither of them is truly alone in their lunacy. At times, my grandfather must think my grandmother's speaking to him through the grate, or maybe he thinks it's God, giving him absolution for all the things he's done wrong in his life—or the Devil, cursing him for them.

Maybe this is his punishment for whatever he did to my father to make him the way he is.

I don't know—but his words ring in my ears. *When was the last time you went to confession, Benny Boy?* How many times did he make my father do that? How many times did he force my father to his knees in front of a false idol made of wood or plaster and make him pray for his salvation.

I reach for the remote control and turn on the television. The sound of it filling up his living room is jarring, and my grandfather suddenly looks around and finds the box with the moving pictures on it. In no time, he's transfixed, so I turn up the sound just a little too much. Maybe it will drown out the voice in the wall, or maybe she'll hear it, too, and not feel so alone.

On my grandfather's kitchen table, I find an empty bowl from breakfast with some dried cereal clinging to the sides. It's still sticky from the milk that's evaporated around it. Next to that is an empty plate which probably held a peanut butter sandwich for lunch and maybe some potato chips. I don't know if we're supposed be watching my grandfather's diet or not. All I know is that between me and my father, we make sure he eats three times a day.

It's the same with Becky. We make sure she eats, too—but that's all.

I take the bowl and the plate, leave my grandfather in front of the television, and quietly go downstairs to the kitchen. There're still a few hours until dinner, so I decide that I'll bring Becky a glass of milk and some cookies. She always liked milk and cookies—any kind, as long as they were chocolate.

We have some Hydrox left in the cupboard. They're those Oreos that aren't Oreos at all, just like Not-Becky's not Becky at all.

I pull a handful of them out of their wrapper and put them on a plate and fill a glass with the milk I bought last night at the BD Mart. As I open the basement door to flick on the light, I look down and count the cookies that I've set out for my sister. There are five of them, not four or six, but five.

There's significance to the number five, and Becky and I are going to have a little talk about that, mostly because I want to know. I want to know why she said, "Five will die," and I'm not going to listen to any more of her crazy talk until I get an answer.

Not this time.

26

THE KEY TO BECKY'S dungeon isn't hanging on the nail at the bottom of the basement stairs. For a moment, fear washes over me. I search the floor, even getting down on my hands and knees to slap at the cement. It's nowhere. What the hell?

I'm about to dash upstairs to search my father's dresser when a flash of light catches my eye. It's the key, sticking out of the bottom lock of Becky's door. It's glinting in the afternoon sun, streaming in from the window well above the laundry machine.

Shit.

I can picture Not-Becky chewing at its own wrists until they are slick with blood, so it can slime free of its chains.

I can picture Not-Becky squeezing itself up against the barred door, its tattered hair stringy and wet with sweat, trying to force its bony arm through the narrow spaces to reach down for the little piece of metal—and freedom.

Who knows what would happen if it got out? I don't want to think about that because all I can see is blood smeared across my mind, threatening to blot out the world.

I stand there, holding the cookies and milk, staring at the head of the key as it sticks out of the door, forcing the rational part of my mind to come up with a plausible reason for why it's there in the first place.

All I can come up with is my father.

Why would he do that? He must have left the key there this morning by accident, when he brought her a bowl of cereal for breakfast and a sandwich and chips for lunch.

Yeah, that must be it. My father just forgot. I shake my head and sneer.

That will be ten Hail Marys for you, Benny-boy. Screw that—make it twenty.

I let out a long breath that I don't even know I'm holding and walk slowly over to the barred door with the milk and cookies balanced in my hands. I can hear my sister inside, muttering something, which is nothing new.

If my family kept me prisoner in the basement, chained to a wall, I'd probably be talking to myself, too. As I peer through the bars, I see Not-Becky crouched in the far corner near the bathroom. The light above the sink is still on, and the little makeup kit, the one she had out yesterday, is still open and sitting on the counter.

"Six," Not-Becky gurgles into the grate in the wall. "Not five." It scratches at its head with its cracked nails, and some of the scabs on its scalp flake off and fall to the floor. "No more five, no more five, no more five." It clutches itself and rocks back and forth. "Six, six, six—that's the number of the Beast, you know. Six, six, six."

My hand that's holding the plate starts to jiggle, and the cookies jitter about as though there's a tiny earthquake underneath my feet.

"Six, six, six. One more for kicks," Not-Becky cackles as it holds the wall with its hands. "Tee hee hee. Tee hee hee. Six, six, six. One more for kicks."

Suddenly, it whips its head around to stare at me through the bars. There are sixes drawn all over its face with eyeliner. Some are upside down, and some are right-side up. Others are tilted sideways.

Across its forehead is that accursed number that everyone knows—666—drawn out in black.

"You got to be kidding me."

"Six, six, six. One more for kicks," Not-Becky screeches. It leaps to its feet, quicker than I've ever seen it move before. The chains clang against the metal bed frame. Before I know what's happening, it's at the door, trying to shove its hand through the bars so it can reach down, grab the head of the key, and twist it free—just like I imagined would happen.

"No," I yelp, quickly setting the cookies and milk down. I bang desperately at its hand with my fist. One of my hits connects, and it squeals and yanks its hand back though the bars.

"Ow," she cries. "Why did you do that?" Becky's speaking now, not the other one.

"You were trying to grab the key," I gasp, my heart pounding in my chest.

"It hurts," she cries as she shakes her hand. She sticks her middle two fingers in her mouth.

"Serves you right," I snap. "What were you thinking? Get back and sit on the bed so I can open the door."

"No," Not-Becky snarls, pulling its hand from its mouth and shaking it again—but I know what it really means is "yes." Reluctantly, it slinks back to the mattress and plops down on the bed with a hateful look on its face.

"I have chocolate," I tell it. "Chocolate cookies."

Its face changes, and now she's Becky again, with an eager smile plastered on her face. She'd wag her tail if she had one. She's painful to see. How can my sister be reduced to this? How could this have happened? The whiplash change of personalities must be excruciating for her.

I know it is for me.

I quickly open up the three locks and drop the key in my pocket. Then I pick up the milk and cookies, step inside the door, and close it behind me. I have to be cautious. I know how quickly things can turn in here.

Lightning fast.

"What kind?" she asks me, meaning the cookies.

"Hydrox," I tell her. I go over and hand her the glass of milk and the plate. She eagerly grabs one of them and shoves the whole thing in her mouth.

"Not so fast," I say as she chews and chews.

"Look," she says and smiles at me with a mouth full of chocolate-colored teeth.

I laugh, a genuine laugh, and so does she, then she takes a long, deep swallow of milk and reaches for another cookie.

"Becky, can we talk?" I ask. She shrugs and scratches absentmindedly at her head. I think it's her medication that makes her itch like that, peeling her skin off her skull, bit by bit.

"That's what we're doing, aren't we?" She shoves a second cookie into her mouth and twists it around so she has a round circle of chocolate surrounded by cracked lips. It's a bizarre vision, and I look away.

"No," I say. "I mean, yeah, we're talking, but I kind of need to know something."

She mashes the second cookie with her teeth and gulps down more milk. As she licks her lips, I pull a set of handcuffs from my pocket. She watches me, rolls her eyes, and reluctantly holds one hand out as she looks the other way. I slip one cuff around her wrist, above the manacle that's attached to the wall by a long chain, and hook the other end to the metal bed frame.

This way she can't get up, even if Not-Becky comes back.

Of course, though, that's exactly what I want to happen. I pocket the small handcuff key and back up until I feel the heavy door pressing against my back. Slowly, I sink down until I'm crouched with my knees bent, balanced on the balls of my feet.

"So?" she says as she pivots her head and stares at me.

"I don't want to talk to you, Becky," I say, staring at my feet instead of at her. "You know who I want to talk to."

She's quiet for a long time. Finally she's says, "Oh," and nothing else, so I wait.

I don't have to wait long.

27

THE FIRST THING Not-Becky does is hock a loogie on the floor near my feet. It's solid and chocolate-green and makes me want to puke—but I won't give it the satisfaction. I need to know how it knows five will die. Actually, I need to know how it knows five will die and now maybe six, because six, six, six—one more for kicks.

"Get out," Not-Becky growls at me through a voice that sounds like its coming from the depths of a sewer.

"I can't," I say. "Not until you answer some questions for me."

"I don't fucking answer questions," it snarls as it lets a copious amount of chocolate saliva drip from its mouth and onto my sister's T-shirt.

"Nice," I say. "Really nice. You used to kiss our grandmother with that mouth." The words sting coming out, and I can feel my chest starting to burn again.

It gurgles and bubbles and licks the slime off of its lips. "And now she's dead," it cackles. "Dead and buried."

I shake my head, afraid that I don't know what I'm doing, but I know I have to try just the same. "Questions," I repeat. "I got a few."

"Get out," it roars so loudly that I can imagine Mrs. Owens from across the street, looking up from her knitting needles, wondering if some sort of strange animal is loose in the neighborhood. I don't move. I just sit there, waiting for Not-Becky to say something—anything of use. Finally, it leans back, dangerously close to the way Margo Freeman leaned back on the living room floor the day she was cut to pieces. Then it chants in a syrupy sing-song:

> *"Four and twenty blackbirds baked into a pie.*
> *Cut yourself a slice of it and you'll get really high."*

"I don't like pie," I say, although a good old-fashioned pie with some 420 baked into it sounds good right about now.

> *"Four and twenty blackbirds baked into a pie.*

Eat another piece of it and you will surely die."

I sigh and stare at the floor. "Are we into nursery rhymes now?"

"Get out, or I'll scratch your goddamned eyes out of your head," it growls. "Just like Claudia Fish."

Crawdaddy Fish.

A long, low rumble issues from its lips, like the one a dog makes when it gnaws on a bone and you happen to stray too close.

"Yeah, let's talk about eyes," I say to Not-Becky. "What do you know about them? What do you know about eyes being ripped out of a girl's head?"

The thing bends its neck all the way to one side, and I can hear the bones crackling. Then it bends it all the way over to the other side, and I fear that something on my sister is actually going to break.

"Six, six, six. One more for kicks," it says to me. "Six, six, six. One more for kicks."

Not-Becky won't answer my question. "Well *you* didn't do it," I say to it. I'm not asking. I'm stating a fact. My sister, or the thing that pretends to be my sister, didn't kill Claudia Fish. Becky's been locked in this room for two years.

"Oh, no?" It purrs in a guttural, fetid way as it brings my sister's head erect. This time, I look up, and its pupils are completely rolled back in their sockets. All I can see are wet, white eyeballs. "Look at me, fiddle dee dee. This is what happens to those who see."

Okay. That's something I can work with. I force myself to stare at the blank orbs, red-rimmed and veiny. "Did Claudia see something?" I ask.

It darts out its brown-stained tongue. "You mean Crawdaddy?" The words crawl out of its mouth like a spider. "Crawdaddy Fish, to die was her wish." A noxious smell is coming from Not-Becky, and I realize that it's freaking taking a dump right in front of me. It smiles because it knows I know. Chocolate cookies are caked between its teeth.

It's all crap everywhere.

I don't know what to do. I'm so far out of my depth that I say the first thing that comes to my mind. "I'm going to call Father Tim," I tell Not-Becky. "I'm going to call Father Tim and tell him to come over right now."

Of course I'm lying. Why would I ever call creepy Father Tim, the man who thinks that having faith is somehow going to cure Becky? I can't even look at him at church on Sunday mornings. He slithers when he walks. The words that come out of his mouth seem to ooze out of him on a slimy stream.

"NOOO," Not-Becky wails and covers its face with its free hand.

I wrap my arms around myself. I can tell that the nightmares will be bad tonight. I might actually see what Not-Becky looks like underneath my sister's skin suit, and it will be terrible.

Terrible and cruel.

"Why not?" I spit out. "Either you answer my questions, or I'm calling Father Tim. It's your choice." My nostrils flare as the smell of shit assaults my nose, but I don't acknowledge it. I'll acknowledge nothing that gives it power.

Not-Becky screams in rage and heaves up another glob of thick mucus to leach out of its mouth. "Ask your questions, boy," it sputters and bubbles. The words are painful to my ears, and the smell in the room is becoming toxic.

"How did you know Claudia Fish was dead, and how do you know more will die?"

Its tongue lolls out of its mouth, and it pulls its legs up so it's crouching on the bed like I'm crouching on the floor.

"She wanted death," it says to me. "I could smell it miles away. She wanted death, so she was granted her wish."

"You're not answering me," I say as I stand up, sweat pouring off my forehead. My heart is pounding in my chest. I feel as though I've run a four minute mile. "How did you know she was murdered? How do you know more will die?"

Not-Becky looks around in frustration. Its blazing eyes finally land on the plate of Hydrox. It curls its free hand into a fist and brings it down hard on the round chocolate cookies, smashing them to pieces. Over and over again, it hits the plate until there is nothing but crumbs.

"We know because we are Legion," it croaks out. "We are Legion. We see everything."

Anger shoots out of my eyes. You can't grow up in a freaking religious household like mine without knowing a thing or two about the gospel. In Mark 5:9 there's a passage about Jesus talking to this guy in the country of Gadarenes. In it, Jesus says, "What is thy name?" and the guy answers, "My name is Legion for we are many."

Creepy Father Tim talked about that passage in study group before I stopped going. I'm not sure what he expected to accomplish by bringing up the fallen angel, but he said in various versions of the New Testament that the name Legion refers to devils or demons.

Becky's no demon. She's just my sick, sick sister.

I look away from it. I don't want to hear any more. Everything about Not-Becky revolts me, and again, I wonder how it ever got to this.

"I've told you what you want to know," it snarls at me, with a nasty, twisted look on its face.

"No—not really," I sigh. "You lied like you always do."

Not-Becky screams and pulls so hard on the cuffs that I fear that my sister's wrist will break. A little trickle of blood drips from where the metal is chafing skin.

"Stop it," I say.

"You'll call the fucking priest."

"I won't. Stop it, and I won't."

Still, Not-Becky writhes and pulls on the bed, the stench of her soiled clothing filling my nose and making my eyes water.

"We're through here," I finally admit and force myself to stand. Not-Becky screams and howls and wails for what seems like hours, but it's only about two minutes. Finally, it's spent.

I wait in silence until I hear a familiar voice.

"Jackson?" she says. I open my eyes and look at her. Her wrist is bloody, but her eyes, scared and questioning, belong to Becky and not the other one. I pull myself to my feet, go to her, and unlock the handcuffs. Thankfully, the damage only amounts to some deep scrapes on her wrist, but nothing serious.

"I'm sorry. Wash yourself up," I say, with as much compassion as I can muster. I take the empty glass and the cookie plate, along with her dishes from breakfast and lunch, and swiftly leave the room.

Only after I close the door and make sure the three locks are secured, do I allow myself to cry. It comes out silently. I shove my fist into my mouth to keep from making noise and let salty water leak down my face.

Six, six, six. One more for kicks. The words run through my mind over and over again. *Six, six, six. One more for kicks.*

More importantly, a question lingers, and it makes me think that I may actually be losing my mind. Is Becky really possessed after all? If not, then how does she know things?

How does she freaking know?

28

BY THE TIME I wake up my mother to tell her she made pizza for dinner, dole out her pills, feed my grandfather, and tentatively go back down to the basement to bring Becky a plate, she's taken a shower and is wearing clean clothes.

Only it's still not my sister—it's Not-Becky.

"Come to gloat," it says to me through clenched teeth. "Rot in Hell."

I roll my eyes. "I've come to give you dinner."

"It smells like shit," Not-Becky growls. "You smell like shit."

I can't deal with this anymore, at least not today. I've done this ride too many times, and I want to get off. "Not me," I say with a certain smugness that only hides the fact that the skin holding my sanity intact is becoming increasingly thin. "Must be your food."

It doesn't acknowledge me, so I shrug again and leave the plate next to the door, along with a glass of fruit juice laced with medication.

The room does smell, though. It's right about that—so I quickly grab the hamper, lock the door, and throw the soiled clothes in the laundry.

When my father comes home, he stays outside and smokes his cigarettes like he always does before pushing open the back door, hanging up his coat, and sitting down for dinner. My mother's dressed and is wearing a hint of makeup like nothing's wrong. We all play the usual masquerade through much of our meal before I put down my pizza and clear my throat.

"I'm walking Annie home from her job tonight," I say, breaking the silence. My mother continues to chew. So does my father. "She's working up at the BD Mart. I told her I would meet her when she gets off work." Still, there's silence from my parents. My mother keeps her eyes focused on her plate. I'm sure that she hasn't heard a word I've said, or if she has, it hasn't registered any more than the far-off rumbling of a train passing by.

My father takes a sip of red wine, because he always has red wine with dinner, and drops the piece of pizza he's holding onto his plate. "I don't want you going out tonight," he says. Frankly, it takes me by surprise, because my father usually doesn't show much interest in me either way.

No matter—he's easy to manipulate.

"Newie's coming with me," I continue, completely ignoring what he said. I don't even know why I need his permission. I'll be eighteen soon enough. It's not like I don't already run the goddamned household, anyway.

My father picks up his pizza and nibbles at the crust. A minute later he grunts, which I take for a yes. After dinner, I watch him go back out the way he came in, smoke another cigarette, and head to the garage. I crane my neck to peek out the back door and see if the garage light has flicked on. Once it does, I realize that he's no longer concerned if I walk Annie home or not.

Back at the table, my mother lights a cigarette and closes her eyes. I wash and dry the dishes, put them away, then go into the pantry and take out the broom and the dustpan to sweep the floor. My mother doesn't move her feet as the heavy bristles collect crumbs and dust around her. I gather a small pile, sweep it into the dustpan, and drop it in the waste basket. When I'm through, I pull the cigarette from my mother's hand, because she's starting to forget that it's there, and gently lead her back down the hallway to her bedroom.

"Mom?" I say, as I push open the door and turn on the light. I notice that at some point while getting dressed for dinner, she's made the bed and folded two blankets at the foot of it as though it's looked that way since this morning. "Did you bake something today?"

She slowly looks at me with glassy eyes. "Bake?" she asks. "Did I miss a birthday?"

"No, Mom," I say. "I was just wondering, because there was some sugar on the counter when I got home. It looked like you were baking something."

My mother blinks her eyes a few times. "No, I don't think so. Please tell me, did I miss someone's birthday?"

I can tell her she's missed everyone's birthday for the past two years, but I figure there's no point. "No, Mom," I say as I guide her to the bed and let her sit down on the firm mattress. "Your cakes are the best."

Her eyes are half-lidded, but she still manages the faint impression of a smile as she slowly lifts her hand and caresses my face—just like

Mrs. Berg and my grandfather. "You're such a good boy, Jackson," she says again, like it's everyone's go-to catchphrase for me.

I smile back, but I don't feel like a good boy at all.

I feel evil. I feel like a boy who lets girls get murdered in the woods and their eyes scooped out of their heads. I feel like a boy who silently conspires with a sullen, distant father to keep his mother drugged, his demented grandfather condemned to the rooms upstairs, and his mentally ill sister locked in the basement.

No—I don't feel like a good boy at all.

"Goodnight, Mom," I say and leave her sitting on the side of the bed. I walk quietly through the house and out the front door. It's starting to smell cold outside.

I pull out my cell phone and text Newie.

You there?

Yup.

With Erika?

No. She's a bitch.

I smile and call him. It rings twice before Newie answers.

"You just figure that out?" I ask him.

Newie snorts. "She didn't even show up for practice. I think she wigged out about Crawdaddy."

"Don't call her that, man. It's rude."

"Why?" he says. "She's dead."

I don't feel like getting into it with him, so I change the subject. "Where you at?"

"Staring right at you," he says. I look up and see Newie across the street, standing in his window on the second floor of their Victorian. I don't see the chief's cruiser in the driveway, but Mary Jane's car is there.

"Fuckwad," I say. "How long were you going to watch me?"

"Who's watching? Nothing to look at."

"Nice, bro. Real nice." Newie only chuckles. "So Mary Jane with you?" I ask like a total douchebag. "I mean her car's out front and all." I'm sorry before the words leave my lips.

"Why the hell would Mary Jane be with me?" he snaps, a little too defensively. I guess I've struck a nerve. It makes me think that no one really knows what happens behind closed doors—even to best friends. Sometimes there are things you don't share with anybody—like fantasizing about screwing your dad's hot girlfriend—or how many people are slated to die in Apple this year.

"Just asking," I begin. "Because her car's . . ."

"Who gives a shit?" he grumbles. "She's out with Asshole."

Enough said. Messing with Newie when he gets all moody is like playing ping-pong with a hand grenade that's about to go off. I switch subjects again. "How did you get home after practice—I mean, if Erika blew you off?"

"Steve Black," Newie grumbles. Steve has it as bad as the rest of us. His old man beats the crap out of him more often than not, so most everyone calls him Steve Black-Eye. His claim to fame is that he has a motorcycle, so he always has one skank or another willing to go for a ride with him. "And, yes, I know that my father would nail me to the wall if he knew I got on a bike with him. I just didn't feel like walking home alone."

"Scared?" I ask him. Normally it would sound like a taunt, but I'm dead serious.

"No," he says. "More creeped out."

"Understandable." I stand there and absentmindedly reach my hand into my pocket. The little present that Mark Zebrowski gave me this morning is still there collecting lint. "Hey, want to smoke a bone?"

"You don't have to ask me twice." His phone goes dead, and a minute later Newie's out his front door, shoving his big arms into his letter jacket.

I check the time on my phone. It's only a little after eight. There's plenty of time to catch a buzz before picking up Annie at the BD Mart. There's plenty of time to get numb.

Numb is good. Numb is exactly what I need right about now.

29

IT'S DARK AND cloudless, but there aren't any stars in the sky because the moon is full. Everything is that weird gray color that you see on television when they pretend that it's night but it's really not.

I grab my jacket from inside the door and meet Newie in the middle of the street. Together we walk down to the end of Vanguard Lane and cut through the shallow woods to the railroad tracks. A graveled hill leads up a short incline to the rails. I have to hold my arms out for balance as we make our way up the stone.

"When's Father-of-the-Year coming home?" I ask Newie as I pull the joint out of my pocket.

"Who the fuck cares?" he says as he sits down on the rusty rails and stretches out his long legs. "They went to Worcester to see a movie or something. I don't give a shit."

"Wow," I say. "You're quite the angry young man tonight, Mr. Anderson. They have drugs for that, you know."

"Yeah, they got drugs for a lot of things." He nods his chin toward the joint in my hand. "You going to spark that or what?"

I sit down next to him and pull out a book of matches with the logo for Nick's Newsstand on them. Old Nick sells cigars and rolling papers in the back of his store, so I always snag a couple books of matches when I'm there. Old Nick's no fool. Whenever we buy rolling papers he drops a book in the bag. Hey, it's free advertising.

"Chillax," I say as I light the joint, suck the sweet smoke into my lungs, and hand it to Newie. I let it eddy around inside before I blow a cloud of smoke out and let my head get fuzzy. "Sorry about Erika," I tell him. "Way to ruin a perfectly good Friday night, huh?"

"No kidding," he says and coughs as he hands the joint back to me. "She gave me this lame-ass excuse about having to work at Tenzar's tonight. They're doing late night inventory or something."

I take the joint from him. "Yeah, I saw Annie's mom. She told me she was working late and asked me to make sure Annie gets home okay. I told her you and me were going to meet her when she's done work."

"Kiss ass."

I shrug and stare down at the joint. The pot's stronger than Ziggy's usual stuff, so I only take one more quick toke and hand it back to Newie.

"I don't want any more," I say. "I've got too much on my mind."

Newie blows on the end until the embers glow, then takes a slow, deep drag and holds it for a long time. It must take twice as much weed for him to catch a buzz. I stare at his legs splayed out on the gravel, practically growing right in front of my eyes. Pretty soon he's going to be seven feet tall, then eight, then nine.

I realize it's a good choice not to smoke anymore. The stuff is too good. Newie blows out another cloud and grinds the joint against the metal track.

"Here," he says as he hands it back to me. "We can save it for later."

The two of us sit there for a moment, listening to the night. There are things moving in the woods—usually normal for around here. Sometimes we've seen deer cross the tracks, and once we even caught sight of a porcupine. It was so random and weird that, at first, we didn't know what we were looking at.

Finally Newie says, "Like what?"

"Like what what?"

"Too much on your mind," he says. "Like what?"

Usually we don't talk about anything more significant than comic books and who we think is hot. Tonight it's different, and the smoke is loosening my tongue. I can feel the words rising up in my throat, and all I want to do is stuff them back down again, only I know they'll find a way back out, so I let the flood gates open and hope for the best.

"Becky told me that five will die this year, or maybe six."

"Becky's crazy," says Newie as he holds his big hand in front of his face, examining his fingers like he's just discovered them for the first time.

"True," I tell him. "But this afternoon something else happened."

"What?" he asks, still staring at his fingers, forcing each one to bend and flex.

I tell him about walking through the woods with Annie and Mark Zebrowski. I tell him about seeing the cops and Mark wigging out on us.

Then I tell him about Officer Randy and the other cops who were looking at the trees and how they found the letters that spell out what was written on Becky's stomach.

Five will die.

"No way," Newie whispers. He's no longer looking at his hand. He's looking at me, and I can tell that the smoke has clouded his brain, too, but he knows this is serious. Still, he's having a hard time concentrating on everything at once, which is nothing new, because Newie often has a hard time concentrating on more than one thing at a time, even when he's not stoned.

"I tried to ask Becky about it today, but she pulled a nutty." I spare him the gory details, like her crapping her pants or practically breaking her wrist trying to wriggle free of the handcuffs. "Now she's going on about how five will die, or six for kicks."

"Huh?" he says. I have to give him credit for being wasted and still trying to take everything so seriously.

"She's saying that six might die this year in town. Six murders, you know?" I take a deep breath and let the words continue to spill out. "And my mother's a basket case, my grandfather's completely de-mented, and my father hides in the garage all night like everything is totally normal." What a whiner. I can't believe I'm dumping this all on Newie. He has his own stuff to worry about.

I'm just about to tell him to forget about everything, because I'm stoned and rambling, and it doesn't matter anyway, when something stumbles out of the woods about a hundred feet down the tracks.

"Shit," says Newie and flattens himself against the gravel hill that leads down into the woods. I do, too. The weed was really strong, and my mind is racing inside my head. I can feel the vague presence of fear scratching at the backdoor of my brain, wanting to come in.

I can't let it—not this time of year—not in Apple.

There's a figure on the tracks. It's not a deer or a porcupine or even a bear, which wouldn't be totally out of the question because there are bears around Apple. It's a person—I can tell that much—standing on the tracks, looking one way then another, trying to decide which way to go.

An owl hoots right behind us, and the figure on the tracks whips its head around and looks in our direction. Slowly, it starts heading toward us, and my heart begins to pound. The door in my head opens wide, and paranoid thoughts flood my brain.

It's the murderer. It's the murderer, and Newie and I are going to be number four and number five. Becky said five will die, and we're going to fulfill her prophecy.

That awful burning sensation erupts in my chest again, and I'm una-ble to move. The figure is coming closer and closer, and I can see that it's wearing a dark jacket and a hat and carrying something that looks like a gym bag.

Both Newie and I lie on the gravel and try not to move. We can see the person clearly now, stooped and walking with a bit of a limp. I rack my brains to think if I know any gimps in town, like maybe one of the bikers from The Gin Mill or a dreg from Millie's Café, but I can't think of anyone—mostly because I'm scared out of my mind.

The figure gets closer, and Newie and I both hold our breath and stay perfectly still. Although it's a clear night and everything is washed in moonlight, I pray that whoever it is won't see us.

Twenty feet, ten feet, five feet away, and I can hear its breath as it limps along the path. It sounds deep and ragged, like a man, but I can't be sure. Right when I think we're dead for sure, the figure passes us and continues down the tracks toward town. We hear its footsteps recede into the night, but we don't move.

Newie and I lie there for at least five minutes before we dare to look at each other.

"What the hell was that?" Newie whispers to me, but even his whisper sounds like he's screaming. My heart starts to beat double time. I'm not stoned anymore. The fear has washed any mellow feelings out of my head, and all that's left is a dull headache.

"I don't know," I whisper back. "But it's someone who's not scared to walk around Apple alone at night."

Newie nods and looks down the tracks to where the figure went, but it has already faded into the dark.

"I almost shit myself," he says.

"You and me both. Let's get out of here."

Quietly, very quietly, we crawl down the embankment and disappear into the woods. I only feel truly safe when we emerge on the other side and see the streetlights and lit-up houses of Vanguard Lane. Of course, I'm not foolish enough to think that home means safety, but at least it's a thin veil between me and whatever lurks in our town.

My thoughts go back to the limping figure on the railroad tracks, and I know it's not safe tonight in Apple.

It's not safe at all.

30

IT'S AFTER NINE by the time I climb up the front steps of my house. Newie says he's going to grab something to eat, because he has the munchies, then we can walk up to the BD Mart and wait for Annie.

I'm cool with that, so I decide to make a peanut butter sandwich for myself, but when I walk in the house, I can immediately tell there's something wrong. Maybe it's a sixth sense—I don't know. There's a heaviness in the air, and I think I know where it's coming from.

Becky.

The house is deathly quiet. I hang my jacket on my dad's coat rack and walk through the living room to the basement door. It's cracked a little, and I can hear a faint noise creeping up from the darkness.

I don't want to go down and look. Still, I think Becky might be crying again—not Not-Becky, but my sister—the one that I love and still care about despite everything.

I slowly open the basement door, turn on the lights, and walk down the steps.

"Jackson?" I hear her whisper through the bars.

"Yeah, it's me. You okay?"

I hear a clicking sound and realize that her teeth are chattering together.

"No," she says. "It's so cold."

It's not cold at all in the basement, and I can't figure out what she's talking about.

"It's not cold," I say before realizing that she's bone-thin and very well might be freezing. "Do you need a blanket or something?" I approach the door and see my sister clutching the bars and staring at me. Her skin seems paler than usual, and her lips look almost blue.

"Co-cold," she whispers through her rattling. "So, so cold."

"Let me get you a blanket," I say, deciding not to try and make sense of her internal thermometer. She nods her head vigorously.

Sometimes, I feel so sorry for Becky when she's herself. Dissociative identity disorder robs her of half her life. I can't imagine slipping in and out of consciousness, not knowing what I said or did when I blacked out.

I can't imagine waking up to a shit-stained room and a bloodied wrist, with the taste of Hydrox cookies in my mouth.

I go back upstairs and quietly walk down the hallway to my mother's bedroom. The door is partially open. She's fast asleep, curled into a fetal position without any covers. I take one of the blankets that are folded up at the end of the bed and quickly leave. A minute later, I'm handing it to Becky through the bars.

"Th-thanks," she says to me as she pulls the material between the dark metal. She drapes the blanket over her bony shoulders and crosses her arms so she's cocooned by the folds of material. "I feel all wrapped and packaged," she says as she sits on the edge of the bed.

It's such a weird thing to say—wrapped and packaged. My head's still foggy from the pot. What's wrapped and packaged supposed to mean?

Suddenly, Becky flips sideways and falls back on her mattress. Her mouth pops open and closed, like she's gasping for air.

"Wrapped and packaged," she struggles to say. "Wrapped and packaged."

She looks like one of those smallmouth bass that you can buy, every once in a while, from the local fishermen down at the Quabbin Reservoir. Sometimes the fish are still alive when they hand them to you, all wrapped and packaged in newspaper, with their tails sticking out of one end and their heads sticking out of the other, still gasping for air—just like Claudia Fish struggled through her last breath as her eyes were pulled from their sockets.

Claudia Fish. Crawdaddy Fish.

I watch in horror as Becky's jerks become more and more futile until, finally, she's just lying there on her side, with her mouth occasionally dropping open, like she's sucking in her last seconds of life.

I back away from the door because I don't want to see any more. Whatever mind game Not-Becky is trying to play, I don't want any part of it. My brain is totally spent, and I don't have any more room in it for bizarre crap. I'm tired, and I need a mental vacation. Even getting stoned with Newie didn't help. That creepy figure on the tracks saw to that.

Still, I stand there in the same spot, staring at the door to her room, not knowing what to do. Finally, I hear Becky whisper, "Goodnight, Jackson. I love you." I don't know if she knows I'm standing outside the door or not, but tears well up in my eyes just the same. In my head I say,

Love you, too, Becks, but I can't manage to bring the words to life.

How much longer do I have to suffer through my sister's madness right alongside her, like it's me locked in a cage with manacles biting into my wrists, instead of her?

How many times do I have to be "wrapped and packaged" into a little box with a note attached to it that says, *Inside is such a good boy—he'll give up his life for you?*

How many Hail Marys do I have to say?

Upstairs, as I stuff the last pieces of a sandwich in my mouth and try to calm a growing anger inside, I hear a light tap at the front door. It's Newie. He's standing on the porch.

"Why the hell didn't you text me?" I snap at him as I grab my jacket and walk out the front door.

He shrugs. "What's the difference?"

"You could have woken up everyone in the house," I grumble, stopping short of saying, "You know, the religious zealot, the vegetable, the guy with the wheels but no brain, and the demon."

Newie shakes his head and walks down the porch toward the street. "Excuse me," he grumbles. "Maybe I'm just a little preoccupied."

"With what?" I mutter.

"Oh, I don't know," he says. "Maybe getting the shit scared out of me by whoever that was out on the tracks? But what the hell. No biggie. Don't sweat it."

"Whatever," I say, using that perfect word—the one to end any unpleasant conversation.

The two of us don't talk as we walk up Vanguard Lane to Main Street. I still can't shake the image of Becky flopping around, all wrapped and packaged, like a piece of fish—that, or why she was so cold.

Nothing makes sense anymore. I feel like we're stuck in a toilet bowl, and everything's swirling around us like one of those enormous dumps you find in public bathrooms. There's so much crap, you can't even flush it away no matter how hard you try. Ever since me, Newie, and Annie found that lifeless body in the woods yesterday afternoon, I feel like we're all in some weird sort of free fall. Annie's cutting herself again, Newie's getting angry, and my whole world is rapidly turning into some sort of puzzle where there are pieces missing.

"I mean, what the fuck?" Newie finally croaks out. "Who *was* that on the tracks?"

"I don't know," I say, because I truly don't.

We walk another minute or so. "Did you see the bag?" he blurts out. "I mean, the dude had a bag."

I close my eyes and think the worst. "We don't know it was a dude," I murmur under my breath.

Newie snorts and waves his hand. "Yeah, well, maybe it was the fucking murderer, and that bag was his tool kit where he keeps his knives and ropes and shit."

I can't hear this right now. I can't hear any of this. "Stop," I snap at him. "Just shut up, Newie." I take a deep breath and lash out with the first thing that comes to mind. "Don't be such a fuckwad, you know?"

He stops talking then. Calling him a fuckwad as a joke is one thing. Saying it for real picks open a scab and lets fresh, goopy shit drip out—the kind you don't want to deal with—not ever.

Just like Claudia Fish. None of us wanted to find her in the woods. We didn't ask for any of this—but now that we have, fresh, goopy shit is dripping over all of us, too.

31

JULIE DOPKIN'S A lesbian, or at least everyone thinks she is. She's really tough, and every other word out of her mouth makes her sound like a trucker. The weirdest thing is that she still wears makeup and does her nails. Her buffed and polished man-hands only accentuate the fact that she's wearing some sort of costume. We all know that the real Julie Dopkin would be way more comfortable in jeans, work boots, and a T-shirt.

By the time Newie and I reach the top of the hill, we're not pissed off anymore. I think we're both just numb, but things get tense again as soon as we get to the BD Mart. Even from the parking lot we can hear Julie yelling at Annie. Annie just looks like she wants to find a hole someplace to crawl in and die.

When we walk in the door, Julie turns to look at me and snaps, "You should teach your girlfriend about cold medicine."

"What are you talking about?"

"You only sell one box at a time," Julie barks as she waves a box of antihistamine in front of Annie's face. "Every loser in Apple knows that."

"Again, what are you talking about?"

Newie snorts. "It's a Ziggy thing," he says.

Julie raises one hand up in the air, and they high-five each other. "The giant gets a gold star," she barks.

I look at Annie. Her mascara's starting to blur the edges around her eyes.

"Drugs, dude," explains Newie. "They use the shit in the capsules to make some of the hard junk."

"Oh," I say, like I know exactly what he's talking about. I guess it pays to be the son of a cop. You learn all the tricks of the trade.

"I'm sorry," Annie says to Julie. "I didn't know."

"Well, now you do," Julie spits. She's being really harsh. It's only Annie's first night. Who the hell does she think she is, anyway?

"Yo, Julie," I say. "Back off. It hasn't been the easiest couple of days."

"I'm the one in charge, and I'm the one who gets screwed for mistakes," she snaps. "I can't afford to lose this job." Julie's parents are really nice and all, but they're about as poor as the Bergs, if that's even possible. Why else would Julie be working nights this time of year?

Hard times call for hard choices.

"What are you doing here, anyway?" she grumbles.

"Walking Annie home."

A sort of sadness washes over Julie's face, probably because nobody ever shows up to walk her home. "Well, you can't hang in here," she says. "Go sit on the picnic table outside or something." She flicks her thumb at the clock. "We still got another forty-five minutes to go."

Newie palms a couple candy bars as we leave. I think Annie sees him do it but doesn't say anything. Julie already has her back to us and is counting the packs of cigarettes behind the counter. She starts explaining to Annie about how she has to count them every night before closing up, because the manager keeps track of stuff like that.

Outside, Newie throws me one of the candy bars he lifted and plops down on one of the plastic picnic tables. He tears it open and stuffs half of it in his pie hole with ease, chewing with his mouth open like a total bottom feeder.

"You're a felon," I say to him as I rip open the wrapper on mine and take a bite of nougat and peanuts.

"For now," he says. "Besides, I think stealing a couple of candy bars is more like a misdemeanor. What's Asshole gonna do, haul me in?"

"Beat the crap out of you," I say.

"He can try," he mumbles through a mouthful of chocolate.

About five minutes before the BD Mart is due to close, a black car pulls into the parking lot and maneuvers uncomfortably close to the picnic table where the two of us are sitting. It's one of those older big cars that nobody drives anymore. It looks like a hearse. The driver's side door opens, and a tall figure gets out.

It's creepy Father Tim.

He looks at us and says, "Good evening, boys." The words ooze out of his mouth.

"Father," I say. Newie just nods his head.

Father Tim's older than dirt, probably older than Mr. Colton or Old Nick, but he's still spry. He's ancient and sinewy, which makes him that much creepier, because he glides through the air when he moves, like a predator honing in on its prey. His spindly arms pump back and forth, giving him added momentum, and his huge Adam's apple bobs up and down.

He looks like a dangerous turkey.

"Aren't you out a little late, Jackson?" he asks me, ignoring Newie. I think he figures Newie's big enough to take care of himself.

"Annie Berg's working tonight," I say. "Newie and I told her we'd walk her home."

Father Tim smiles in that creepy-ass way that gives me the willies. "That's nice of you," he says as he shuts his car door. "And they say chivalry is dead."

"What about you, Father?" asks Newie. "You're out pretty late, yourself."

"Me?" says Father Tim. "Once you get to be a certain age, you don't sleep much anymore."

Yeah, I think to myself. *Like a freaking bat.*

"Besides," he says. "I have a sweet tooth tonight. I'm hoping I can find something here to cure what ails me. Maybe ice cream or some pastries."

"Sugar's bad for you," says Newie.

"There are a lot of things that are bad for you, Mr. Anderson," says creepy Father Tim as he raises one eyebrow. "How's your father and that girlfriend of his? The . . . the talented one?"

I can feel the Father's words punch Newie full in the gut. It takes him a second to recover. Newie stretches out his long arms and cracks his knuckles. "They're a couple of regular lovebirds, Father," he says.

"Ah," says creepy Father Tim. "It's nice to hear that. These are troubling times. The chief deserves a little slice of Heaven." The Father smiles at the two of us as we sit there on the plastic table, most likely waiting for us to squirm—even a little. I've always known Father Tim likes that kind of power, but I won't give him the satisfaction. Neither will Newie. After an uncomfortably long time, he says, "Goodnight," and leaves us to slither into the BD Mart.

Once he's out of earshot, Newie chuckles and shakes his head. "What a freak," he says.

I don't disagree.

A few minutes later, Father Tim comes back out holding a box.

"Apple pie," he says and licks his sharp teeth. "That'll do the trick." He opens his door and is about to get into his car when he stares directly at me and says, "It's good to know that gentlemen still walk young ladies home at night. You're such a good boy, Jackson."

I flinch at his words. I wish I hadn't heard them before, but it seems that everyone has had the same impression of me over the past few days.

My face gets hot. "Goodnight, Father," I say. Newie only lifts his hand a little. We watch as the big black sedan pulls out of the parking lot and disappears into the night.

"The dude's a vampire," says Newie.

"Or something," I say.

Annie comes out about twenty after eleven looking a little flustered. She sits down next to me, and I drape my arm around her.

"Well, that sucked," she says.

"No kidding," says Newie. "That's why they call it work."

"Yeah," she says. "That Julie's a bitch."

"Wow," says Newie. "Someone's got a potty mouth."

"I know," says Annie. "I'm sorry. I don't have my head on straight. Everything seems so weird."

I don't know if I'm scared or relieved that Annie feels the same way as I do. Things *are* really weird.

Uber weird.

Freaking weird.

"I keep thinking about those letters in the trees this afternoon," she says. "What kind of person does that?"

I shrug. I don't feel like rehashing the whole thing again, and I certainly don't want to crawl inside the mind of a murderer. People who leave little mementos at their crime scenes are crazy.

Crazy—just like Becky.

Besides, Annie needs to forget about all this weirdness for a while. She has work to think about, and her new little hobby to get under control—stat—but Newie opens up his big mouth and says, "We saw some strange guy out on the railroad tracks earlier."

Annie leans forward, her eyes wide. "What do you mean, 'strange'?"

He shrugs. "Some weirdo."

"Who was it?" she asks.

"We don't know," I tell her. "We didn't catch a good look. We were both a little buzzed and got all freaked out because, well, it's autumn."

Annie shakes her head. "Who walks around the woods in Apple alone at night?"

"Someone with a death wish," says Newie ominously. "Or some-one doing the killing."

"Shut up, Newie," I say to him, although I'm thinking roughly the same thing.

"Or stupid idiots getting baked," she says and smirks at both of us. "I hope you saved some of that joint for me."

I reach into my pocket and pull it out. Most of it's still there. "It's really strong," I say. "We both only took a couple hits."

"Strong's good," Annie says. She takes it from me as we leave the BD Mart with Julie Dopkin still inside.

None of us think anything about leaving her there by herself.

Why would we?

32

IT'S AT LEAST A half hour walk to Annie's house from the BD Mart. We could cut across the top of the hill, but that means walking behind a lot of backyards, a little stretch of woods, and still ending up at the top of High Garden.

None of us want to walk through the cemetery tonight.

We each share a few more hits off the joint, and it burns down quickly. By the time I snuff it out there's only a quarter of it left. I give it to Annie and smile. I figure she needs it more than me or Newie. She pockets it and entangles my fingers in hers.

It's so natural being Jacksannie that I don't notice right off that Newie's being extra quiet. I suppose it sucks to be a third wheel, but I don't think that's what's causing the silent act. I think there's something more going on at home than he's letting on. We all have our demons—me, maybe literally—but Newie has something altogether different.

We walk down Main Street, each lost in our own thoughts. No doubt Annie's thinking about what kind of animal she may find when she gets home and praying he's not too bad tonight. Newie's probably fantasizing about Mary Jane, which is just so wrong on so many levels.

As for me, my thoughts are still on Becky.

Everything's so different with her lately. I suppose things are always different when it comes to Becky, but she seems extra ramped up, like something is about to explode, and all I need to do is find the lit fuse and put it out to keep it from happening.

It's not that Becky's my responsibility, but either the joint we smoked or the hard reality of my situation is making it abundantly clear that no one is going to take over for me if I stop worrying about everyone.

While I'm having my little self-imposed pity-party, a cop car speeds by going toward the far side of town. Its lights are flashing red and blue, but there's no siren. It can't be Newie's dad, because the chief's out with Mary Jane tonight.

Still, we all stop—and just when we start to think we're being way too paranoid, the cop car slows down and does a U-turn in the middle of the street. It heads back in our direction.

"Fuck," says Newie. "I'm really high."

"Well, snap out of it quick. Every cop in town knows who you are."

"You'll be fine," says Annie, but it comes out of her mouth so lilting and ethereal that she sounds more stoned than not.

"This sucks," he says.

The cruiser slows down on the other side of the street and stops. The door opens, and someone gets out of the car, looks both ways, and strides across the pavement toward us.

Before whoever it is even has a chance to speak, Newie blurts out, "Why are the lights on? Is there something going on?"

"I don't know, you piece of shit. You tell me." A booming voice shatters the night. It *is* Newie's dad after all.

Fuck.

Fuck. Fuck. Fuck.

I'm so stoned I see two of the chief instead of one—two giants who are going to grind me into dust.

"Ugh . . . ugh . . ." babbles Newie, but that's all he can manage. He shrinks into that little boy again, like he always does when he's around his father. Before we know it, the giant monster-cop is on us. With one great, sweeping arc he backhands Newie across the face with such force that Newie falls to the ground with a thud.

Annie yelps and clings to me, her nails digging into my arm.

"What the fuck are you doing, Newton?" the chief bellows. "Mary Jane and I come home early, and you're not even in the house? No note, no nothing?"

I almost let out a sigh of relief. This is a "break-your-curfew" smackdown, not something way worse.

Newie doesn't say anything. He's stoned, and his father's a freaking lunatic.

"Mr. Anderson . . ." I begin, but he cuts me off.

"Shut up, Jackson. This is between me and my son." The chief reaches his calloused, mammoth hand down, grabs Newie by the hair, and drags him to his feet. I'm scared for my friend. I feel like there's something I should be able to do, but there's not. There's just the chief and Newie, and Annie and I are so insignificant at that moment, we might as well not even be there.

"Well?" he roars with his hand still curled in Newie's black mop.

"What the fuck do you have to say for yourself?"

All of a sudden, the chief stops short. His nostrils flare, and I think some sort of invisible flame shoots out of his eyes. He knows we got stoned. He can smell it. I'm sure of it—and now we're truly screwed.

From some well of courage deep down inside himself, Newie gets up the balls to push his father's hand away. "Get off of me, you fucking asshole," he barks at him.

I'm stunned. I'm beyond stunned. You never say words like that to your parents. You can go to Hell for saying words like that to them—the fire and brimstone Hell that creepy Father Tim preaches about. The seven-level Hell that my dad prays to avoid.

What's even worse is that Newie sounds exactly like his father, and knowing that's your future is a torturous Hell all its own.

It's deathly quiet on the sidewalk.

Chief Anderson takes a step closer and bends down so he's right in Newie's face. "You touch me again, and I'll break your fucking arm, you little turd," he hisses as spittle flies from his mouth.

"Go ahead, big man," whispers Newie. "It wouldn't be the first time."

I close my eyes. All I can remember is when Newie broke his wrist in the winter of eighth grade.

It was a week before Christmas. The two of us were stoked about the various hills in town we were going to conquer with our sleds over winter break. Then one morning he was sick and didn't come to school. The next day, he showed up with a big cast on his right arm, signed by a couple of the nurses who put it on.

His face was banged up a little, too. He told everyone that he was being stupid and fell down the stairs at his house. It was totally understandable because they're really steep. Still, every time someone came up to him that day and signed his cast, and he had to retell the story of what happened, his words sounded plastic—like he had to grit his teeth to convince himself that what he was saying was the truth.

We didn't get to conquer any of the hills in town over that winter vacation because Newie had to heal, and when he did heal, he was quiet for a long time—almost an echo of himself.

As we stand on the sidewalk—me, Annie, Newie, and the chief—with the memory of his broken wrist flooding into my baked brain, I realize a simple truth about my best friend and his father.

It's something I don't want to know, but now it will always be there at the edge of my brain—just another thing I'm going to have to worry about.

"Um," I say, trying to diffuse the tension, which is dark and thick. "Annie has to get home." Newie and the chief keep staring at each other for a long time. The chief's hands are squarely on his hips, and his eyes are blazing. Newie's not budging, probably for the first time ever.

Finally the chief spits and says, "The three of you, get in my car." I don't know if that means he's going to bring us in for being high or what. I suppose he can only assume we're stoned because of the smell, unless he searches Annie and finds the roach I gave her.

"Wh . . . Why?" Annie squeaks.

He glares at her and at me. "I'm driving you all home," he growls and lumbers back across the street.

Newie lowers his head, deflates his chest, and follows his father. Annie and I follow after them, afraid to get into the cruiser with Chief Anderson, and afraid not to.

33

I HEAR THE SIREN at 6:15 the next morning. It's only for a moment, then it trails away and disappears, and I think that I'm still dreaming.

I lie in bed with my eyes closed, going over what happened last night, replaying everything in my head. We got into the back of the chief's cruiser, and he drove Annie home, not saying a word as she got out of the car. He glared at her as she murmured a "thank you," before quietly letting herself into her house. The lights in the shabby windows were dark, and I remember hoping that her father was passed out drunk.

The chief turned the cruiser around and drove us back home, not even stopping in front of my house to let me out. He pulled into his own driveway, parked, pulled the keys out of the ignition, and got out of the car.

It was scary seeing him so quiet.

"Are you going to be okay, man?" I whispered to Newie, but he didn't say anything—just like his dad. I got out of the car, mumbled something that I don't remember, and walked across the street to my house.

The kitchen light was on when I came in.

My father was sitting at the table, his leg up on one of the chairs with an ice pack on his ankle. I stood in the shadows, wondering if I could be stealthy enough to creep down the bedroom hallway and slide into my bedroom without him noticing.

"I told you not to go out tonight," he said without turning around to look at me.

"We walked Annie home," I said. "Me and Newie. We talked about it at dinner." I couldn't pull my eyes away from the ice pack. I couldn't stop thinking about the figure limping down the tracks.

He took a deep breath, noisy and surreal. "You have no respect for your father," he said. "Not one lick." I didn't want to argue with him. Besides, he was right. I didn't.

"Becky needs to be in a hospital," I blurt out. There were a million things that could have come out of my mouth, but that's the one that bubbled to the surface first.

"Don't you tell me where your sister should be. She's safe right where she is."

"No, she's not." I think it was the lingering weed that was talking, not me.

He turned around and snared me in his gaze. His eyes were blood-shot, and his skin was almost gray. Each day in our house seemed to age him a year. "When was the last time you prayed, Jackson? When was the last time you talked to God?"

I didn't know what to say. I didn't know how to tell him that I didn't believe in his God. "In church," I said. "This past Sunday." I licked my lips, refusing to look away from him. "What's wrong with your leg?"

"Nothing," he muttered. "I slipped on the stairs out on the porch."

He turned away from me, just as I was sure my heart was going to beat right through my chest.

"She's sick," I said, but he shot his palm in the air, lightning fast, forcing me into silence. There was no point in talking. There was only my father, a sprained ankle, and the memory of the figure on the tracks.

A minute later, I was undressed and lying in my bed with my head still in a pot-fog and my mind in a knot of confusion.

At some point, I drifted off to sleep without even brushing my teeth. The next thing I knew, the siren was waking me up way too early on a Saturday morning.

My phone dings, and there's a text from Newie.

There's another murder.

I don't think he expects me to answer right away, but I'm already up. The siren was Chief Anderson's cruiser as he sped down Vanguard Lane and headed off toward the center of town.

How?

Newie doesn't answer, so I wait. It's starting to get light outside, and I can already tell it's going to be one of those dullish days where the fall colors are muted, and everyone acts like it's already winter, though the snow is still months away.

I look down at the little screen on my phone, waiting for it to bleep with a response from Newie. Finally, I text him again. *How?*

His message comes back quickly. *Tenzar's* it says. Nothing more.

A murder at Tenzar's? How can that be? How the hell can someone get murdered in a supermarket? Aren't there tons of people around? I pull myself free of my sheets and sit on the side of my bed. A mossy fur has grown on my tongue overnight, and it tastes terrible. As I smack my dried lips together, I remember the joint and wonder how bad Newie got brutalized when he was finally alone with his dad.

I stand but immediately fall back down on the hard mattress with my head pounding. A minute later, I stand again and steady myself against the edge of the bed. I need to brush my teeth. They feel like felt against my tongue, and I want to wash the memory of last night away. I open my door and cross the hall to the little bathroom that Becky and I once shared, but now is basically mine. I pull my toothbrush out of the right-hand drawer, notice that the bristles have started to split and fray, and make a mental note that I have to get a new brush. No one else is going to buy it for me.

Besides, rotten teeth are a common sight in town. They mark the fact that you're Apple born and bred.

As I stand there, staring at myself in the mirror, my thoughts wander to Becky. I wonder why she was so cold last night. I hope there isn't something wrong with the boiler, or worse, that we have to get more oil. Everyone knows that the price of oil's going up, and between what my dad pulls in from the farmer's co-op and what he shells out for medication and food and stuff, I hope he doesn't come to me and hint around that I have to get a job—like Annie.

Maybe he can sell some of the crucifixes he makes, instead. You have to admit, they *are* beautiful. You can see they've been crafted with reverence and awe, as though they were made to work holy magic by the skilled, practiced hands of a pious man—the hands of my father.

My dad gave one of the crucifixes to creepy Father Tim a couple years ago. It was after the Father said he couldn't do anything for Becky. Father Tim hung it in the rectory and one Sunday morning announced that my father had made it. There were hushed whispers throughout the congregation, mostly about my tragic family, but no one came up to my dad after the service to congratulate him on his work.

It was just as well. My father thinks hubris is a sin.

A sin—just like he thinks it's a sin that I don't believe in the things he and my mother believe. Honestly, I can't say for sure if there's a God or not, but I know that going to church every Sunday morning, or getting on my knees in front of his beautiful pieces of crossed wood hanging all over the house, won't help me to believe any more or less than I already do.

I do believe in evil, though. Not the supernatural kind, but the kind that festers in our minds like rotted meat. It makes people like my mother fall into the dark pits of their souls. It creates things that look like my sister but aren't.

Maybe that's what happened to Becky. Living in Apple fed her inner evil until it needed to be expressed.

Just when I'm sinking into my own little pool of depression, a stray thought flits by, and cold fingers dance up my spine.

Annie's mother had to work late at Tenzar's last night.

No.

No. No. No.

I have my jeans and a T-shirt on before I can let the stray thought form into something cohesive. Seconds later, I'm out the door and running across the street to Newie's house.

There's been enough death connected to us.

Too much.

34

"YO, CHILL," NEWIE says to me as he stands in his front hallway in only his sweatpants.

"I've texted Annie like ten times," I tell him. The frustration in my voice is palpable. "She's not answering."

"Maybe her phone's off. It's friggin' seven in the morning on a Saturday."

How can he not understand what's happening? My guts are churning inside, and I can tell there's something terribly wrong. You don't live in a house like mine, day after day, without developing a feel for these things.

"What did your dad say?"

"About what?"

"Jesus, Newie." How can he be so freaking obtuse? "What did he say about what's happened at Tenzar's?"

Newie shrugs and lumbers down the hallway to the kitchen. "Just that someone's dead." He opens the refrigerator and pulls out a jug of milk. "Asshole got the call this morning. That's all I know." Newie begins chugging the milk, the plastic collapsing in on itself each time another swallow gushes down his throat. "Ahhh," he says when he's done and the jug is spent. He belches, loud and long. "Why?"

I feel the blood drain completely out of my face. I'm probably as pale as the milk Newie sucked down. "I think it's Mrs. Berg," I say hoarsely. Her weary face and sad smile float behind my eyes.

"Shut up," he says. "Why would anyone kill Annie's mom?"

"I don't know," I say. "Why would anyone kill Claudia Fish or Ruby Murphy or even Ralphie Delessio? Why would anyone kill Margo Freeman and cut her into pieces?"

"Yeah, that was messed up," he says. "She was hot."

"Jesus Christ, Newie. Really?"

"Okay, okay," he says, starting to slip into cop mode. "Why Mrs. Berg?"

I shake my head. "She had to work late at Tenzar's last night," I whisper.

Newie wipes his mouth with his hairy arm and drops the plastic jug into the wastebasket. "So did Erika," he says. "So did a lot of people. Erika said that they were doing inventory or something."

I don't get how he can be so callous about the whole thing. Someone's dead—maybe someone we know—and I need my best friend right now, because I can feel in my gut that Mrs. Berg's the one.

I don't know how I know—I just do. There's a strange emptiness inside of me that wasn't there before. It's the same kind of emptiness I felt when my grandmother died—like part of me was chipped away with a hammer and chisel. That's what I'm feeling now—that another part of me has been taken away, leaving me a little less whole than I was before.

"Let's ride our bikes down there," I say to him. "I have to see."

"No fucking way," snorts Newie. "Asshole will kill me. The only thing that stopped him from beating the shit out of me last night was Mary Jane—but he'll get around to it, don't you worry. He'll come home tonight, and he'll be all moody and obsessed because there was another murder, and he'll stare at those creepy pictures like he always does. Then right in the middle of it, he'll stop what he's doing, come find me, and wail on me. I know the drill. I've lived it enough times."

I clear my throat, but no words come out. I'm not sure what I'm supposed to say.

"One of these days I'm gonna hit him back," he mutters. "I just want to make sure that when I do, he doesn't get up. You know what he always says to me? 'Don't throw the first punch in a fight, Newton. Throw the last one.' Well, one of these days I'll hit him back when I know I'm throwing the last punch. Then we'll see who the fuckwad is—that's for damn sure."

I look anywhere but at Newie. He's got major life issues, and I know I need to be there for him, but I can't take on one more person right now. I just can't. One more piece of straw, and my back is going to break.

"I have to know about Annie's mother," I finally say. "I'm riding my bike down there."

Newie rolls his eyes. "You're a pain in my ass," he growls. "If I get the shit kicked out of me by Asshole, it's your fault. Give me two minutes." He flies up the stairs, and I'm relieved that I don't have to ride to Tenzar's alone.

Five minutes later, we're peddling down the street on our bikes. Newie looks a little like something out of a circus because he's so big, and his bike's so little.

Town is quiet. Most of the stores won't open for another hour or two, except for Dippity Doughnuts and Tenzar's. The supermarket's always busy on Saturday mornings, because that's when all the working mothers go to cash and spend their weekly paychecks. Too many have to spend the cash quick, before their baby-daddies can use the money at the liquor store or maybe down at the Indian casino in Connecticut. I'm not quite sure what actually goes on at a casino. All I know is that my father thinks gambling is a sin.

Sometimes he acts like breathing is a sin, too.

Newie has to stand on his bike as he peddles. If he sits, his knees are too high, and they bang against the handlebars. I do the same, because I feel as though standing on my bike, instead of sitting, will get me there faster. I hold my phone in my hand, because I'm hoping it will ring or ding, and it will be Annie, wondering why I'm acting so crazed—but I know that's not going to happen.

Annie's not going to call. She's going to wake up with the same foggy headache that I woke up with, stumble downstairs, and make herself something to eat. She'll never even notice that her mother didn't come home last night. It won't be until later, when her father gets up, reaches for his first beer of the day, and yells for Mrs. Berg to come and make him breakfast, all the time scratching himself and calling her a useless bitch.

And the whole time that my mind is racing with these thoughts, another thought is sidling up right next to them. It's quietly whispering in my ear that all of this is just in my head, and Mrs. Berg is fine. Someone else was killed at Tenzar's, like one of the managers or maybe even Erika, which would be equally as horrible but somehow a little easier to take.

When we see the lights of the police cars up ahead, flashing red then blue, red then blue, all I want to do is cry.

35

OFFICER RANDY WANTS to know why we're at the supermarket. There's a small crowd of employees outside, and most of them look gray. An older woman is crying. She has her arms around a young guy with greasy hair, who looks like he might be the manager, or at least the junior manager.

"My girlfriend's mom worked late last night," I gasp breathlessly. Sticky sweat plasters my hair against my forehead. "I just want . . . I mean, I just hope . . ."

He doesn't say anything. Instead, he waddles back inside Tenzar's and leaves us there with the rest of the growing crowd. Newie and I sit silently on our bikes and stare at the double glass doors, waiting for someone to come out, but after ten minutes, nobody does.

Off in the distance, I hear a siren, and I rightly guess that it's an ambulance. It's coming from further down the street past the market. The wailing gets louder and louder, and right when I think that a white van with red lettering and flashing lights is going to turn into the parking lot, the ambulance speeds by toward the center of town.

Newie looks at me questioningly.

"Bad things come in threes," I say. "Whoever got murdered, whoever needs that ambulance, and one more thing."

"That would be Asshole killing me," he says and turns back to the double glass doors. "That's one more thing."

On some level, I know he's serious. Newie just tightens his jaw and waits for someone to come out of Tenzar's and tell us anything.

Finally, Officer Randy comes back through the doors, followed by Chief Anderson, and I feel that all-too-familiar burning in my chest again, because the chief's not looking anywhere but at the two of us. There's something in his face that's not anger. I can't tell what it is because the chief's always angry.

Newie puts his nails in his mouth as he stares at his dad.

"Fuck me," I whisper under my breath. Newie doesn't say anything. Neither does he move when his father begins to come towards us. It's all happening in slow motion, and somehow I already know that whatever the chief says, it's going to be like he's yelling through a wind tunnel. The words are going to be muffled and far away, because the only thing I can really hear is the blood pounding in my head.

That's when I really do start to cry. It's not great, heaving sobs—only a trickle of salt tears that I barely know are there, until a gust of wind blows by, and I feel them grow cold against my face.

"Guys," says Chief Anderson as he rubs the back of his neck and stares at the pavement. He doesn't ask why we're there. He doesn't seem angry. If I had to guess, I'd say he seems as sad as I am and a little at a loss for words.

"Who?" I croak out, breaking Apple protocol by asking "who" instead of "how."

The chief looks anywhere but at the two of us. He surveys the crowd, then he looks across the street, but I can tell his eyes are glassy. He doesn't want to say the words, because if he says them, they'll be real.

Finally, he sighs, and his nostrils flare a little. "Carla Berg," he says. "I'm sorry."

I feel like I've been stabbed. Newie's mouth falls open, but nothing comes out. He stares at his dad like the chief is staring at us. Everything we're supposed to say is being said with our eyes instead of our mouths.

Annie's mom. Mrs. Berg. Why her? Why now?

I swallow, and that Apple word finally bubbles up out of me, simple and finite, but I need to know. "How?" I rasp.

Chief Anderson rubs his chin. He's not supposed to say anything. I know that. I watch murder shows on TV like everybody else. Saying something will supposedly compromise his investigation, but this is Mrs. Berg. She's one of us. She's connected to Annie, and Annie's connected to me, and I'm connected to Newie. We're family, sort of.

Family has a right to know.

"How?" I ask again, but the chief can't bring himself to tell us.

"Shit," he whispers under his breath.

"Please."

His nostrils flare, and he rolls his eyes, because he knows he's not supposed to tell—but he does anyway. "In the fish section," he says quietly. "On the ice."

I remember Mrs. Berg once complaining about how the fish section at Tenzar's was one of the toughest places to work, because every night, after the store closed, all the fish had to be taken off the ice and put into refrigerators. The next morning, it all had to be taken out again and placed back on the ice in little displays of layered filets.

Only this morning, whoever went to Tenzar's early to open up the store and lay the fish out on the ice found something already there.

Something cold and dead.

The double glass doors to the market open again, and Erika Tenzar comes out wrapped in a blanket. She's pasty-white and shaking. That white-haired cop, the one who looked like he wanted permission to shoot me yesterday, is by her side. Erika's crying, and her face is screwed up into a horrible grimace that seems permanent—and all I can think is that I have to know.

I have to know now.

I drop my bike to the ground and push past Chief Anderson to where Erika's been deposited in the open back seat of one of the cop cars. She's sitting sideways, and her feet are pigeon-toed on the tar.

"Erika?" I say to her. She doesn't move. Newie appears next to me, and the chief is behind both of us, but not stopping me from doing what I need to do. "Erika?" I say to her again, and this time she slowly raises her eyes and looks at me. She blinks a couple of times as if she doesn't quite know who I am. Then her gaze passes beyond me to Newie.

"I saw it," she whispers to him.

Newie gets down on his knees in front of her, but still, his head towers above Erika's. "What do you mean?" he asks as he gently takes her hand. "What did you see?"

"I saw a murdered person," she whimpers, her lower lip pouted and trembling. "I've seen death."

"What happened?" I blurt out, although I already know that I don't want to hear the answer. Still, I need to hear her say the words.

"All wrapped and packaged," she gulps. "On the ice in the fish department. She's all wrapped and packaged."

It takes me a second to realize what she means.

Then it actually hits me that it's Annie's mother she's talking about. She's laid out on the ice, all wrapped and packaged like a smallmouth bass from one of the fishermen at the Quabbin.

Wrapped and packaged.
Wrapped and packaged.
Wrapped and packaged.

I close my eyes and clench my fists.

Meanwhile, Erika realizes how awful the words are that are coming out of her mouth, quickly lowers her head, and pukes all over the pavement in front of Newie. He doesn't move or say anything stupid like

Newie always does. He holds her hair as she coughs and sputters. When she's done, she accepts a tissue from the white-haired officer and wipes her mouth.

When she looks up, her eyes search Newie's, and I can tell she sees safety in them.

Her gaze moves to me.

"She looked co-cold," she says. "She looked so, so cold."

A shiver rushes through my body. It's not because of what Erika says. It's because of what Becky said to me last night.

"Co-cold," she whispered through her chattering teeth. "So, so cold."

36

ERIKA IS SITTING in the back of the police car with Newie. He has one arm wrapped around her shoulder, and she's leaning up against him. He's biting his nails like he always does.

Meanwhile, the chief is standing next to me, talking on his cell phone. I can hear him, but whatever he's saying isn't quite registering. The only things that stick with me are the names "Berg" and "Dunhill Road," where Annie lives. Other than that, there's only one thought that keeps running through my head over and over again.

Becky.

Last night when Not-Becky was hiding somewhere in the depths of her brain, Becky told me she was cold. Then she flip-flopped around in the folds of her blanket and called herself wrapped and packaged.

How did she know it would happen that way to Annie's mom? How the hell did she know?

The chief keeps talking, but his words mean nothing to me. The only thing that means something is my sister and her connection to the murders this year. Somehow she knows. Somehow, from the prison of a bedroom where she's been locked away like a princess in a tower, she knows.

For the first time in a very long while, I want my mother—not the person who huddles in her bed all day with her cigarettes burning to ash between her fingers. I want my mother from before Becky got sick. I want my mother from before my grandmother tumbled down the stairs to her death. I want the woman who scooped me up into her arms when I was a kid and smothered me with kisses and sometimes made pancakes from scratch on school days just because, and who read me bedtime stories before I went to sleep.

Hell, I need my mother right now, because Annie's is gone, and I have to somehow make sense of it all.

My brooding thoughts are interrupted by the chief's gruff voice. "Annie Berg?" he says into his cell. "You gotta be shitting me."

I turn and look up at him as he clutches the phone to his ear. His eyes are shut, and he looks even more concerned than before. When he opens his eyes they find mine.

"Yes," he says. "I'm looking right at him."

His thumb clicks the off button, but he still holds the phone to his mouth. The giant cop stares at me almost as though he's afraid. If I didn't know any better, I'd say he has the look of someone who wished he didn't wake up this morning.

"What?" I whisper. I don't think I actually make a sound when I say it, so I clear my throat and say it again. "What?"

"We need to talk," he says.

I look back at Newie and Erika. Newie's slowly chewing away at his hand. Erika's eyes are shut, and I think she might be crying. "Um . . . sure," I say, because there isn't anything else I *can* say. After all, this is the cop who caught me stoned last night with his son. This is the cop who's holding my fate in the palm of his baseball-mitt-sized hands.

Chief Anderson jerks his head to one side and motions for me to follow him.

We walk deeper into the parking lot, past Tenzar's, with its autumn corn stalks and pumpkins set out front and bushels of apples that have come from one of the local orchards.

There's a place a little outside of town called Apple's Apples where most of the local crop comes from. On weekends, tourists come and pick bushels there, eat cider doughnuts, and sometimes go on haunted hayrides. If you're lucky or stupid enough to take a seasonal job there, you can get ten bucks an hour to wear a sheet and hide in the trees until the hay cart rambles by, filled with wide-eyed kids and folks from other places.

Then you can scare the crap out of them, if you aren't already scared yourself.

There was a murder in the Apple's Apples orchard last year. It was one of the biker dudes who used to hang out at Millie's Café. Someone used a hammer and nails on him so that his braided ponytail was fixed to the tree where he was found sitting, leaning against the gnarled bark. His eyes, nostrils, and mouth were nailed shut, too, and spikes were driven into the ground in the middle of his feet. His arms were left spread wide.

Sort of like a crucifixion.

The chief grabs an apple as he walks past one of the overflowing bushels. It's totally stealing, but I don't say anything. He shoves it into his mouth and takes a huge bite. By the time we pass the grocery store, a discount bakery that sells yesterday's fresh goods at half price, and a dollar store, he's done with the apple and tosses the spent core into a trashcan.

Suddenly, he stops and turns around. I involuntarily take a step back, because I'm that freaked out. He rubs his chin again as he looks down at me. Finally he takes a deep breath and says, "We have a problem."

"I'm sorry about last night," I blurt out. I'm more than a little scared, and the thought of getting busted for smoking a joint is more than I can handle right now.

"What?" he says. Then he realizes what I mean and shakes his head.

"Don't worry about last night," he grumbles, and I'm genuinely shocked. "Consider it a freebie."

A freebie? What does he mean? Is he giving me a warning instead of a ticket because I'm his son's best friend? Maybe he feels sorry for me because my girlfriend's mother was just murdered in the fish department at Tenzar's and left there, wrapped and packaged?

Wrapped and packaged.

"Okay," I say to him, but he can see the concern in my eyes as much as I can see the concern in his. Only then do I realize that he doesn't want to talk about last night. That's not why we're here.

He wants to talk to me about something else.

"Annie's being taken to the hospital," the chief says in that deep baritone voice of his. The side of my lip curls up, and I squint, because I don't quite get what he's saying.

"Annie's being taken to the hospital?" I say, repeating the words slowly.

"I'm sorry," he says.

Terror slaps me in the face. "Is she dead?" The burning in my chest that I didn't even know was rekindled becomes a bonfire.

"No," he tells me, but his words sound thin. "That's all I know for now."

As I try and process what the chief is saying, I hear the wail of the ambulance that passed by when Newie and I first got to Tenzar's. It's the ambulance that I thought was coming for Mrs. Berg. Sunlight splashes off its windshield as it speeds past, its siren tearing into the morning.

"I don't understand."

"She's asking for you," he says. "She doesn't know about her mother yet."

"But . . ."

"If you want to go to the hospital, I'll have one of the officers drive you, okay?"

"Okay," I say, but I think I only nod my head. For a second, the world seems to turn sideways, so I take a deep breath and force it right-side up. I can't break—not now. If I let myself stop to take in everything that's happened since I woke up this morning, even for an instant, I think I might die.

I think I might surely die.

37

OFFICER RANDY drives me in his cruiser. Newie doesn't come. He stays with Erika Tenzar because Erika isn't herself and needs someone with her who can tether her to reality. I'm sure that in the back of Newie's mind he's expecting that, someday soon, he's going to get into her pants. I can understand that. Sometimes Newie's priorities are messed up.

I sit next to Officer Randy as he pulls out of the parking lot and turns left down Main Street. Wang Memorial is Apple's hospital. It's perched on a hill that overlooks the Quabbin Reservoir. Everyone makes fun of the name, but somehow the thought of "yanking my chain at Wang" doesn't strike me as funny today.

A million years ago, Wang was an orphanage. After that it was a boarding house. Somehow, Apple got up enough funding to turn the place into a hospital, but everyone knows that you only go there if you want to get your finger stitched or if you have a twisted ankle. If you have anything worse than that, you have to go to one of the bigger hospitals in Worcester or Springfield, where they know which end of the thermometer goes into which end of the patient.

"Annie Berg," says Officer Randy. "She was the redhead with you the other day, right? When the three of you found that Fish girl?"

He isn't really asking. He's only trying to make conversation, because he thinks talking is better than silence right now. Besides, he saw her as a blond when we were in the woods yesterday.

I thought cops were supposed to be observant. Maybe Apple cops are just numb to the details.

"She's blond now," I say to him. I watch Main Street whiz by in a blur. "And her name was Claudia, not 'that Fish girl.'"

Officer Randy turns and stares at the side of my head. I can feel his eyes boring into me. He waits another minute. "You guys a thing?"

I don't answer—a silent cue for him to shut the hell up. I just want to see Annie and make sure she's okay, although I know she's not, because her mother's dead and all wrapped and packaged.

Officer Randy reaches down and flips on the radio, pressing the buttons a few times before hitting on a song he probably thinks I'll like.

I don't give a crap. I'd be just as happy in silence, because in silence I would be able to hear my thoughts better, which are jabbering away at warp speed.

I feel like there's a giant puzzle in my head with a bunch of pieces missing, so I can't exactly tell what it looks like yet. There are familiar parts, and there are parts I don't understand. The picture it's making keeps moving in and out of focus, and if I concentrate on it too long, it disappears altogether.

It's almost as though I have to look at the picture sideways to actually see it for what it really is.

I know I'm not ready yet. I know that I don't want to see the picture, because if I do, everything's going to change, and I'm not sure I want that to happen.

Officer Randy makes a right and pulls past a small dairy farm that stinks during the summer and sells crappy ice cream made out of goats' milk. He then turns left and keeps winding farther up the hill. This is where most of the nice houses are. Anyone who has money in town lives on the hill. Their houses have things like granite kitchen countertops and automatic lawn sprinklers.

In my fantasies, hill kids don't have problems at home like me, but I'm not stupid enough to think that's true. There are secrets behind everyone's door, and some of them are probably worse than what I have to deal with.

I'm sure there are drunk single parents up here, or dads who go on coke benders to re-live their glory days. I even have it on pretty decent authority, meaning Newie, that some of the worst parties up on the hill—the ones the cops have to break up—are the ones that mid-life-crisis people throw.

I think that's sad. What do they have to party about? Don't they know they're living in a ticking time bomb, and any moment it could explode? When it does, any one of them could become another Apple statistic.

No one's immune.

Officer Randy palms the wheel, and we turn a corner. Wang Memorial looms ahead of us like something out of a horror movie. Its spires and round corners make it look creepier than it should. Juxtaposed against all the creepiness is a fairly new electric sign that welcomes visitors and points drivers in the direction of the Wellness Center and the

Emergency Room.

"I'll stay with you," Officer Randy says to me as he pulls into a special spot reserved for the men in blue.

"You don't need to."

He stops the car and pockets his keys. "I know," he says, his hands still gripping the steering wheel. "But I'm staying, anyway."

I can't tell if he's trying to be nice, or if he's a little leery of me. After all, I'm connected to two people who have died in the past two days, and Margo Freeman from two years ago. Now, a girl—my girl—is hurt. Maybe he thinks I'm somehow to blame.

It's the first time that thought dribbles into my mind, and I wonder if that's what's going on here. Maybe the chief wants me watched. Maybe he thinks that I'm some sort of suspect.

Maybe I am.

For some reason, I can't shake the feeling that everything's my fault. Even though the rational part of me knows that's not true, the irrational part keeps telling me that nothing's rational about my life.

I sit there, in the passenger's seat of Officer Randy's car, staring at the double entrance to the emergency room. There's a cement ramp leading up to it for handicapped people to use and two huge sliding doors that look as out of place next to the dark brick of Wang as the electric sign in front of the hospital.

Someone probably thought the new sign and the new doors would make Wang look all up-to-date. That's a joke. The inside of the hospital is as dank and old as the outside.

"Ready?" he asks me. I'm not, but I find myself opening the door and sliding out of the cruiser. Officer Randy walks a few steps behind me. I slowly cross the parking lot to the cement ramp and purposely zigzag up the handicapped gauntlet to the sliding doors.

He doesn't follow me that way. He walks up the few stairs and waits for me so that we can go through the emergency room doors together.

When we do, I see a couple people sitting in dingy upholstered chairs, reading magazines that have probably been there for decades. We don't sit in the chairs, though. Officer Randy points me toward a desk with a woman sitting behind it, popping her gum. She's twenty-something and trashy looking, with too much makeup on her face. She smiles when she sees us, and I can see that some of her red lipstick is on her teeth, making them look as bloody as my world has turned since finding Claudia Fish in the woods.

"Sheila," says Officer Randy like he knows her a little too well.

"Randy," she says back and smiles at him broadly. "What can I do you for?"

About fifty bucks, I think. Maybe twenty-five.

"This is business," he says. "We're looking for a patient who's probably still in the emergency room. And don't give me any of that crap about only family members being able to see patients, yada yada."

"Okay, okay," she says and snaps her gum again. "You don't have to get all official about it. What's the patient's name?" she asks, absent-mindedly rubbing her fingers across her teeth and moving the lipstick stains from her molars to her hands.

"Berg," I blurt out. It's the first time I say anything to her at all, and she shifts her gaze from Officer Randy to me and does a quick once-over, like she's judging me at a 4-H show.

"Which one?" she asks, as she looks at her computer screen.

"What do you mean?"

"Berg," she says again. "Which one? We brought two in. Anthony Berg and Annie Berg. I think they're father and daughter."

38

WE WAIT LESS than five minutes, but each minute seems like a life-time. Officer Randy goes to the vending machines at least twice, and I endure watching him eat like Newie after a game. For some reason, listening to his lips smacking together is making me sick. I turn away from him, stare at the wall, and try not to think horrible things.

I need to find out what's wrong with Annie. I don't know if she's dead or alive, and I don't know anything about her father—although Mr. Berg being dead wouldn't be such a bad thing.

Every time the second hand winds around the clock on the wall, my shoulders tense up. Finally, I'm about to explode. "Who found them?" I ask Officer Randy.

"Huh?"

"Who found Annie and her father?"

"Oh," says Officer Randy. "One of the officers went to the Berg residence to inform them about, well, you know, and found the door open."

I nod and turn away again, right as he's reaching out to offer me a mini powdered doughnut from the vending machine. I don't want it. Like I said, doughnuts and cops always seem to go together—doughnuts and cops and death.

Finally, Officer Randy and I are let into the triage area by a jolly nurse who seems way too happy. I want to lash out at her for being so freaking normal. Doesn't she know we don't do normal in Apple? Didn't she get the memo?

Triage is the place where they check you over and try to figure out what's wrong with you. The jolly nurse—the one I want to smack upside the head—immediately ushers us to the central desk. Another nurse, with thin skin stretched across her hatchet face, looks up from whatever work she's doing, but it seems to me like she's not doing anything much but reading a fat novel. Her glasses are perched on the edge of her beak.

"What?" she snips.

"This is Jackson Gill," says Officer Randy.

Her eyes widen. "Jackson Gill?" She nods her head toward the far corner of the room. "You're all that little girl's been asking for since she's come in here. 'Jackson Gill. Get me Jackson Gill.'"

"Well, I'm here now," I say, letting the words burn in my mouth like acid. I want to punch a wall. I want to scream. Most of all, I just want to see Annie.

"What's with the patient?" asks Officer Randy.

Hatchet Face leans in and pretends she's whispering a secret, but she's not whispering at all. "Pills, honey," she says. "Lots of pills. We didn't have to pump her stomach, though. She's pretty groggy. We're letting her ride it out."

I don't know what happened to Annie last night after Chief Anderson dropped her off, and I don't give a crap about her father. All I know is that Annie's not a pill-popper—she's a cutter. We all have our preferred methods of self-torture. Mine's just on the inside. Besides, me, Newie, and Annie never got into doing pills. Ziggy Connor has the market cornered on that sort of stuff, and his prices are out of our league.

Ka-dunk. Something clinks inside my head—a puzzle piece in the picture I can't yet see.

They use the shit in the capsules to make some of the hard junk. That's what Newie said last night. *They use the shit in the capsules to make some of the hard junk.*

The nurse comes out from behind the counter and motions for me to follow. Officer Randy follows us, too. I want to yell at him to back off, but I can't. It wouldn't do any good, anyway.

Annie is in a cubicle, sectioned off by drab beige curtains, but the front is wide open because I think she needs to be watched.

"She's talking," says Hatchet Face. "She's just confused."

"Five minutes," Office Randy says to me. "That's it. Then I need to have some words with her."

Thankfully, Officer Randy and the nurse stand outside and let me see Annie alone. I get the sense that he's probably breaking some sort of rule by doing that, but I think the police break a lot of rules in Apple, just so they can cope with how ineffective they are.

I wait until they are safely in a conversation by themselves, mere inches out of earshot, before I say anything to Annie.

"What happened?" I whisper to her as I stand next to the bed.

Annie's curled into a ball on the small industrial cot with her back turned to me, but I'm sure she can hear every word.

"They say I took pills," she whispers hoarsely. "Like an overdose."

She rolls over to face me. "I didn't take pills, Jackson, but no one will believe me."

I'm not sure I believe her, either. Her eyes are vague, and it seems like she's looking right though me.

I'd like to think I know Annie better than to believe she would swallow a handful of pills, but the truth is, sometimes everyone has dark thoughts about how it would be so much easier if they were asleep.

It kills me that I can't say anything to her about her mother. It's bad enough that she's already tried to kill herself once today. I don't want to give her a reason to try and do it again.

I can't think of anything that won't sound horrible, so I say, "What now?"

"I dunno," she murmurs. The words sound like butterflies fluttering out of her mouth. "I think it's bad."

"How bad?"

"Lockdown bad."

"Shit," I say, because I know she's right. When her tox-screen comes back and it shows anything in her system more noxious than pot, which it probably will, they won't release her. That means she'll be stuck at Wang for a while. First, they'll keep her on some sort of suicide watch, to make sure she's not going to try anything stupid like biting herself or yanking tubes out of her arm. After that, they'll move her someplace else for observation. It'll be a group home or an institution. They'll spend days shrinking her, until she finally breaks down and has to talk about why she took so many pills.

That's a freaking good question. Why?

I sit down on the edge of the bed, next to Annie, and hold her hand. We both don't say anything for a moment. Finally, I get up the courage to ask, "Where did you get the pills, Annie? Mark Zebrowski? Ziggy?"

A tear rolls down her cheek. "I told you. I didn't take any pills."

I bite the inside of my lip. "What about your dad?"

"I don't know," she whispers. "What about my dad?" I can see a hint of fear growing in her eyes. "What about my dad?"

I realize that she doesn't know. "He's here, too."

Annie spaces out for a moment. Finally she asks, "Why?"

I don't know why. I look at my feet and shrug. Annie closes her eyes, and another tear spills out. Finally, she says, "I had a dream last night. I had a dream, but it was so real."

"About what?" I ask her as my fingers gently rub her hand.

"I had a dream that the doorbell rang. It woke me up. I couldn't figure out who would be ringing our bell. I thought it might be the chief coming back to talk to my dad—but when I opened the door there was no one there."

Annie drifts off for a moment, and a little bit of drool falls from her mouth. "There was an apple pie," she says. "I remember there was an apple pie on the kitchen table."

A sick feeling gnaws at my gut as I remember what creepy Father Tim said to me and Newie last night when he was getting into his car at the BD Mart.

Apple pie . . . that'll do the trick.

"What are you talking about, Annie?" I ask her. "Is this real, or were you dreaming?"

She swallows and sucks in some snot. "I don't know," she whispers. Another tear pools at the corner of her eye and drips onto the pillow. "It feels like a dream, but it might have been real." She wipes both eyes with her fists. "There was a note that said *Carve her up—Mom*, sitting next to it. I only had a little piece," she whispers. "It tasted like McIntosh and cinnamon and caramel . . . and something else . . . something funny." Annie sniffs and looks up at me with her glazed expression. "I don't remember anything after that," she says. "It was a dream, Jackson, wasn't it?"

No, I think. *It wasn't a dream at all. It was a nightmare.*

39

I FEEL SICK TO my stomach and have to reach down to steady myself on the cot. The burning in my chest—the burning that always comes like hellfire whenever I get scared or stressed or angry bursts into feverish life underneath my skin. Not-Becky's chanting comes flooding into my brain as clear as day.

> *"Four and twenty blackbirds baked into a pie.*
> *Cut yourself a slice of it and you'll get really high.*
> *Four and twenty blackbirds baked into a pie.*
> *Eat a bigger piece of it and you will surely die."*

Along with that sick singsong rhyme comes something else. Annie said the pie tasted like McIntosh and cinnamon and caramel—just like my house smelled yesterday after school, when I found the candle lit.

I hear Hatchet Face talking to Officer Randy. She lowers her voice and says, "Look, I'm not supposed to say anything, and I don't have the toxicology report on this one and her dad yet, but the guy's barely holding on. It looks like he took a boatload of prescription pills— anti-depressants and tranquilizers—enough to kill a horse."

Antidepressants and tranquilizers? The words roll around in my head as Annie floats away on a cloud.

Antidepressants and tranquilizers.

That's what my mom and Becky take. That's exactly what they take.

Ka-dunk. Another puzzle piece snaps into place in the picture inside my head.

"I need to ask a few questions," says Officer Randy as he suddenly materializes by my side. Thankfully, he doesn't notice that I've probably turned green since I feel a little woozy, myself.

Annie opens her eyes. She sees Officer Randy and nods. I guess there's some sort of comfort in him being there. He's always been there—at the school, in the library, at the playground.

"I know you're tired, Annie," he says. "But I need to know. Your dad likes his beer, but"—he licks his lips—"what else does he like?"

"Huh?" says Annie.

"You know," Officer Randy continues. "Percocet, OxyContin, Valium, Clonazepam." He's spews out a litany of drugs.

"My father doesn't use pills," Annie says softly to Officer Randy.

"What about your mother?" he asks, and I wince. He steals a quick glance at me, probably to make sure that I won't say anything.

I won't. I'm sure there's a protocol for telling Annie that her mother's gone. A social worker and a psychiatrist probably need to be involved, but for now, she's pleasantly in the dark. Whatever she took is still washing through her system. I see her face relax, and she closes her eyes and sighs.

"She doesn't take pills, either," Annie murmurs before drifting off.

"Mr. Berg's a drunk," I say to Officer Randy. "That's all. He drinks like a fish."

"I know all about Tony Berg," says Officer Randy. "I just want to know where he got those pills, because it's starting to look like he never wanted to wake up."

I'm tempted to tell Officer Randy about creepy Father Tim and Annie's dream of eating a poisoned apple pie, but I don't. One thought keeps distracting me, banging against the wet insides of my head.

How did Becky know? How?

"Let's let her rest," Officer Randy says as he escorts me away from her bed. None of this seems real. None of this seems right. "I'll drive you home, okay?"

"What about Annie?" I ask, but I'm pretty sure I already know the answer.

"Annie's going to be here for a while," he tells me. "I'm sure she'll be fine." Then he says it again for emphasis, or to make himself believe that what he's saying is true. "I'm sure she'll be fine."

"Thanks," I say, trying to hide the pained look that I know is painted on my face. I must be doing a good job because Officer Randy seems not to notice. He brushes by me and pushes through the doors to the waiting room. The lady who was snapping her gum is still there, and she winks at Randy as we walk by.

It grosses me out. I don't know why, but it all seems so fucking inappropriate—like saying "fuck" all the time.

That seems fucking inappropriate, too.

It's after twelve by now. My father's working at the farmer's co-op today. There's a big fall sale, and all the tourists will want to buy something that means "Massachusetts." Crap like postcards, or T-shirts, or coffee mugs with pictures of moose. Also, planting season is coming to a close. All the hobby-gardeners are getting in their last bulbs for fall. My father has to be around for that, especially if they need an extra hand at the registers or for loading up cars and pickup trucks from the warehouse.

I wonder how he's going to do all that with a twisted ankle.

I slipped on the stairs out on the porch.

Ka-dunk. A third puzzle piece fits into place inside my head, but I don't want to look at the picture being made. Not yet. I need to make sense of why Annie and her father are doped up on pills—the same kind of pills that my mother and Becky take.

Ka-dunk-dunk. The picture in my mind becomes almost clear, like a knob is turning inside my head, bringing everything into focus, one notch at a time.

Suddenly, I know what I have to do when I get home.

I know exactly what I have to do.

40

MY MOTHER DOESN'T bake—not since Margo Freeman was dismantled all over town, and not since Not-Becky came to live inside my sister's head. My mother doesn't make cookies or pies or homemade muffins. Gone are the days of pancakes from scratch and waffles made on a greased waffle iron and served with whipped cream on top.

My mother doesn't bake, so why the hell was there sugar all over the kitchen counter and in the cabinet where we keep her depression pills and Becky's anti-psychotic stuff?

Why?

As Officer Randy drives me home—down the winding hill, away from Wang Hospital, and across the top of Glendale Road past the high school and the middle school, I can't stop wondering why there was sugar all over the counter in the kitchen when my mother doesn't bake.

"You doing okay?" asks Officer Randy as he cuts down a street that I've never noticed before. The big houses on either side of the road are foreign to me. People with money live in them. They're the ones who hire cleaning women to wipe up their sugar in their kitchens.

I don't answer him, which is as good as saying, "Leave me the hell alone. I don't want to talk." We pass by a house that's already decorated for Halloween, with so many tacky things on the front lawn that it makes my eyes hurt.

Officer Randy snorts as he sees a blowup sculpture of a Frankenstein monster with a tiny head next to a chorus of little cloaked figures with skeleton faces, all standing in a semi-circle. "That's a crowd pleaser," he says, but I still don't respond.

A few minutes later, he turns right where the BD Mart and the gas station face off against each other on opposite corners. I stare at the plastic picnic table where Newie and I sat last night, waiting for Annie to get off work. I think about Julie Dopkin and her rant against Annie for selling too much cough medicine to one person, and I think about creepy Father Tim buying that freaking apple pie because he had a sweet tooth.

My eyes narrow into slits. Officer Randy maneuvers his cruiser down the hill and stops at the corner of Main Street.

"Let me out here," I say, reaching for the door handle.

The wrinkles on his forehead accordion together, making them more pronounced. Eventually they relax, and he presses the button on the electric locks. I guess I'm not a suspect after all. "Okay," he says. "But why don't you take it easy today. You've been through a lot."

He's right. I have been through a lot—today and yesterday, and all the days going back for a long, long time.

I open the door, get out of the cruiser, and watch as he pulls past me down Main Street and back toward Tenzar's. As he goes, the red and blue lights on his roof begin to flash, but with the siren off.

After a minute, I pull my phone out of my pocket and text Newie. *Annie's okay.*

He answers me right away.

U yank your chain at Wang?

Fuckwad. *I'm home. U?*

Still with Erika. She's a mess.

K. Later.

I close the phone and stare across the street at the entrance to Vanguard Lane. There was a time when my street meant safety and security and home. Now it's just dark and gloomy with bad memories and mental illness.

I don't want to go home. I want to put off what I'm going to find when I get there. One thing's for damn sure. Whatever I find will be part of the out-of-focus picture in my head.

I wait a couple minutes, shifting back and forth on my feet, before finally crossing Main Street and slowly walking down Vanguard Lane to the two-family house that's the only home I've ever known.

My father's car is gone. The driveway seems like a lonely stretch of highway leading off into a gloomy wasteland. At the end of the wasteland is my father's garage. I stare at it, pushing away the thought that I may very well discover another piece of the puzzle there, but for right now, I have to focus.

I'm concerned with the kitchen and what I'll find in the cabinets.

With one hand shoved deep in my pocket, I blow a gust of air out of my mouth, push open the gate, walk up the stairs, and through the front door.

The house is quiet inside. The air is thick with questions. I don't even take off my coat and hang it on my father's coat rack. Instead, I quietly make my way through the living room to the kitchen. I stop at the linoleum floor, only because I know once I step onto it, there's no going back.

Still, I need to know, and that need propels me forward.

The cabinet with the medication in it looms in front of me, larger than life. I stare at the handle as it silently beckons me to pull it open so it can vomit out its secrets, but before I can reach my hand out to grasp it, I hear a creak somewhere in the house.

Could it be the old man upstairs? Is my mother up? Could it be Becky downstairs, huddled against the wall and spewing filth into the decorative metal grate, so that she can pick apart what's left of my grandfather's already-addled brain?

I wait and I listen, but I hear nothing else. Maybe it's only the sound of the house settling. Old houses do that sometimes. After a while, their bones become brittle and sometimes crack. They let out short, involuntary moans, which are only their foundations settling into the holes that will someday be their graves. Old houses are just like old people, who come to realize that the bag of skin that holds their insides in will eventually turn to dust and decay.

No more strange sounds come, so I grip the handle on the cabinet door and pull it open.

Before me are the orange bottles of medication for both my mother and my sister. Most of them are less than half full because the end of the month is near.

I pull the bottles out of the cabinet, tear off a double piece of paper towel, lay it on the counter, and set the medications on top of it.

Then I do what I know I need to do, although I already know what I'm going to find.

41

SUGAR.

Goddamned sugar.

Capsule after capsule is filled with sugar—not that granulated stuff that my dad scoops into his coffee, teaspoon after teaspoon, but the powdered crap that sifts and cakes like flour.

This is what was all over the counter before I cleaned it up. This is what was on the medicine bottles, giving me the briefest of hopes that my mother actually woke up out of her stupor and baked cookies or a pie.

These little red and yellow tubes are supposed to hold the cure for my mother's depression. Tiny granules of medication should be inside, each expertly engineered to react with her brain so that she doesn't think everything around her is so bad.

These pills are supposed to erase the crippling depression that holds her encased in a wall of stone, unable to get out and unable to interact with her family or the rest of the world.

Now I know she's been robbed of their help.

Each time she's been given a pill, it's been a fraud—a clever ruse to disguise the fact that she's not being given medication at all. She's been given sugar. Her illness has gone unchecked for who knows how long and has left her all but paralyzed, a vegetable trapped in human form—trapped in the malnourished dirt of her own brain.

I stare at the white powder on the paper towel before dabbing my finger in it and putting it to my mouth to confirm what I already know. The sickeningly sweet taste blooms on my tongue and makes me angrier than I've been in a long time.

Also in the cabinet are Becky's medications—two bottles' worth. I know they're both filled with tranquilizers, one for the morning and one for at night, so I start with the evening pills. They look different from my mother's. These are solid blue. I twist them in two and am surprised to find them filled with her medicine. I take apart several of them before I realize they haven't been touched.

I can't say the same for her morning pills.

Each time I open one up, more powdery white sugar falls to the paper towel.

They're useless. Becky isn't being given the medication that she's supposed to take every morning. Without it, Not-Becky hasn't been silenced during the day. While I'm at school or in the tobacco fields in the summer, it must howl and berate and torment the ones in my house who can't escape—my mother and my grandfather. Only after I mash the evening pills into its food does it quiet down.

Only then does it sleep.

I clench my fists as the ruined capsules lay in front of me like dead soldiers. My mind reels with this new revelation, adding bits and pieces to the picture in my head and rearranging the image over and over again in an attempt to make it clearer—but clarity still doesn't come.

Instead, the questions explode in my head like paintball bullets. Why are the pills being tampered with? What possible reason could there be to keep my mother and sister sick instead of well?

Who the hell has done all this?

Something whispers in my ear, forlorn and loving, like a soft and deadly kiss.

The only person who could have done this is your father.

The thought barrels into me with such force that I momentarily lose my breath. I gasp, sucking deeply on air as though it might be the last breath I'll ever take. Quietly, I find myself saying the words out loud.

"The only person who could have done this is my father." The sentence echoes in the empty kitchen as though I'm standing in a room full of granite, carved through millennia by a stream trickling endlessly within the bowels of the earth.

It makes no sense.

It seems so right.

There aren't any other choices.

Becky's chained in the basement. My mother's a dry and withering husk, and my grandfather's a living corpse who drags himself around his rooms by his heels, looking for a woman who tumbled down the stairs two years ago.

I say it again. "The only person who could have done this is my father."

The words seem more grounded this time. They seem real—and as they solidify into something of substance, I will myself to move. My hand sweeps across the kitchen counter, throwing everything away in the yellow wastebasket under the sink.

Then I walk down the hallway to my mother's bedroom and quietly push open the door.

There she is, under her blanket, hiding in the dark so she doesn't have to face the day. More than anything, I want to go to her and hug her and tell her that everything's going to be okay, but I know she won't hear me. She'll just ask for a cigarette and let it fester between her yellowing fingers until it burns her skin.

Instead, I back out of her bedroom and gently click the door closed.

My chest starts to burn again—fear or stress or anger fueling the flame like it always does.

Freaking pills. Goddamned freaking pills.

As I start back down the hallway, my sneakers creak against the hardwood floor. From somewhere beneath me, I hear the beginnings of thick, phlegmy laugher, but I force myself not to listen. I'm not concerned with Not-Becky.

I'm concerned with the garage.

What's inside my father's workshop? What's so damn important that he hides there all night long, leaving me alone to handle our miserable excuse of a family?

I go out the back door, pushing the screen open so hard that it hits the railing. Halfway down the stairs, I almost fall, because one of the steps is loose. A coffee can filled with cigarette butts that's sitting on the stairs topples over, rolling onto the cracked pavement of the driveway.

I leave the butts lying there as I tighten my face and push ahead.

As I edge closer, a chill whips up in the air and swirls around me like the questions swirling in my head. I start to shake. Wave after wave of icy tendrils lash out at me, causing my skin to tingle and making me feel alive and scared and alone, all at the same time.

I have to see what's inside my father's garage. He's never locked it or forbidden me to enter. It's more that he's placed an invisible unwelcome sign over the door. This is his place. It's where he can hide and do whatever he wants and not have to think about my mother or Becky or my grandfather.

Or even me.

A few more steps down the driveway, and I stop to look both ways to see if any of our neighbors are in their backyards watching me—but there's nobody there to see me commit the unthinkable sin of believing that my father's somehow evil.

I continue on.

At the door to the garage—not the one that my father hasn't lifted in years to put his car inside, but the other door to the right that he uses to get into his workshop—I pause. I'm not sure why, but I feel like I'm betraying something sacred by going into his space.

Still, I have to. If what I suspect is true, he's betrayed us all for years.

I touch the knob on the door, tentatively caressing the rusted metal. That knob has probably been there since my great-grandfather first bought this house. It's seen my grandfather grow up here and start a family of his own. It's seen my own father as a little boy, a teenager, and an adult with a wife and children.

If it could speak, the knob would probably be wise beyond its years.

The knob probably knows things—dark things—things that might fit into the puzzle that's being pieced together in my mind. Unfortunately, now isn't the time to reminisce. Now is the time for finally doing something.

I take a deep breath and twist. At first, I think my father's locked the door, because it doesn't seem to turn. After a moment, it slowly gives way, and I push inward into the darkness of my dad's lair.

The windows haven't been cleaned in years. Any light that manages to creep its way through the grime and dirt is brown and muted. From memory, I know there's a switch somewhere on the wall to my right.

I find it and turn it on. Only then are my eyes assaulted by what I find.

42

THE GARAGE IS filled with upside down crosses. Every type of wood, every color, is represented. There are big ones and small ones. Some are adorned with crude shapes of a man, carved out of wood or sculpted out of screws and nails and held together with wire and drippy white glue.

In the center of the garage is a stepstool next to a huge crucifix, almost like the anchor of a great ship. I can tell that he still hasn't finished it, because some of the wood needs to be sanded and polished. I can picture my dad working late into the night, a cigarette growing out of his mouth, as he grunts and sweats to will it into being.

The crucifix reaches almost to the ceiling and is tied to one of the heavy wooden rafters by thick rope. The excess of the knotted cord drapes from the ceiling to the floor. On the cross is the suggestion of a life-sized figure made out of blocky wood, with its legs crossed and its arms outstretched, but like everything else in the garage, the figure is pointing downward.

Something about it makes my throat tighten and my inner fire burn.

I remember one Sunday morning a long time ago, before everything changed, and Becky and I were still kids. Creepy Father Tim had finished his service, and everyone was outside the church exchanging pleasantries. My mother was clutching her rosary beads in her hands as she talked to the Father. A tiny cross had draped over her knuckles and was dangling upside down.

Becky pulled at my mother's hand. "Mommy, your cross is upside down," she said. She really hadn't meant anything by it, but Father Tim smiled a toothy, shark-like grin, as though she had cut herself in the ocean and he smelled blood.

"Do you know who Satan is?" he asked her. My parents were right there and my grandparents, too. We both looked at their faces. My mother was a little taken aback by his question. My father was stoic. It was my grandfather who said something.

"Go on," he urged Becky, almost proud. "You can tell Father Tim."

My sister, all red hair and freckles, puffed out her chest like she knew the answer to a particularly difficult math problem written on a blackboard. "He was one of God's favorites," she said to Father Tim, her eyes bright with wonder. Even then, Becky saw creepy Father Tim as an extension of God. I never did. I don't know why. To me, he was just a scary man in black.

"That's right," he said to her. "And what happened to him?"

She sucked in her lip. "He disagreed with God," Becky said, her voice lowering to a whisper. "He disagreed, so God sent him away and turned him into the Devil."

"The Devil," my grandfather echoed.

"Very good, Rebecca," Father Tim said to her. "That's exactly right." He bent over her like a big black spider about to trap a fly in its web. He scared me, and I shrank back from him. "An upside down cross is a symbol for people who worship the Devil," he said.

I was holding my father's hand, and he squeezed it so tightly that I pulled away from him and wrapped my arms around my grandfather's leg instead. "It's the sign of someone who has lost faith."

My sister brooded for a moment, sticking two fingers in her mouth and sucking on them. Finally, she pulled her fingers out of her mouth, looked up at my mother with her upended rosary wrapped around her hand, and asked, "Mommy, have you lost faith?"

My mother got all flustered, and her face turned red. She shooed Becky away, telling her to go play with her friends. I stayed there, hugging my grandfather's leg.

I remember my quiet father shaking his head and saying, "With all due respect, Father, an upside down cross does not represent the Devil. It pays homage to Peter, one of the first twelve chosen by Jesus to be a disciple. He was crucified upside down by Nero."

Father Tim sort of chuckled, clapped his hand on my father's back, and left us to greet some of the other parishioners. He completely dismissed what my dad had to say.

I remember my father grumbling something under his breath. He turned to me and reached out his hand. I took it, and he picked me up in his arms. "Peter was a fisherman," he said, his nicotine breath tickling my nose. "He fished on the Sea of Galilee."

"What's a sea?" I asked him. "Is it like the reservoir?"

"Something like," he said to me.

I smiled and imagined my father fishing the reservoir, as reverent and holy as Saint Peter because he was doing the divine work of God.

My grandfather snorted, and we both looked at him. "I don't know where you get your special brand of horseshit," he snapped at my father. Then he fixed his eyes on mine. "An upside down cross is the sign of Lucifer," he said to me in a coarse voice. "Lucifer—God's angel—and don't you forget it, Jack."

I looked from my father to my grandfather. They were both angry, but I didn't know why. "Wha . . . What's horseshit?" I asked, but by then my grandfather had taken my grandmother by the arm and hobbled away.

I remember that morning like it was yesterday. It's still clear in my mind—a loose piece of the past too stubborn to melt into oblivion. Some memories are like that. They stick to you like flypaper, and you never know why.

As I stand in my father's workshop, replaying that moment in my mind, a question comes to me. Is the forest of upside down crucifixes the sign of Saint Peter who was crucified by Nero, or do they symbolize Lucifer—the fallen one? I suppose the answer all comes down to a matter of belief. I can believe that my father is good and righteous and devout, or I can believe he's doing Lucifer's bidding.

I shake my head, trying to make my thoughts stop spinning faster and faster like a killer tornado. Nothing about what's happening is making sense. Nothing that's happening to the people in my life is fitting together into anything other than a Salvador Dali painting—all messed up, drippy, and insane. The upside down crosses, Annie and her dad almost overdosing on the same medication that my mother and Becky take, the sugar, the lit candle that smelled like baked apple pie—the same apple pie that Annie imagined was left at her door. Four and twenty blackbirds—all of it.

I can't puzzle everything together. There are still missing pieces, and if I can't find them and fit them into the picture in my head, I might actually go insane.

My eyes fall on a Bible marked and opened on my father's work-bench. He worships that book. He reads it and quotes it and tries to live his life as best he can by it. I can't imagine that he's been broken by it, too.

I tighten my face and take a few steps until I'm in front of his book. There are dozens of pieces of paper sticking out of it, most likely marking his favorite passages—the ones he recites at dinner—the ones he repeats on his knees when he prays.

I reach down and flip through the pages, feeling almost guilty for touching his holy relic.

The first passage I stop at is from St. Luke 8:30. It says, "And Jesus asked him, '*What is your name?*' And he said, '*Legion.*'"

Legion.

That's what Not-Becky called itself when I gave my sister the Hydrox cookies.

I turn the pages to another marked section, put my finger beneath the words, and slowly read them. My lips move, but no sound comes out. This one is from St. Mark 5:4-20. Some of the words don't make sense to me, but five of them leap off the page like they've been magnified a thousand times over. "Bound with shackles and chains."

I pull my finger away like it's been burned. Shackles and chains—just like Becky.

The passage goes on further. I'm almost afraid to read it, but I do, anyway. ". . . and the chains had been torn apart by him and the shackles broken in pieces, and no one was strong enough to subdue him. Constantly, night and day, he was screaming among the tombs and in the mountains . . ."

Or in the basement, I think. Not-Becky screams in her tomb in the basement.

My hand moves on its own, an independent part of my body. I'm only a spectator as I watch my fingers reach for the edges of the pages and turn them over. My eyes fall on a third passage. I don't notice where it's from, because all I see are words circled in red, and I pray the red isn't blood. They say, "I command thee, in the name of Jesus Christ, to go out from her."

I read the sentence again and again.

I command thee, in the name of Jesus Christ, to go out from her.
I command thee, in the name of Jesus Christ, to go out from her.
I command thee, in the name of Jesus Christ, to go out from her.

Suddenly, the door to the garage bangs open, and one of the panes of glass shatters. Becky is standing there, her chains broken and the manacles bloodied around her wrists. Her eyes are filled with evil. It isn't my sister at all. It's Not-Becky, and it's laughing.

It's laughing and gasping, and saliva is dripping from its mouth. Its lips are shredded where it's bitten itself, and blood is pouring down its chin.

"Do you like my redecorating?" It giggles hysterically. "Crosses always look so much better upside down." In a flash, Not-Becky disappears from the doorway.

I run, only to catch a glimpse of it as it bounds up the back porch and through the screened door into the house.

43

MY BLOOD RUNS cold in my veins. I stand there holding the frame of the door, trying to comprehend what just happened.

I play it back in my mind in slow motion. Not-Becky hurdled across the backyard like a crazed animal. At one point, its arms reached to the ground as it grabbed handfuls of straw-like turf for purchase, to propel itself forward. When it reached the back stairs, it scrambled up them, lizard-like, and disappeared out of sight.

The image burned into my brain is so unreal, but the pounding in my chest is telling me that it's very real, after all.

Not-Becky's chains are broken. It's out, and now that thing—that creature—is alone in the house with my mother and my grandfather. How many days has it been free to roam with them? How many times has Not-Becky tormented them even more than they've been tormented by their own illnesses?

The thought is almost too much to bear, and all I want to do is run after it into the house and confront it. The problem is that I can't seem to will my feet to move. I stare at my sneakers, silently willing them to take the first step.

Move forward, I think. Be a man—but I simply can't. I'm hobbled by fear.

It's slow going. I put one foot in front of the other—carefully, cautiously—until somewhere along the way, the glue that's binding me gives way, and I find myself sprinting across the yard to the back porch, to where Not-Becky disappeared into the house.

I stop at the bottom step. From inside, I hear crazed laughter. It's the sort of laugh track corn you hear inside a cheesy funhouse. There are gut-wrenching howls and clown-like hoots that sound like they're coming from a giant painted mouth filled with sharp fangs. They spill out through the tiny holes in the screened door. It's the laughter of a lunatic. It's the mirth of murder.

How many times has she been loose?
Is Not-Becky the murderer?

The thought is ludicrous. The murders have been happening in Apple for sixty years.

I stand at the bottom of the steps with my hand on the railing and wish someone, anyone, could tell me what to do, but there's no one to help me.

I blink my eyes, and my heart skips a beat. I'm sure when my father left for work this morning all the crosses in his workshop were upright. It was Not-Becky who rearranged his collection, making them an obscenity. The thing is, my father doesn't think that upside down crosses *are* an obscenity. He thinks they're a symbol of Saint Peter who was crucified upside down by Nero. He thinks they're a symbol of one of the original disciples of Jesus.

So why did Not-Becky turn all his crosses upside down?

I hear creepy Father Tim's voice from that Sunday so long ago. "*. . . an upside down cross is a symbol for people who worship the Devil. It's the sign of someone who has lost faith.*"

My father hasn't lost faith. He's desperately trying to use his faith to make sense of Becky's condition. He thinks she's possessed. Building the crucifixes only serves to confirm his religious convictions.

Another puzzle piece falls into place, and with it, another question. Is this a subconscious message from my sister, like when she tried to warn me about Mrs. Berg by saying she was cold and all wrapped and packaged?

Is Becky trying to tell me that someone has lost faith?

The question stops me in my tracks. Has someone lost faith?

I certainly have, but I never had faith to begin with. I've spent my entire life going through the motions for the sake of my family. I've sat on hard pews for countless Sunday mornings at church. My family has grasped hands around our kitchen table for as long as I can remember, as my father recites memorized words out of his book—but all those things have meant nothing to me.

They've only washed up against my atheism like the ocean against a stony cliff.

I've never had faith. No—it can't be me.

Is it my mother? Has she lost faith? I can't really say. She's been hidden behind her depression for so long, I wouldn't be able to tell. Besides, before Margo Freeman was killed and Not-Becky appeared, my mother was about as faithful as they come.

It can't be her, either.

Who else is there?

I hear cackling again from inside the house, so I dash up the steps and throw open the screen door. As soon as the doorframe bangs against the porch railing, the maniacal laughter stops. It's as though someone's lifted the needle off of an old-fashioned record player.

We have one of those in our living room. It stands in a corner, collecting dust. There's a crank on one side. I remember my grandfather telling me that you only need to turn it twenty times to make the spring tight enough to carry a thick seventy-eight through an entire song. I've never tried to do it myself. I was always afraid that I'd break the record player, and part of my family's past would be gone forever—like my grandfather's lost memories are gone forever from his addled, mixed-up brain.

My grandfather.

The words linger silently inside my head.

My grandfather.

Ka-dunk. Ka-dunk. Ka-dunk. Ka-dunk. Ka-dunk. Several more pieces of the picture in my head fall into place.

44

I STAND IN THE kitchen, frozen like a statue. I close my eyes and reach out with all my senses, mentally picturing every nook and cranny of the house, mapping out where the corners are and imagining the places where Not-Becky could be hiding from me.

The house is silent, save for a vague creaking upstairs. The sound is most likely coming from the wheels of my grandfather's chair as he slowly pushes himself back and forth with the heel of his foot while he watches television.

I cock my head sideways and listen as hard as I can. If I try, I think I can hear the faint sound of a game show host babbling something nonsensical above my head, speaking to the man in the upstairs rooms.

My grandfather.

Is my grandfather the one that Becky's trying to show me? Is he the one who has lost faith? All those years ago, after creepy Father Tim dismissed my father, my grandfather called my dad's beliefs horseshit. *"An upside down cross is the sign of Lucifer,"* he said. *"Lucifer—God's angel—and don't you forget it, Jack."*

My grandfather believes in Lucifer, the beloved one whom God cast out of his kingdom.

There's a scampering of feet in the living room, and I hear freakish laughter again. I'm not sure what to do. On the kitchen counter is a blocky knife set that my mother bought at Three Penny's a few years ago. It's black, and where the black lacquered paint has chipped, my father's filled it in with dark Magic Marker.

I stare at the handle of the butcher knife on top. It holds a sacred place on the pyramid, with the small steak knives on the bottom followed by a serrated bread knife and a paring knife for fruit. The butcher knife, thick and brutal, stands alone at the pinnacle of the triangle.

I slide it out of the wood with a quiet *whoosh*.

I hear giggling now, and in my mind's eye, Not-Becky is sitting on the landing of the stairs where my grandmother made a swan dive to her death. I imagine both hands over its face, with its vile tongue darting through the open spaces—impressed with itself because it managed to lure me into the house.

"Becky," I shout out, slipping her name in between the laughter, filling up the moments that she's gasping for breath. "Becky," I yell again into the house. My words echo in a cavern a thousand miles deep.

"Becky who?" I hear Not-Becky snarl, followed by a fetid, putrid snicker. I squeeze the handle of the knife a little tighter, and it begins to shake in my hand.

"Honey?"

A soft moan creeps down the hallway. My mother is in her bedroom, in the dark. Just as I remember that she's there, the faint stench of cigarette smoke makes my nostrils flare.

I stand with my legs tense and my arms outstretched, not sure what to do. Then my eyes fall on the heavy butcher knife trembling in my fist.

What am I thinking? I may do a lot of questionable things, but I don't stick pointy edges into people, sixteen times over, and watch them bleed. I don't hang degenerates in tobacco barns and slice their throats. I don't cut out the eyes of sad, lonely girls who are destined to live out their lives unnoticed. I don't cut up sweet, poor, hard-working moms and leave them all wrapped and packaged on ice for others to find.

My thoughts carry weight. All of a sudden, the knife in my hand seems impossibly heavy, and I fling it from my grasp. It sails across the linoleum, twirling around a few times before coming to rest underneath one of the kitchen chairs.

I don't want it. I don't need it.

I refuse.

"Honey?" my mother calls out again, but this time her words are punctuated by a slight cough.

Without thinking, I leave the knife underneath the chair and walk straight through the kitchen to the hallway and down to my parents' bedroom. Not-Becky could be right behind me. It could crawl, spider-like, into the kitchen, pick up the knife, and follow me down the hall with its hot breath creeping around my neck like a moist hand.

I don't care.

I keep walking until I reach my parents' door and push it open without stopping.

My mother is sitting on the side of the bed in the dark. She's nothing more than a gray shape, but I see her put her hand to her mouth. The tip of a cigarette springs into red hot life.

"I had the strangest dream," she says.

"What about?" I ask as I move into the room and gently shut the door behind me.

"I can't remember," she says and rubs her head with the hand that's holding the cigarette. "I think I was talking to your sister." My heart begins to beat faster.

"Dreams are weird like that," I hear myself say. "They're hard to remember once you wake up."

My mother shrugs and waves her cigarette slowly in the air as though she's dismissing what I'm saying.

"No," she says to me and shakes her head. "I mean, yes. I usually don't remember my dreams when I wake up."

Behind my head, I hear a shuffle from the other side of the door. Very quietly, long, barely audible scratches come through the wood—a vampire wanting to be invited across the threshold—a vampire that knows that if I don't make the invitation, it can't come in.

Right now, I almost wish that were true. I wish I had that mystical power over Not-Becky, so that I could stop it from barging into my mother's dark world.

My hands are clasped behind my back. Slowly, I back up against the door and search around desperately with my fingers until I find the skeleton key that always rests in the lock. I close my eyes, twist the key, and listen as the lock clicks into place.

Immediately, the scratching on my mother's door stops, and I hear bare feet slapping against the hardwood floor in the hallway, fading away into nothingness.

"So strange," says my mother again, her head shaking back and forth.

"What is?" I ask her as I move away from the door to her bed.

"My dream," she says again. "The one with your sister."

"Why?" I ask, not really caring what she has to say. My mind's mentally following Not-Becky through the house.

"It's what she said," my mother says to me. She sighs and flicks ashes from her cigarette into a stained coffee cup she keeps on her nightstand.

"What did she say?"

My mother takes another deep drag on her cigarette then mumbles softly into the darkened room. "It's silly, really," she muses. "She said, 'Five will die or six for kicks.' Do you know what that means, Jackson?"

Unfortunately, I do.

45

THE THOUGHT OF Not-Becky standing over my mother as she vegetates in her room is enough to make me want to puke.

At some point in the last few hours, maybe even the last few days, Not-Becky has come into my mother's room and whispered vile things to her. My mother, a hollow shell, hasn't been able to tell if what she's heard has been her own imagination or a tangible thing, murmuring filth.

I can't think about that right now. All I can be thankful for is that my mother hasn't been physically hurt.

"Why don't you lie down for a little bit," I say as I take the cigarette out of her hand. "You need your rest, right?"

"I suppose," she mumbles and closes her eyes. My mother allows me to push her gently back into bed. Her head sinks into the pillow, and she sighs. I watch her for almost a full minute before I go back to her door and put my ear to the wood. I hear nothing, so I take a deep breath and reach down for the skeleton key. My hand finds it, and I gently turn the slender rod until it clicks.

Then I open the door.

Not-Becky is standing right in front of me. Its eyes are angry and insane, and it's holding the knife that I left on the floor in the kitchen. "This is pretty pretty," it sneers at me in a voice that's pure evil dipped in sugar. It's holding the blade in front of its face like a medieval warrior who is readying for battle. It smiles—a wicked, hateful grin—and rudely licks the sharp metal, probably sampling how much pain the blade can inflict. A wash of blood appears on its gray tongue. Not-Becky laps at it, then spits onto the wall to my right.

Red saliva splatters everywhere.

I'm rooted to the floor by fear, but somehow I find my courage. "Go back downstairs," I bark at the monstrosity, adrenaline fueling my anger.

"No," it croaks and swings the knife wide. I dart backwards as the silver metal sails by me and wedges in the wall to my right, smack in the middle of the splatter of blood.

We both freeze and stare at it.

In that moment—a second that seems to last forever—I realize my sister is truly gone. Suzie Zickle is gone. The obsessive nun is gone, too. The only creature left is Not-Becky, and even if my sister were to somehow come back, her personality would be the fake one.

I react quickly, grabbing for the handle, my fist closing around the heavy wood. Not-Becky grabs for it, too, raking its ragged, sharp nails across my knuckles.

I stifle a howl as we struggle in silence over the butcher knife—but Not-Becky is small, and I'm heavier. I maneuver my body and use my shoulder to shove, low and hard. With a wrench, the blade pulls free of the wall and out of my hand—onto the wooden floor.

"Mine," Not-Becky wails and throws itself on top of the butcher knife. It's bony and quick. Somewhere beneath its frail body, Not-Becky grabs hold of the handle and scrambles to its feet so that its back is to me.

It looks over its shoulder, and for a quick second, I see Becky flicker in its eyes. "Help me," she whispers. She looks frightened, like a person afraid of heights at the very top of a rollercoaster that's about to plunge to the ground.

I don't care.

I don't believe it anymore.

Creepy Father Tim says the Devil lies.

In an instant, Becky's gone again, and Not-Becky spits out, "Mine." It runs down the hall in a hunched-over gallop. "Mine. Mine, mine, mine, mine, mine."

Not-Becky disappears into the living room, leaving me alone and breathless. The bloody scratches across my knuckles ache. My eyes travel back and forth between the empty hallway, my parents' bedroom, and the ruined wall next to me.

"No fighting," my mother murmurs dreamily from her bed. She sounds absurd.

I close her door behind me, leaving my mother in comfortable oblivion beneath her bed covers. Then I wait and listen. After a moment, I hear a creak that sounds like wood settling, and I know what it is. Not-Becky is on the fronts steps. It's placing its bare feet carefully on each tread, trying to be quiet, but I know it wants me to follow.

That's what it's always wanted.

I take off my sneakers, leaving them on the floor underneath the blemish of blood on the wall, and quietly steal down the hallway to the kitchen.

The back stairs, the ones in the little alcove between the kitchen and the porch, wind in a steep curve through the guts of the house. I slowly climb them, my stocking feet gliding smoothly between the piles of old paper. For the past two years, ever since Becky got sick and my grandmother died, I've been bringing my grandfather his meals up these winding stairs—day after day, month after month, up and down to the man above our heads.

As I climb, I begin to hear the voice on his television set. My grandfather's probably sitting in his chair, snoozing—blissfully unaware that Not-Becky is sneaking closer and closer to him with a butcher knife.

As horrible as it sounds, I'm happy it's going after my grandfather instead of my mother. He's had his life. His days and nights are now mixed up together in his head, and his dreams and reality are one and the same. If I ever make it to be that old, I hope I don't end up like him. I want my memories. I want to be able to sift through them when I'm ancient and feeble, so that I can find the good ones amidst all the bad and drink them in like aged wine.

They say that bad memories fade away, and that's why women go through childbirth more than once. I hope there's some merit to that, because the last few days of my life should be parceled together and thrown away someplace deep and dark so they'll never be found.

A few steps further, and I'm standing at the back door to my grandfather's apartment. It's closed, and I hear the television through the door. I can't make out the words. Carefully, I grasp the old-fashioned glass knob, its cut and polished surface smooth against my skin. I softly turn it until the door dislodges from its frame, and I can sneak inside.

My grandfather should be in the living room. If I can just make it to the front door of the apartment before Not-Becky finishes her climb, I may be able to lock it and protect the old man.

Quickly, I move through his kitchen, only barely registering that there are apple peels on his kitchen counter, along with a pie rack and the faint smell of McIntosh, cinnamon, and caramel in the air.

I'm moving too quickly to piece those final images into the puzzle in my head. Instead, I'm more focused on the fact that the front door to the apartment is wide open.

Not-Becky is sitting cross-legged at my grandfather's feet, crimson dripping from its bloodied mouth and manacled wrists. The television is off. There's no game show host.

My grandfather is talking to Not-Becky, and it's staring up at him with wide, attentive eyes. The butcher knife is upended and balanced on the floor, and Not-Becky is slowly spinning the blade on point as it listens intently to him.

I stop. It's not because of Not-Becky. It's not because of the blood or the knife or the fact that my grandfather is talking. It's not even because the entire apartment smells like apple pie. I stop because my grandfather's not sitting in his wheelchair. He's standing above my sister, slightly bent, exactly like creepy Father Tim was that day that Becky asked him about the upside down cross.

My grandfather's standing. It's a miracle.

Only it's not.

46

MY MOUTH FALLS open. "You'll catch flies, boy," he says to me with a grin, not unlike Not-Becky's.

"How . . . how are you standing?" I whisper. Still, my voice cracks like it did a few years ago when I hit puberty and everything turned adult.

"On. My. Feet," he says to me in very short, clipped words. Drool stained with blood spills from Not-Becky's mouth in a thick stream. It pools on the floor. Not-Becky laughs, though, when he says that, and its shoulders jump up and down like they're attached to marionette strings.

"But . . ." I say. "But you can't stand. You haven't stood for two years."

He takes his old, gnarled hand, covered with age spots, and softly pats my sister on the head like a dutiful dog. Not-Becky's bloody tongue hangs out of its mouth.

"I've stood plenty," he says to me. "I've done plenty."

I've done plenty.

Ka-dunk, dunk, dunk. Those words, those last three words, are the final pieces of the puzzle for me. They form together inside my head and fit neatly into the picture I've been building there. I know it's finally time for me to look at it, so I can see it for what it really is—and when I do, everything begins to make sense.

"It's you," I croak.

One of his eyebrows lifts up. "It's me, what?" he says, shifting on his feet and taking two quick steps toward me. He limps as he moves, slight but noticeable, like the figure on the tracks that Newie and I saw—the one that was carrying a bag—a bag filled with the things needed for a night's worth of evil.

"You," I say again as my world turns on its head like the crosses in my father's workroom. Everything I've ever known to be true is a lie.

For sixty years, the town of Apple has been plagued with murders, unspeakable things, every September and October. My grandfather would have been only a few years older than me when they started. He lived in this house then, with his parents. They were staunch, devout people.

Just like my parents.

But my grandfather wasn't like them, was he? I see it now. The boy who lived in this house so many years ago had turned away from the beliefs of his mother and father. Whether by fate or design, he somehow cleaved to a different God—a cast-out God.

The God of lies.

The crystal clear picture swims behind my eyes. I see a boy praying to his false God in secret. I see him waiting in anticipation for the dead leaves to come each year so that he can pay homage to the death of the earth with deaths of his own—to please the fallen one, the horned one.

Lucifer.

"It's you," I say again as I see the picture in all its hideous glory. I see my grandfather sneaking out at night, first as a young man, then as a husband and a father. I see amazing kills in ritualized fashion, from skinnings to beheadings to awful, hideous disembowelings.

Then I see the years piling on top of him, until he can no longer bear their weight alone. I see his tributes to his God coming from closer and closer to home. First there was Margo Freeman, and this year there were people from my school like Ruby Murphy and Claudia Fish—because death was her wish—and finally, people from my life—Mrs. Berg and almost Annie and her father.

He drugged them with the contents of the pills—the contents of the pills that were replaced with sugar. He baked the drugs into a pie, secreted it into their house—probably stepping over a passed-out Mr. Berg in the process—and left a note saying it was from Mrs. Berg. Then he rang the doorbell, making sure to wake someone up. Making sure they would find his poisoned pastry.

Carve her up—Mom.

The contents of my empty stomach start to boil into my throat. I back away from him, my head shaking from side to side, not wanting to believe what I now know is the truth.

Not-Becky sits on the ground, watching both of us as it spins the butcher knife round and round. Finally it croaks, "Show him the book," like a groveling henchman. More blood dribbles to the floor as it closes its eyes in blissful, painful ecstasy. "Show him. Show him."

"Ah," my grandfather says, holding up one finger in the air like he's just heard a capital idea. "The book. Yes." He limps over to his couch, the one that he hasn't sat on for years, and reaches for the lumpy pillow that I almost used to block the grate in the wall. "My treasure," he says as he unzips the flowered print and sticks his hand inside its puffy white guts.

He pulls out a black book. It's worn like my father's Bible. My grandfather pats the cover with his wrinkled hand and carries it back across the room, stopping just far enough away from me so I don't bolt down the stairs like a mouse fleeing a cat.

He holds the book out to me.

There's an upside down pentagram on the front cover. I know what that represents, and it holds no more meaning for me than the gold-embossed crosses on the front covers of the books that sit behind each pew at church.

It's only a symbol. It's meant to represent a belief. My father's cruci-fixes represent what he believes to be everything good and safe and righteous in the world.

My grandfather's upended pentagram is the polar opposite. It means evil. It truly is the sign of the Devil.

"What is it?" I ask nervously. My hand finds the back of one of the chairs in his dining room. I hold on to it tightly as I stare at the book between his withered fingers. He stretches his arm out, offering me his prize, but I'm afraid to take it. I'm afraid of what I might find inside.

He grins and waits for me. He knows that my overriding curiosity will eventually win out over my fear. He knows that I'll take it from him, so he waits—and he smiles.

Behind him on the floor, Not-Becky suddenly stops twirling the knife. It stares at the dull metal for a moment as if it's not sure what it is. Then it pulls its hand away, and the knife tips over and falls. Not-Becky blinks its eyes a few times and looks around the room, and suddenly she's not that thing anymore. She's Becky, and she seems as though she doesn't know where she is.

"Take it," my grandfather urges me on. "It's time that you know."

Becky suddenly realizes that she's sitting on the floor in my grandfa-ther's living room, covered in blood, with a butcher knife at her feet.

She looks up at the two of us, and I see her eyes grow wide as the old man extends the book out to me. Becky shakes her head back and forth and mouths the word *no*. I can see the fear in her eyes, and sud-denly I understand something that I've never understood until now.

It was never Not-Becky, huddled against the grate in her room in the basement, speaking horrific things through the walls to my grand-father.

I had it all wrong.

He's been the one whispering madness to her.

He's probably been feeding her filth her entire life, provoking and nurturing the divisions in her head. Out of pure terror, she must have created the childlike Suzie Zickle personality, always looking to play games—to just be normal. Then, the obsessive nun appeared, reading the Bible over and over again to wipe her thoughts clean of my grandfather's obscenities.

Finally, when my grandfather killed Margo Freeman, the horror was so great that Becky was hacked apart once more.

Not-Becky was born—a demon created out of the ashes of my grandfather's madness.

"I don't want to take it," I say to him as the book halves the divide between us.

"But you must," he says and takes another step forward. "Don't be an ass like your father and cling to his Bible of lies. It's a fool's folly, Jack. It's a work of fiction."

They are blasphemous words coming out of a blasphemous man—even for me, who has no belief at all. I feel the sting of what he says as surely as if I've been struck across the face by God himself.

From behind him, I see Becky grab the sides of her head. She's trying desperately to hold onto herself, instead of letting Not-Becky come through. She wants to be present in the here and now. She wants to be present for me.

Becky takes one arm and rubs it across her ruined face, pulling back a sleeve soaked with blood. Her mouth curls as she stares at the red gore. Her eyes fill with horror.

"I don't have to do a fucking thing," I say to my grandfather and push myself away from the chair and walk quickly around the table so that the ancient polished mahogany is between me and him.

He sneers. "You dare use that language under my roof?"

"Yeah, I fucking dare, you murderous piece of shit." I try to dredge up the worst possible words in the world. I want to pummel him with my fists. I want to break him apart for breaking my family—for breaking Becky.

My grandfather is a completely different person from the one that I thought he was when I woke up this morning.

Now I know that everything about him has been a lie, just like the pills that my mother and my sister were supposed to be taking have been lies. The man who's standing before me isn't broken or ready to take his last breath. He's vibrant and alive, with a gleam in his eye that's worse than anything that I can ever imagine seeing in the eyes of creepy Father Tim.

"Take it," he growls, and the glint in his eye sparks fire.

"You filled Mom's and Becky's pills with sugar," I blurt out.

"Had to," he says. "They were both beginning to understand the way of things."

"What's that supposed to mean?"

Becky's still on the floor, but she's listening to us now. Not-Becky has disappeared into the back of her mind.

"It seems we were starting to have a crisis of belief in this family," the old man says to me. I can't think of him as my grandfather anymore. All I can see in front of me is a creature wrapped in a skin. It looks like my grandfather but is really something dark and evil.

"Besides," he says and grins again in that horrible way. "Your poor excuse for a mother was always meant to wallow in her own depression. I only let it happen." He turns for a moment and steals a glance at Becky. "As for my granddaughter?" he says. "Well, I have high hopes for her. What good is she to me drugged? I let the pills take her at night, but during the day? No-sir-ee-Bob. The daytime has been for studying." His words bubble out of him covered in thick, oily slime. "Someone has to be the keeper of tradition."

"Tradition?" I gasp.

"Yes," he says and drops the book on the table. "Tradition—the festivals to honor the true God, cast out of heaven—the Sacrificial Rituals."

I feel as though the room is tilting on its side. I stare at the book in front of me. The binding is old and worn, held together in places with tape. Brittle paper sticks haphazardly out of the top and sides—newspaper clippings that are too large to fit on the pages.

Sixty years' worth of newspaper clippings.

I want desperately to run my fingers across the cover. I have to open it. I have to look inside.

"Don't," I hear Becky say. She's standing now, a little unsteady on her feet. She's not hunched over like Not-Becky. "You mustn't look," she says.

"He must," snaps my grandfather.

"No," she pleads with him. "Not him. He doesn't need to know." She stands behind my grandfather, and for the first time I see that the butcher knife isn't on the floor anymore. It's in her fist, the blade sharp and gleaming, yearning to be brought to life.

My grandfather doesn't look at her. He stares straight at me. "For years, your grandmother knew nothing, then she found my book two years ago, and I had to cast her out. It was what my God commanded of me. Don't you see? It's what he commanded."

The words come back to me once more as if he's speaking them now for the very first time.

I cast you out. I cast you out. I cast you out.

He wasn't trying to cast Not-Becky out of his home. He was casting out his own wife. He pushed her out the door, and she tumbled down the stairs to her death, and all this time, we thought it was my sister who killed her.

It wasn't. It was my grandfather.

"Please, no," says my sister again. There is a sadness in her voice and a sort of resignation that I can't identify.

"He needs to understand the work I've done," snaps my grandfather. "He needs to see how one pays tribute to the true Lord." He licks his lips with anticipation, waiting for me to open the book—waiting for me to see his life's work in newsprint.

Murder after murder after murder—year after year after year.

"You promised you would leave him alone if I listened," Becky cries. "You've always promised." My grandfather's eyes are locked on mine. He just waves his wrinkled hand behind him, willing her to shut up.

"Liar," she screams. "Liar, liar, liar."

With a swift motion, she brings the knife down hard, burying the blade deep into my grandfather's neck all the way to the heavy wooden handle. The old man's eyes grow wide. He reaches up, not sure what's just happened, trying to grasp where the pain is coming from—but by then he's already gurgling, and blood is bubbling out of his mouth. He sways back and forth, back and forth, not sure where to fall.

When he finally does, hitting the floor with a great thud, Not-Becky fills my sister up again. "Five will die," it cackles. "Five will die or six for kicks."

It laughs out loud and grabs the book off the table, then disappears down the front steps before I can even process what my sister has done. As it hops away from me, bent over and evil, I hear it scream those hateful words again. "Five will die or six for kicks. Five will die or six for kicks."

My grandfather was the fifth.

47

A POOL OF BLOOD is spreading across the floor. As the last of the old man's life leaks out of him and seeps into the hardwood, I wonder who will clean it up. I wonder why it happened in the first place. Then I wonder if it was self-defense, because Becky couldn't take his abuse any longer.

I see him replacing the contents of the pills with sugar, to keep my mother a zombie and Becky deranged during the day. I see him setting her free from the basement while I'm at school and my father's at work, bringing her up to his apartment, so he can continue indoctrinating her into what he believed to be true. He probably showed her the contents of that damn book hundreds of times, gloating over each article and reciting the names again and again.

I can imagine him telling her that he'll hurt me, or the rest of the family, if she doesn't promise to listen, and I can imagine Not-Becky soaking up his lies and becoming more demented and evil with each passing day.

It's been the dissociative identity personality that he's been fertilizing with his filth. It's been Not-Becky who's been growing and growing, and my sister becoming nothing more than a shadow.

With that realization, it becomes clear to me what I have to do. Becky saved me. I see that now, so now I have to save her. That's what she would do if she were me.

"I love you, Becks," I whisper softly as I step over my grandfather's lifeless body.

It's funny how the love that you feel for someone can evaporate as quickly as morning dew. Once you peel back the layers and see the darkness that boils beneath the surface, it has a way of deadening love. As for me, I feel nothing when I look at the wrinkled sack of flesh in front of me. It was twisted and psychotic, and now it's dead.

In a way, what Becky did was humane. Now it's my turn.

I go to the top of the stairs and stand there, turning my head to one side and closing my eyes so I can hear what's going on below. There are no creaks of tiptoeing footsteps slinking through the house. There's no laughter. There's only silence.

Each step I take seems hindered by a thick dread. Is Not-Becky going to be waiting at the bottom of the stairs for me, holding the butcher knife that's stained with my grandfather's insides? Maybe it will be crouching behind the couch in the living room, or worse, maybe Not-Becky is already by my mother's bedside, staring at her with a freakish sort of detachment, getting ready to whisper bloody, awful things to the woman who bore it.

No.

By the time I reach the bottom of the stairs, I know where my sister is.

All of the crucifixes in the living room are turned upside down. It's as though whatever's left of Becky is blazing a trail for me to follow, and I know where I have to go.

My father's garage.

I'm no longer afraid for my mother. My sister isn't in the house anymore. She's already out the screen porch and down the steps, across the yard, and into the doorway to my father's private place. I'm as sure of it as I am in the belief that there's no God and there's no Satan.

There's only good and evil—and crazy somehow mixed up between the two. I don't know how my father never saw it before, or if he did, why he chose to ignore it. All I know is that I'm as true to my convictions as my father or my grandfather ever were in their own beliefs.

I don't know why, but I shove my middle finger up in the air at the crosses hanging on the wall. Maybe it's because of all the harm they've done to my family, or maybe it's for all the people who've been destroyed in Apple over the past sixty years.

Sixty years. Ever since my grandfather was a young man, insane enough to think that whatever he was doing every fall was somehow the right thing to do.

I walk through the house to the little alcove with the backstairs leading up to where my grandfather's corpse is bleeding out on the floor and out the screen door.

Across the lawn, my father's workroom door is open. I'm meant to go there. My sister has something to show me, and in the pit of my stomach I know what it is. It's like the real final piece of the picture in my head. It's the five-hundred-and-first piece in a puzzle that's only supposed to have five hundred pieces.

It's the final thing that must happen in all this madness—and I know. I know what I'm going to find.

I cross the yard, step by step, like I am being propelled forward by an unseen hand pressed against the small of my back. It pushes me with purpose.

I know I'll be strong. I've been strong my whole life and even stronger since Margo Freeman died and everything went to hell.

I'm strong and I'm here, and that's what I keep telling myself as I cross the yard, grasp the doorknob, and pull the door open wide. I step inside without even a glance ahead of me.

The lights are on, and that's a good thing, because I can see the forest of upturned crucifixes all around me. The great crucifix is in the middle of the room, tied upside down to the rafters with the thick cord that looks like a fisherman's rope, and Becky's there—not Not-Becky, but my sister. She's standing on my father's stool, the one he sits at when he studies his Bible, and she's knotted the rope that drapes over the rafters into a noose, and has slipped her thin, ratty head into it.

Her eyes meet mine, and they are Becky's eyes. She's holding the butcher knife in her hand and has the sharp blade against her wrist.

"I can't be like this anymore, Jackson," she says as she strokes the rope with one hand and rubs the edge of the blade gently over her wrist with the other. "I can't be like this anymore, and I need you to help me."

I know what she's asking me to do. It seems I always knew it was going to come to this. I knew I would have to take all the puzzle pieces and own the picture that they make—but I can't do it. A new horror begins to dance across my face. I can't do what she's asking me to do. It would be a mercy. It would be an act of love—but I can't do it.

She's always been the strong one, not me. I know that now.

"I . . . I can't," I whisper.

She sighs. "All right."

"All right?"

She nods and drops the knife to the floor. Then she twists her body around so she's facing away from me. The rope makes that terrible tearing sound as little fibers of horse hair rip under the pressure of her weight.

"Six is for kicks," she whispers, and she says it again. "Six is for kicks."

My sister kicks the stool out hard from beneath herself. It twirls on one leg and falls to the floor. There's a wet snapping sound and the groan of the rafters and more tearing of rope.

"Six is for kicks," I say as I turn and walk out the door, flipping the light switch as I go.

Only when I am halfway across the yard do I stop, and I stand there staring into space for what seems like hours.

Six is for kicks.

Six is for kicks.

Six is for kicks.

Epilogue

ANNIE WAS SENT to live with her aunt in Springfield after Becky and my grandfather died. I saw her at her mother's funeral, but I was on the other side of a crowd of people from where she was standing. She was flanked on one side by Officer Randy and on the other by a flabby, superior social worker with her arms crossed over her chest.

Mr. Berg survived, but he wasn't there that day. I think everyone agreed he wasn't going to get within ten miles of Annie ever again.

I kept staring at her until she looked up and found my eyes. I mouthed *I'm sorry* to her, and she did the same to me.

She wasn't saying she was sorry because of our mutual tragedies. She was saying sorry because of the bandages on my arm.

The bandages were courtesy of a last minute decision on my part. After I stood in the backyard for what seemed like days, I snapped myself out of it and realized that my grandfather and Becky were truly gone. I went inside the house, dumped the rest of the pills down the toilet, then took the butcher knife and sliced my arm without hesitation. I made my cut ragged and angry, as though I were fending off an attacker. Then I dialed 911 and started crying hysterically. The crying wasn't pretend. It was as real as the blood that was dripping down my arm and soaking my jeans.

An ambulance and a police car were sent. They found me sitting in a sea of red on the floor in the kitchen. My head was woozy. I was barely able to speak. Still, in my stupor, I told them that my sister had killed my grandfather, destroyed my mother's pills, attacked me with a knife, and killed herself in my father's garage.

It was easy to lie, because I wasn't lying. It was the truth. Mostly.

I remember flashes of what happened after that, like me staring at the ceiling of the ambulance, or the white shirts with red patches that the paramedics wore while they kept telling me that everything was going to be okay.

I remember the slew of stitches in my arm, and my dad wanting to light a cigarette in the hospital, but a nurse telling him he couldn't because it was a safety hazard.

My father chose to cremate my grandfather and Becky and have a private service. I barely remember it, except for creepy Father Tim, who I somehow couldn't help feeling a sick sense of resentment toward.

I blocked out his words and concentrated on the throbbing in my arm until everything was over. Then we went back home to our house, minus two fifths of my family.

Annie and I talked a lot on the phone those first few months. Her aunt made her get real help for her cutting, and she finally stopped. She told me she was going to get her GED and go on to junior college. Things worked out great for her at her aunt's, and she blossomed there, a thing that would have never happened if she stayed in Apple.

Eventually, our calls slowly tapered off until they turned into texts that went from daily to every few days, to once a week, to less than that, then nothing. I was happy for Annie. She got out, and that was the important thing.

They say if you love something you should set it free. If it comes back to you, then it was meant to be. I hope Annie comes back to me some day, but I don't think she'll ever come back to Apple.

Newie was a different story. I don't blame him, but he just didn't know what to say to me after everything happened. It was like someone had taken a sledgehammer and smashed apart the bond we had forged together over the years. I guess the next best port in the storm of his life was Erika Tenzar.

They started dating, and what I mean by dating is screwing like rabbits every chance they got. Newie and I stopped hanging out altogether. It was strange at first, but I got used to it. I even got used to seeing him in the halls at school, holding hands with Erika and not saying hi to me when I walked by—or me him.

I think sometimes life gets too painful, and the best way to handle it is not to look at the pain.

Actually, around Valentine's Day, I found out from Mark Zebrowski that Erika was knocked up. Of course, that was taken care of over a sick day, and Newie showed up at school with a black eye, courtesy of his father. I think the chief had a boatload of his own issues to work out, anyway, because Mary Jane got knocked up, too, and moved out.

My mother started on real depression pills and broke free from her dark prison after a really long sentence. She began walking, then talking, then even smiling. Things started happening in the house that never used to get done unless I did them. Grocery shopping happened, although the fish case at Tenzar's was closed for months, and if you could afford fresh fish you had to drive to the supermarket in Bellingham. Dinners were made before I got home from school, and laundry was washed and folded.

Sometimes even candles were lit in every room.

Through everything, my father was the one who really didn't change at all. He still worked hard every day, came home, led the three of us in prayer over whatever my mother cooked for dinner, and spent his evenings in the garage.

Eventually, he finished the big cross that Becky hung herself on. It was planted right-side up in the backyard come spring.

We all went to church every Sunday, and I continued to tune out everything that creepy Father Tim had to say, but somehow, people started being a little nicer to our family. I'm not sure if it was out of pure Christian charity, or because they felt bad for everything that happened to us.

My father was even asked to make a few custom crucifixes, which he solemnly agreed to do, but I know it secretly made him happy.

As for me, I spent so much time up in my grandfather's rooms, reading his book over and over again, that my parents finally told me I could move up there, if I wanted. I was going to need my own place come graduation, anyway, and you couldn't beat the rent. Up there, I felt free and alive, with no one looking over my shoulder as I pored over the years of my grandfather's sadistic reign, all without ever telling a soul.

There was no one left to tell, and no good would come of it, anyway.

Right after graduation, my mother told me that Mary Jane, the chief's old girlfriend, lost the baby she was carrying, which I think was a huge relief to the chief. He wasn't the best at being a dad.

Newie started bagging groceries at Tenzar's and told anyone who would listen that he was going to marry Erika when he finished the police academy.

I took a summer job in the tobacco fields. Most of the other guys kind of stayed away from me, probably for the same reason that Newie and I drifted apart. No one knew what to say. I can understand that.

I ended up reading a lot. I asked creepy Father Tim for a Bible, which made him almost pee in his pants with excitement, and I spent a lot of time examining the words, blackening out with a pencil the ones that I thought were complete and utter bull, and circling the interesting ones.

I started carrying around a gym bag with me with both books nestled inside, so that I could read them when I wanted—the one from Father Tim and the one that my grandfather had created. Over that hot summer while I picked tobacco, a new picture started to form in my head.

I couldn't see it clearly for the longest time, and it bothered me. Even after I left tobacco to take a full-time job in the cider mill at Apple's Apples, every waking moment was consumed with that picture. It took the first leaves of autumn to start falling for it to finally come into focus so I could understand what it was.

I had a belief. It wasn't my grandfather's, and it wasn't my father's. It was my own, and I knew that everything would be okay.

Late one night, after my mother and father went to bed, I took a walk down the street to the dead end with my gym bag in tow. I pushed through the tangle of woods and came out at the railroad tracks.

Underneath the clear, moonless sky, I gathered some dead leaves together and stuffed them inside the gym bag all around both books. I piled some twigs into a little teepee and put the gym bag on top of it and lit a fire.

That flame was for everyone my grandfather had ever murdered. I lit a fire for Claudia Fish and Ruby Murphy and Mrs. Berg and horrible Ralphie Delessio. I even lit a fire for my grandfather, but mostly that fire was for Becky.

I missed my sister terribly, but she was at peace now, and I could handle that.

After I watched all the horrors of the years burn to nothing, I said a silent forever-goodbye to the past and slowly walked home.

The next day after dinner, I went upstairs, picked up the phone, and punched in familiar numbers.

"Hello?" said a voice on the other end.

"Hey, fuckwad."

"Hey, back," Newie said. "Are you over yourself yet?"

"Yeah, I think so."

"Good," said Newie. "What are you doing? Wanna go to the tracks and smoke a bone?"

I laughed. "Aren't you, like, a cop or something?"

"Not yet," he said.

Some things never change. "How about we just go to the tracks and talk."

"Or that. What about the freaky guy with the gym bag?"

"That was last year," I said. "I think everything's okay now."

"If you say so," Newie snorted and hung up the phone.

Yeah, I say so. I grabbed my jacket off my father's coat rack and headed out the front door.

Everything would be okay.

Two days later, the first body of the year was found on the Giant Steps in High Garden.

The End

Acknowledgements

As always, I would like to thank David Gilfor for reading over my shoulder, chapter after chapter, to make sure my story and my characters remained authentic.

I would like to thank Shira Block McCormick for assuring me that, indeed, she had to leave her house after she finished my transcript because it freaked her out that much.

I would like to thank my readers, Tamara Fricke, Lauren Levin, Sherrie Gilfor, Jeremy Gilfor, and my mother, Joline Odentz, for wading through the smorgasbord of creepy that is the fictional Apple, Massachusetts.

In addition, I would like to thank Lois Winston, Ashely Grayson, Debra Dixon and the team at Bell Bridge Books for their tireless support, especially Danielle Childers who coined the phrase, "Poodles—you can't eat just one."

Finally, I would like to give a special thanks to my eighteen-year-old nephew, Nicholas Gilfor, who is the most brilliant, brutal copy editor I could ever hope to have. His dedication to keeping my writing grammatically correct and my story grounded in reality was both humbling and inspiring. I hope to have as good a grasp of the English language as he does when I grow up. One can only dream.

About the Author

Howard Odentz is a life-long resident of Western Massachusetts. His love of New England, along with the lore of the region, usually finds their way into his stories. Influenced by decades of reading thriller and horror novels, his writing often delves into the more psychological aspects of those who are thrown into unique or otherworldly circumstances. In addition to writing fiction, Mr. Odentz has penned two full length musical comedies. *In Good Spirits* is inspired by the real-life ghostly experiences of a local community theatre group and their haunted stage. *Piecemeal* tells the backstory of Victor Frankenstein's Hollywood-created protégé, Igor.

Howard's first novel, *Dead (A Lot)*, was released in 2013.

Visit with the author on Facebook and at howardodentz.com.

CPSIA information can be obtained at www.ICGtesting.com
Printed in the USA
BVOW07s0054101214

378662BV00001BA/2/P